新编
美国文学史及选读

朱玉英 / 主　编

许晓萍 / 副主编

NEW AMERICAN LITERATURE:
A SHORT HISTORY AND SELECTED READINGS

浙江大学出版社

Preface

When I first heard that one of my friends was busy writing a book, I thought such kind of work was far from my life. It never occurred to me that I would finally undertake such a demanding job. Anyway, I was lucky to teach American Literature early in my life, which exposed me to a wider world that I had not known as a student.

Despite the fact that its history is comparatively short, American Literature has contributed a lot to world literature since the 19th century. Under the influence of philosophy, religion, art, science and even history, numerous literary works have come into being, which not only enrich American Literature but also help the whole world to know the United States, this country, and its culture better. This book mainly covers two parts: a short history of American Literature and selected readings. At the beginning of each period the historical background is presented so that it becomes easier to grasp the mainstream of literature. To introduce a writer and his works, his life is involved, which serves to shed light on his works. All those selected readings are classic and short, suitable to analyze and even to recite. To have a full understanding of American Literature, I have read some reference books and borrowed some ideas from them. And in some aspects, it is not perfect and still needs improving. Therefore, both sincere criticism and constructive suggestions are welcome.

I am deeply grateful to the Foreign Languages Department at Hexi University for offering me the opportunity to further my pursuit of literature. My special thanks go to my dear friends, Xu Xiaoping, who has encouraged me to restart this formidable task, after my computer was attacked by a terrible hacker and all my files were encoded. I should also extend my thanks to those who have supported me all the way. Without their constant help, it would be impossible for me to finish this book.

Zhu Yuying
December 2016

CONTENTS

Part One

The Literature of Colonial America

Historical Background

Christopher Columbus, an Italian explorer, made a famous voyage in 1492. Afterwards many European settlers came to American continent to escape religious persecution and to build a new Garden of Eden. Finally the first permanent English settlement in North America was established at Jamestown, Virginia in 1607. In the early period, American literature began with the orally transmitted myths, legends, tales and lyrics (always songs) of Indian cultures. The Indians also made a contribution to American vocabulary. Some Indian words are still used in everyday American English today such as "canoe," "tobacco," "potato," "moccasin,""persimmon," and "totem."

American Puritanism　Puritans was the name given in the 16th century to the more extreme Protestants who thought the English Reformation had not gone far enough. They wanted to purify their national church. In the 17th century many Puritans emigrated to the New World, where they sought to found a holy Commonwealth in New England. Puritanism remained the dominant cultural force in that area into the 19th century. Puritans believed in the doctrine that John Calvin, the great French Theologian preached in Geneva.

- Predestination: God decided everything before it occurred.
- Original sin: Human beings were born to be evil and this original sin can be passed down from generation to generation.
- Total depravity: Man is completely depraved.
- Limited atonement: Only the "selected" can be saved.

Puritans were convinced that human beings were predestined by God before they were born. Some were God's chosen people while others were predestined to be damned to hell. They also believed that everyone had a calling, which was given by God. The success of one's work or the prosperity in his calling was the sign of God's elect. Therefore, working hard and living a moral and thrifty life were their ethics.

It can be safely concluded that without some understanding of Puritanism, there can be no real understanding of America and its literature. Optimistic puritans have exerted a great influence on American literature. The Puritans dreamed of living under a perfect order and worked with indomitable courage and confident hope toward building a new Garden of Eden in America. Fired with such a sense of mission, the Puritans looked at even the worst of life in the face with tremendous optimism.

American Puritanism contributes to the development of symbolism[1], a widely used

---

Note [1] symbolism: the use of symbols in literary works. A symbol refers to something that represents or stands for abstract idea and deep meaning.

technique. To the pious Puritans the physical, phenomenal world was nothing but a symbol of God. Besides, Puritans thought that all the simple objects existing in the world connoted deep meaning.

With regard to their writing, the style is fresh, simple and direct. The rhetoric is plain and honest, not without a touch of nobility often traceable to the direct influence of the Bible.

William Bradford (1590–1657)

William Bradford, who signed the Mayflower Compact while aboard the *Mayflower* in 1620, was an English leader of the Separatist[1] settlers of the Plymouth Colony in Massachusetts. He was elected to be the Plymouth Colony governor for about thirty years. His journal published as *Of Plymouth Plantation* describes early settlers' life from 1621 to 1646. It can be regarded as a retrospective account of his recollections and observations. In this work, Bradford was mainly concerned with the spiritual pursuit of the Plymouth group. More than once he compared the Puritans in Massachusetts to the Israelites led by Moses in the Old Testament. Bradford is also credited as the first civil authority to designate what popular American culture now views as Thanksgiving in the United States.

John Winthrop (1588–1649)

John Winthrop, born into a wealthy Puritan family, once attended Trinity College, Cambridge. Later he worked as a lawyer, but was forced to resign the position due to a crackdown on Nonconformists under King Charles I. Then Winthrop led the first large wave of migrants from England in 1630 and became one of the leading figures in the founding of the Massachusetts Bay Colony, the first major settlement in New England after Plymouth Colony. He had even served as the governor for twelve years. His writings and vision of the colony as a Puritan "city upon a hill" has exerted a great influence on the government and religion of neighboring colonies. He is now known for *A Model of Christian Charity* and *The History of New England*.

Anne Bradstreet (1612–1672)

Anne Bradstreet was the first colonial female poet to be published in the New World. She was both the daughter and the wife of Massachusetts Bay Colony governors. As an accomplished poet, she set a good example for other female writers to follow in an era when women generally tended to family and domestic matters. Through her poetry she eloquently expressed her concerns with Puritans' religious experience, family life and early settlers' lives. Bradstreet's first volume of poetry was published as *The Tenth Muse Lately Sprung Up in America* in 1650. Today she is recognized for

---

Note [1] separatist: Puritan who wants to break free from the Church of England

her *Contemplations*.

＼ Edward Taylor (1645–1729)

Edward Taylor, born into a nonconformist family in Leicestershire, England, immigrated in 1668 to the Massachusetts Bay Colony after the restoration of the monarchy and the Act of Uniformity under Charles II. Soon she was admitted to Harvard College and upon graduation in 1671 became a pastor and physician at Westfield, on the remote western frontier of Massachusetts, where he remained until his death. Edward Taylor wrote his poetry during the last years of the Puritan theocracy and some are considered the finest poetry written in Colonial America. His poems were concerned with the inner spiritual life of Puritan believers. In his poems, Taylor hoped for a "rebirth" of the "Puritan Way."

The Witchcraft Trials in the 1690s

In the 17th century, the Puritan community was greatly troubled by witchcraft trials from time to time, since the supernatural could not be explained in a natural way. Gradually many people began to associate some bizarre events with the Devil, thus witchcraft hunting and trials in New England became widespread. Some young girls and lonely old women were arrested and put on trial as witches. A number of these people were even put to death for "selling their souls" to the Devil.

Among these trials, the most notorious might be the Salem witch trials, which involved a series of hearings and prosecutions of people accused of witchcraft in colonial Massachusetts in 1692. When a group of young girls began to have strange behaviors, the bewildered community believed that it must have something to do with Satan. Consequently, some innocent people were condemned to death in these trials. The Salem witch trials showed the psychological environment of the time and the Puritans' strange beliefs: To many Puritans of the time, witchcraft and other forms of evil were an absolutely real part of everyday life.

Part Two

The Literature of Reason and Revolution

Historical Background

Enlightenment Movement   The 18th-century American Enlightenment was a movement marked by an emphasis on rationality rather than tradition, scientific inquiry instead of unquestioning religious dogma, and representative government in place of monarchy. Enlightenment thinkers and writers were devoted to the ideals of justice, liberty and equality as the natural rights of man. The colonists who would form a new nation were firm believers in the power of reason. They were ambitious, inquisitive, optimistic, practical, politically astute and self-reliant.

Sir Isaac Newton (1642–1727)   Due to the great achievement of Sir Isaac Newton, Newtonian ideas can be seen as a general symbol of world outlook in Enlightenment thinking. Through the Newtonian prism, the universe is seen as a mechanism operated by a rational formula. Mankind is supposed to have the ability to discover and unfold all "Nature's Laws." Newtonian assumptions also help to shape a new image of God, different from that of Puritanism. This God is revealed in nature, not in the Bible. Besides, he argued that man can be perfected through education. In this religious thinking, all men are created equal. This idea would eventually appear in *The Declaration of Independence*.

Thomas Hobbes (1588–1679) and John Locke (1632–1704)   Revolting against the intuitive philosophy of medieval scholasticism, both Thomas Hobbes and John Locke continued to influence people in the 18th century. Thomas Hobbes, an English philosopher, is best known today for his work on political philosophy. His *Leviathan* (1651) established social contract theory, the foundation of later Western political philosophy. To Hobbes, men are by nature enemies and at war with each other. Humans agree to accept certain laws of nature out of fear and the need for mutual protection. As men enter into a social contract to escape the state of war and to keep peace, they submit to the sovereign, whose power must be absolute. Hobbes also argued that government was not created by God, but by men themselves.

John Locke, an English philosopher, is widely regarded as one of the most influential Enlightenment thinkers. Apart from his contribution to epistemology following the tradition of Sir Francis Bacon, he also exerted a great influence on political philosophy. Locke believed in man's natural rights of life, liberty and property. His observation of human nature is somewhat different. He argued that every person was born with a blank slate, upon which experience inscribed its lessons. In addition, men are equal and they enter into a social contract by reason. Here Locke's understanding of social contract also differs fundamentally from that of Hobbes. Locke argued that the institution of government must be established with the consent of those who subject themselves to government. He further emphasized that the social contract must involve the individual's consent to submit to the will of the majority. Some of these ideas are finally reflected in *The Declaration of Independence*.

Deism　Deism, a natural religion, prevails during the Age of Enlightenment. Deists believe in the existence of God, on purely rational grounds, without any reliance on revealed religion or religious authority or holy text. They reason that God is indeed the creator of the universe, "the maker of the clock." The best way to worship God is to study his handiwork, namely, the natural world and the human world, and to do good things to mankind. This is a new concept of the universe which was radically different from the dominating Christian position of original sin and predestination. Jean-Jacques Rousseau (1712–1778), a French deist, declared to a bewildered world that man is by nature good and free in his famous *Social Contract* (1762) for example. Deism simplified the Christian religion in such a way that the rights of religion became consistent with the rights of government and rights of the individual. Thus deism was an integral part of the American Constitution and was embraced by the American Founding Fathers, especially Benjamin Franklin and Thomas Jefferson.

American Revolution—The Independence War (1775–1783)　By 1733 Great Britain had established 13 colonies in North America, but strict rules made by English government hampered the economic development of the colonies. The British wanted the colonies to remain politically and economically dependent on the mother country, which led to the colonies' intense strain with England. The conflict became fiercer, after Britain began to impose more and more taxes on the colonies to pay the cost of fighting the Seven Years' war while refusing to offer them a seat in British Parliament. Consequently the colonists united together to protest with the slogan "no taxation without representation." The Boston Tea Party in 1773 was the culmination of the resistance movement against the Tea Act passed by the British government. The first shots were finally fired in Lexington, when some British soldiers went to Concord to search for weapons and "rebels" in 1775. Thus broke out the American War of Independence.

During the Revolution, the writers held vitally important places in the movement for American independence. The 13 original American states were persuaded to become a single nation by the arguments of statesmen and men of letters. Freedom was won as much by their fiery and inspiring speeches and writings as by the weapons of Washington and Lafayette.

Benjamin Franklin (1706–1790)

Benjamin Franklin, America's "first great man of letters," embodied the Enlightenment ideal of human rationality. When Franklin died, one of his fellow Americans said, "His shadow lies heavier than any other man's on this young nation."

Benjamin Franklin was born in Boston, Massachusetts. At the age of twelve, he started as an apprentice with his older brother. Ten years later, he opened his own printing shop. His newspaper, the *Pennsylvania Gazette* became very popular and profitable. A few years later, *Poor Richard's Almanac*[1] was released and soon became the best selling book in the colonies. Soon he became the most active printer and was appointed the official printer of Pennsylvania. Afterwards Franklin and some fellow printers, known as the Leather Apron Club (because most of them wore leather aprons) started a lending library that was open to everyone. They would pool their money and buy books, which people could borrow. In 1731 the first lending library in America opened. And other towns began to imitate the library, until reading became fashionable. When he was forty-two, Franklin retired from printing to explore his other interests. He was not only devoted to inventing but also experimenting, of which the most fascinating one is how he got electricity with a kite.

During the fight for independence, Franklin, as a statesman, was sent to Europe to represent the colonies. He signed *The Declaration of Independence* in 1776 and the *Treaty of Alliance with France* in 1778. When the colonists won their independence in 1781, Franklin helped negotiate the peace with England and signed what ultimately became known as the *Treaty of Peace with Great Britain* in 1782.

Franklin published *Poor Richard's Almanac*, an annual collection of proverbs continuously from 1732 to 1758. Its main features are as follows:

- practical and useful
- interesting by creating the character "Poor Richard"
- continuation of simple but realistic story about Richard, his wife and family
- including many "sayings" about saving money and working hard, some of which are known to most Americans today:

God helps them who help themselves.

Early to bed, and early to rise, makes a man healthy, wealthy and wise.

Diligence is the mother of good luck.

Autobiography is an introduction of his life to his own son, including four parts written in different times. It is the first success story of self-made Americans.

Apart from his literary achievement, Franklin played an important role in establishing the University of Pennsylvania, the Pennsylvania Hospital and the American Philosophical Society. He was also called "the new Prometheus who had stolen fire (electricity in this case) from heaven." Everything seems to meet in this one man—"Jack of all trades." Herman Melville thus described him as "*master of each and mastered by none.*" In many ways, Franklin's life illustrates the impact of the Enlightenment on a gifted individual. Self-educated but well-read in John Locke, Joseph

---

Note [1] Almanac: a popular form of practical literature containing much useful information for farmers and sailors

Addison and other Enlightenment writers, Franklin learned from them to apply reason to his own life and to break with tradition, in particular the old-fashioned Puritan tradition, when it threatened to smother his ideals.

As an author, Franklin's style is quite modern, and his works show a return to their "plain style." At the same time, there is something "anti-literary" about Franklin. He had no liking for poetry and felt that writing should always have a practical purpose. In the language of his writing, Franklin admirably reflects both Locke's psychology and Locke's political theory, and influences other writers in their choices of language, subject matter and worldview.

Selected Reading

The Autobiography

An Excerpt from Part Three

I had begun in 1733 to study languages. I soon made myself so much a Master of the French as to be able to read the Books with ease. I then undertook the Italian. An Acquaintance, who was also learning it, used often to tempt me to play Chess with him. Finding this took up too much of the time I had to spare for Study, I at length refus'd to play anymore, unless on this Condition, that the Victor in every game should have a Right to impose a Task, either in Parts of the Grammar to be got by heart, or in Translations, etc., which Tasks the Vanquished was to perform upon Honor, before our next Meeting. As we play'd pretty equally, we thus beat one another into that Language. I afterwards with a little Pains-taking, acquired as much of the Spanish as to read their books also.

Thomas Paine (1737–1809)

As a pamphleteer, Thomas Paine supported the American War of Independence with his powerful writings.

Thomas Paine was born in Thetford, England. At the age of 37, he came to America, with a letter of introduction from Franklin. In his adopted country, the United States, Paine stood on the side against his native country. He studied pamphlets Americans had written in opposition to British policies in the colonies and soon established himself as a revolutionary journalist and pamphleteer. Paine went to France to participate in the French Revolution in the 1790s. It was Paine who famously declared: "Where liberty is, there is my country."

Published in 1776, *Common Sense* helped to inspire the nation to support the war. Many at the beginning were still uncertain about the need for independence. *Common Sense* persuaded many to support the revolution in their own way. Paine made these points in it: He denounced monarchies as outdated and advocated a new form of government called republicanism; he argued that the colonists were not English and should not want to be considered English; he encouraged Americans to build a new country where freedom prevails and where immigrants are welcome.

The American Crisis (1776) was a collection of articles written by Thomas Paine during the American Revolution. After the shots were fired at Lexington, Massachusetts, Paine shouldered a gun and joined the army. But after a series of losses of battles, desertions from the Revolutionary Army increased. George Washington retreated across the Delaware and a defeat seemed imminent. A week before Christmas, he said in a letter to his brother: "I think the game is very near up." Paine, however, faced up to the situation. On December 19, he published the first of the *Crisis* papers. The paper boosted the morale. Enlistment in the army increased. Washington ordered that the paper be read to every regiment.

In defense of the French Revolution Paine wrote and published *The Rights of Man* (1791). In it, Paine advocated four key rights: *liberty, property, security and resistance to oppression*. Paine also assumed that the right to engage in revolution is inalienable. He made his argument for democracy from the state of nature and from the Bible. To see God and Nature as Reason, as we remember, is a legacy of Enlightenment.

The Age of Reason (1794–1795) systematically criticized the organized religions (the Church of England) and many of their doctrines and beliefs, promoted deism as "the one true religion," and emphasized philosophy and scientific study as the only source of true knowledge.

Paine's approach to writing is pragmatic. He responds to contemporary events in order to inspire, not to be original. His style may be simple but powerful.

Selected Reading

The American Crisis
An Excerpt

These are the times that try men's souls. The summer soldier and the sunshine patriot will, in this crisis, shrink from the service of their country; but he that stands by it now, deserves the love and thanks of man and woman. Tyranny, like hell, is not easily conquered; yet we have this consolation with us, that the harder the conflict, the more glorious the triumph. What we obtain too cheap, we esteem too lightly: It is dearness only that gives every thing its value. Heaven knows how to put a proper price upon its goods; and it would be strange indeed if so celestial an article as FREEDOM should not be highly rated. Britain, with an army to enforce her tyranny, has declared that she has a right (not only to TAX) but "to BIND us in ALL CASES WHATSOEVER" and if being bound in that manner, is not slavery, then is there not such a thing as slavery upon earth. Even the expression is impious; for so unlimited a power can belong only to God.

✎ Thomas Jefferson (1743–1826)

Thomas Jefferson served as the third President of the United States. As one of the Founding Fathers, Jefferson advocated democracy, republicanism and individual rights, which motivated American colonists to break from Great Britain and form a new nation.

Thomas Jefferson was born on the Virginia frontier and graduated from William and Mary College. He read widely in the classics. Like Franklin, Jefferson exemplified the ideals of his time. He accepted the main tenets of deism. And he believed in natural rights, political equality and natural altruism. He was deeply interested in science and agricultural experiments. He was also an architect, a scholar and an educator. Indeed, he established the University of Virginia and even drew the architectural plans. In his political thinking, he believed that the best government was the government that governed least. Early in his life, he had an interest in poetry and novels, which he later gave up.

The Declaration of Independence, drafted in June, 1776, was at once a national symbol of liberty and a monument to Jefferson as a statesman and author. Embedded in the political philosophy which Locke and the continental philosophers had expressed, Jefferson summarized this philosophy as "self-evident truths" and set forth a long list of grievances against King George III in order to justify the separation of the colonies from Britain.

It consists of 5 sections: the introduction, the preamble, the indictment of George III, the denunciation of the British people and the conclusion. On July 4th, 1776, the *Declaration* was officially adopted by Congress "…We hold these truths to be self-evident, that all men are created equal…"

Selected Reading

The Declaration of Independence
An Excerpt

We hold these truths to be self-evident, that all men are created equal, that they are endowed by their Creator with certain unalienable rights, that they are among these are Life, Liberty and the pursuit of Happiness[1]. —That to secure these rights, Governments are instituted among Men, deriving their just power from the consent of the governed.

Note [1] Life, Liberty and the pursuit of Happiness: based on the natural rights as those to "life, liberty and property" identified by John Locke in *Second Treatise of Government*

—That whenever any Form of Government becomes destructive of these ends, it is the Right of the People to alter or to abolish it, and to institute new Government, laying its foundation on such principles and organizing its powers in such form, as to them shall seem most likely to effect their safety and happiness.

Philip Freneau (1752–1832)

Philip Freneau, one of the American poets, found new subject matters for American literature and left a body of poetic work which exerted great influence upon his immediate successors.

Philip Freneau, born in New York, was raised in New Jersey. In 1768 he entered the College of New Jersey (Princeton University), where he wrote the poem "The Rising Glory of America" in collaboration with Hugh Henry Brackenridge, a future novelist. After graduation, Freneau traveled to the West Indies, where he was indulged in the beauty of nature and wrote "The House of Night" (1781) anticipating the Gothic mood of Poe and Coleridge. In 1778 he returned to America and fought the American Revolution. Unfortunately, he was captured and held on a British prison ship for about six weeks. This unpleasant experience furnished him with enough materials to produce "The British Prison Ship" (1781) and "To the Memory of the Brave Americans" (1781). When he worked as an editor of and contributor to the Freeman's Journal between 1781 and 1784, he advocated the essence of Jeffersonian democracy—decentralization of government, equality for the masses, etc. Later, encouraged by Jefferson, he established the anti-federalist paper, the *National Gazette* (1791–1793). In his later years, he became a heavy drinker, lost much of his property, and died in a blizzard.

As a poet, Freneau is called "Poet of the American Revolution" since most of his poems are political satires or patriotic revolutionary verses with democratic ideas. Freneau is also regarded as "Father of American Poetry," in that he tries to avoid imitation of English poems, dedicated himself to describing American subject matter: American landscape, American images, hatred toward the British colonists, and resentment toward slavery. "Pioneer of the Romanticism" goes to him, because some of his themes and images anticipated the works of such 19th-century American Romantic writers as Cooper, Emerson, Poe and Melville. This is best illustrated in his nature poems, such as "The Wild Honey Suckle" (1786) and "The Indian Burying Ground" (1788).

As to his style, Freneau's poetry tends to be natural and simple. Satire is employed as a poetic device and political weapon against the British during the Revolution.

Selected Reading

The Wild Honey Suckle[1]

In "The Wild Honey Suckle," the central image is a native wild flower, Honey suckle, instead of rose or daffodil, which makes a drastic difference from elite flower images typical of traditional English poems. It is "wild" just to convey the fresh perception of the natural scenes on the new continent. The poem shows strong feelings for the natural beauty, which is the characteristic of Romantic poems.

Hyperbole is a figure of speech in which the poet consciously exaggerates in order to heighten an effect. The line "the space is but an hour" contains a hyperbole stressing the transience of life. Flowers are born, bloom and decline to repose, and human beings would exist in exactly the same way. Thus a philosophical meditation is indicated by the description of the fate of a trivial wild plant.

In this poem the poet expressed a keen awareness of the loveliness and transience of nature. He not only meditated on Mortality but also celebrated nature. The poem implies that life and death are inevitable law of nature.

The Wild Honey Suckle

Fair flower, that dost so comely grow,
Hid in this silent, dull retreat,
Untouched thy honeyed blossoms blow,
Unseen thy little branches greet:
No roving foot shall crush thee here,
No busy hand provoke a tear.

By Nature's self in white arrayed,
She bade thee shun the vulgar eye,
And planted here the guardian shade,
And sent soft waters murmuring by;
Thus quietly thy summer goes,
Thy days declining to repose.

Note [1] The Wild Honey Suckle: then the popular name for a familiar shrub, sometimes "swamp honeysuckle"

Smit with those charms, that must decay,
I grieve to see your future doom;
They died—nor were those flowers more gay,
The flowers that did in Eden bloom;
Unpitying frosts, and Autumn's power
Shall leave no vestige of this flower.

From morning suns and evening dews
At first thy little being came:
If nothing once, you nothing lose,
For when you die you are the same;
The space between, is but an hour,
The frail duration of flower.

Part Three

American Romanticism

Historical Background

The Romantic Period, one of the most important periods in the history of American literature, stretches from the end of the 18th century to the outbreak of the Civil War. It started with the publication of Washington Irving's *The Sketch Book* and ended with Whitman's *Leaves of Grass*. Being a period of the great flowering of American literature, it is also called "the American Renaissance."

The Romantic Movement in England and Europe proved to be a decisive influence on American Romanticism. Many English and European masters of poetry and prose made stimulating impact. In addition, the development of the American society nurtured "the literature of a great nation." The young Republic, devoid of a heavy burden of the inherited past and history, was flourishing into a politically, economically and culturally independent country. Historically, it was the time of westward expansion. The western boundary had reached to the Pacific by 1860; the number of its states had increased from 13 to 21; its total population had increased greatly, too. Economically, the whole nation was experiencing an industrial transformation, which affected the rural as well as the urban life, including the use of steam power, the erection of factories and the technological inventions and innovations. Politically, democracy and equality became the ideal of the new nation, and the two party system, Republicans vs. Democrats, came into being. Culturally, the Americans struggled for cultural independence: American writers try to create a distinctive literature separated and different from English literature. Thus, with a strong sense of optimism and the feeling of "feeling good" of the whole nation, a spectacular outburst of romantic feeling was brought about in the first half of the 19th century.

The American national experience of "pioneering into the west" proved to be a rich source of materials for American writers to draw upon. They celebrated American's landscape with its virgin forests. The wilderness came to function almost as a dramatic character that symbolized moral law. The desire for an escape from society and a return to nature became a permanent convention of American literature. The American Puritanism as a cultural heritage also exerted great influence over American moral values. One of the manifestations is the fact that American Romantic writers tended more to moralize than their English and European counterparts. Besides, a preoccupation with the Calvinistic view of original sin marked the works of Hawthorne, Melville and a host of lesser writers. In addition, the "newness" of the Americans as a nation can not be ignored. The idea of individualism and political equality, and their dream that America was to be a new Garden of Eden for man were distinctly American. The feeling of "newness" was strong enough to inspire the romantic imagination.

Early Romanticism

American Romanticism did not achieve its most powerful articulations until Poe, Emerson and some others writers. Slightly earlier were Irving, Cooper and Bryant, who are regarded as pioneers of American Romanticism. Thus, their works and the works of others constitute what is called "early Romanticism."

Romanticism celebrates the triumph of feeling and intuition over reason. It is suspicious of the rational explanations of the universe and human nature as derived from the Enlightenment. A philosophical cornerstone for the Romantic resistance to rationalism was laid down by the German philosopher Immanuel Kant in his *Critique of Pure Reason* (1781). Since Romantic writers placed a higher value on the free expression of emotion and on the power of imagination, they showed great interests in the psychic states. As a result, characters in Romantic stories sometimes revealed extremes of sensitivity, such as fear of dark and the unknown. Besides, Romanticism exalts the individual over society, thus showing a strong disliking for the bondage of convention and customs. As it is sometimes the contradiction, nostalgia for the past traditions is also a Romantic strain. What's more, Nature is believed to be the source of goodness and the antithesis of society as society tends to be corrupt. A related manifestation is the moral enthusiasm exhibited in some Romantic writers.

✎ Washington Irving (1783–1895)

Washington Irving, one of the first American writers to gain an international reputation, is regarded as Father of the American short stories.

Washington Irving was born in New York's lower Manhattan, the youngest of eleven children. His father was a moderately wealthy Scottish hardware merchant. He grew up in a household filled with federalist sentiments. Throughout his life, Irving remained a man pleased with upper-class tastes and a federalist in politics and in culture. His aristocratic sense of pleasure with the details of life was a far cry from the ethical ideals of Puritanism. As a child, Irving was frail in health and was precocious. His earlier education was received from various seminaries in New York. In his formative years, Irving experienced intimately the literary and cultural vitality of New York and studied law as well.

In 1803 he interrupted his work as a law clerk to travel through the frontier of upper state New York and eastern part of Canada. In 1804 he went to Rome where he met the American painter Washington Allston and developed an interest in art. He returned from Europe with a sharpened sensitivity to American provincialism. Then came out *A History of New York* (1809), with which Irving gained not only financial success but also international fame. In 1805 he made his second trip to Europe, where Irving resolved to recreate the rich European cultural heritage in American settings. *The Sketch Book* (1819–1820) represented his efforts in this respect. With it, Irving's literary fame further increased both at home and aboard.

The Sketch Book of Geoffrey Crayon, Gent was published in serials between 1819 and 1820. It won Irving international fame on both sides of the Atlantic. The book contains familiar essays on the English life and Americanized versions of European folk tales like "Rip Van Winkle" and "The Legend of Sleepy Hollow." The main theme of "Rip Van Winkle" is loss of identity. After Rip awakened from his long sleep and returned to the village, he did not recognize the people he encountered and none of them knew him either. What's more, the look of the village underwent great change: It was larger, with rows of houses he had never seen. His wife was dead, while others left the village. Everything was different and nothing was as it had been. Faced with so many changes, Rip had difficulties in regaining his identity.

Irving lived the life as the recognized man of letters and remained a bachelor. His works are characterized by humor, his sense of irony and his finished style. Thus, he is worth the honor of being "the American Goldsmith" for his literary craftsmanship.

Selected Reading

Rip Van Winkle

In a village at the foot of the Catskill Mountains of New York lives a simple, easygoing man named Rip Van Winkle, when New York is an English colony. Because of his kindness, Rip is popular with all of his neighbors, especially with children. However, his wife takes advantage of his meekness and regularly nags him.

Besides, He is always ready to help a neighbor with hard work and frequently runs errands and does odd jobs for housewives. But when it comes time to tend his own farm and keep up his own property, he is of little use. The only plants that thrive on his farm are weeds. Consequently, he has the least productive and least attractive farm in the area. Whenever Dame Van Winkle begins to blame Rip for his failings, Rip will shrug and go outside, out of range of her scolding tongue. She treats his dog, Wolf, in the same way, which resembles Rip in submissiveness. Rip often seeks refuge with a village group that convene on a bench in front of an inn to gossip, to tell stories, and occasionally to discuss events reported in a newspaper left behind by a traveler. Unfortunately for Rip, Dame Van Winkle sometimes comes to the inn for him and hauls him off, all the while her tongue lashing him and his compatriots.

To escape his wife and the drudgery of his farm, Rip sometimes heads into the woods with Wolf and his gun. One day, high in the Catskill Mountains, after he hunts squirrels for a few hours, he feels tired and decides to lie down for a rest on a green knoll. When it is time for him to return home, a man comes up the mountain, calling Rip's name. As the man approaches, Rip notices that he is short and squat, with a beard and bushy hair, and wears old-fashioned Dutch clothes. He is carrying a keg and beckons for Rip to help him. Thus, Rip, with the man, ascends the mountain to a hollow, where, Rip sees bearded men, all dressed like his companion and all of odd appearance, playing ninepins. His companion opens the keg and empties it into flagons, then motions Rip to serve the players. After the strange men drink the liquor and resume their game, Rip decides to sample the brew. He drinks one after another until he falls into a deep sleep.

When he wakes up to a sunny morning, he is on the same green knoll upon which he rests when he first sees the man with the keg. He recalls what happened to him the night before—the men, the ninepins and the liquor. Dame Van Winkle will give him a severe scolding this time. He reaches out for his gun but is surprised to find its barrel rusted and its stock eaten away by worms. Wolf is nowhere to be found. He also finds that the path he has walked with the strange man is now a mountain stream. Moreover, at the place where he enters the ravine, there is now only a wall of rock. Dumfounded, he returns to the village but is further puzzled when he sees people he does not recognize, all wearing strange fashions. Stroking his chin in bewilderment, he discovers that he has a beard a foot long.

The village is larger than when he left it, with more people. He sees strange houses with strange names over the doors. Dogs bark at him and children make fun of him. When he reaches his house, he sees an old, deteriorating dwelling with broken windows and a collapsed roof. An old dog outside—is it Wolf? Inside, he looks about but finds only emptiness. Immediately, he walks over to the inn, but it is gone. In its place is a ramshackle building with these words painted on the door: "The Union Hotel, by Jonathan Doolittle." There are men outside, but none of whom he recognizes.

Soon the men gather around him and eye him, for he is a strange sight to them. Women and children from the village also come to look at the peculiar man with the long beard and odd clothes. Confused by their questions, Rip tells them, "I am a poor quiet man, a native of the place, and a loyal subject of the king." At that, they declare him a Tory and a spy. When Rip tells his story to others, it is also said that the discoverer of the region, Hendrick Hudson, visits the area every twenty years with his crew. Once they were observed playing ninepins in the mountains and a thunderous sound was heard. It is finally confirmed that he is indeed Rip Van Winkle and that twenty years has passed by since he left. Rip then goes to live with his daughter and her farmer husband. Rip's son has been hired to work the farm but spends all his time on his own interests.

When Rip begins sitting on the bench in front of the Doolittle's Hotel, the villagers look upon him as one of their patriarchs. In time, he learns that there has been a revolutionary war in which the country has broken away from the Great Britain and that he is now a citizen of the United States. Overall, he is a happy man and is especially pleased to be free of the tyranny of Dame Van Winkle.

An Excerpt

He now hurried forth, and hastened to his old resort, the village inn—but it too was gone. A large rickety wooden building stood in its place, with great gaping windows, some of them broken and mended with old hats and petticoats, and over the door was painted, "the Union Hotel, by Jonathan Doolittle." Instead of the great tree that used to shelter the quiet little Dutch inn of yore[1], there now was reared a tall naked pole, with something on the top that looked like a red night cap[2], and from it was fluttering a flag, on which was a singular assemblage of stars and stripes[3]—all this was strange and incomprehensible. He recognized on the sign, however, the ruby face of King George[4], under which he had smoked so many a peaceful pipe, but even this was singularly metamorphosed. The red coat[5] was changed for one of blue and buff[6], a sword was held in the hand instead of a scepter, the head was decorated with a cocked hat[7], and underneath was painted in large characters, GENERAL WASHINGTON.

...

Rip's heart died away at hearing of these sad changes in his home and friends, and finding himself thus alone in the world. Every answer puzzled him too, by treating of such enormous lapses of time, and of matters which he could not understand: war—congress—Stony Point; —he had no courage to ask after any more friends, but cried out in despair, "Does nobody here know Rip Van Winkle?"

"Oh, Rip Van Winkle!" exclaimed two or three, "Oh, to be sure! That's Rip Van Winkle yonder, leaning against the tree."

Rip looked, and beheld a precise counterpart of himself, as he went up the mountain:

Note [1] of yore: in the old days
Note [2] red night cap: close-fitting cap adapted during the French Revolution as a symbol of liberty
Note [3] stars and stripes: the American national flag
Note [4] King George: King George III
Note [5] red coat: uniform of the British Army
Note [6] blue and buff: colors of the Revolutionary Uniform
Note [7] cocked hat: a three-cornered hat with turned-up edges

apparently as lazy, and certainly as ragged. The poor fellow was now completely confounded. He doubted his own identity, and whether he was himself or another man. In the midst of his bewilderment, the man in the cocked hat demanded who he was, and what was his name?

"God knows," exclaimed he, at his wit's end; "I'm not myself—I'm somebody else—that's me yonder—no—that's somebody else got into my shoes[1]—I was myself last night, but I fell asleep on the mountain, and they've changed my gun, and every thing's changed, and I'm changed, and I can't tell what's my name, or who I am!"

James Fenimore Cooper (1789–1851)

James Fenimore Cooper, a prolific and popular American writer of the early 19th century, is best remembered for the historical romances of the frontier life.

James Fenimore Cooper, born into a rich land-holding family of New Jersey, was one of the few American authors who did not have to worry about money. He was sent to Yale at 14 but was expelled in his junior year because of improper behavior. He went and spent five years at sea. Then, while still in his early twenties, he inherited his father's vast fortune and settled down to a life of comfort and even luxury. Cooper's career as an author began quite by accident. Reading an English novel one day, he was so disgusted with it that he threw it down and said he could do better. His wife challenged him and he became serious about it. And succeed he did. After a mild success with his first book, the second one, *The Spy* (1821), a novel about the American Revolution, proved to be an immense success. However, he was best known in his own day and remembered today as the author of the "Leatherstocking Tales," which is concerned with the frontier life of American settlers.

In fact, the Leatherstocking series consists of five novels: *The Pioneers* (1823), *The Last of the Mohicans* (1826), *The Prairie* (1827), *The Pathfinder* (1840) and *The Deerslayer* (1841), among which *The Last of the Mohicans* is often regarded as his masterpiece. *The Last of the Mohicans* is the sequel to *The Pioneers* and the prequel to *The Prairie*. It is set at the time of the war between France and England in North America. The five Leatherstocking novels chronicle the life of Nathaniel "Natty" Bumppo, who lives in the frontier (which moves steadily westward with each successive novel) at the intersection of European and Native American culture. Bumppo is a hybrid of these cultures; in each book, he has a different Native American name, and it is by these names that he is known. These books offer a lucid and insightful study of the encounter between wilderness and civilization, from the point of view of a man who manages to straddle the divide between them.

Cooper also produced other types of novels. Set against the American Revolution, *The Spy* is

---

Note [1] got into my shoes: became me

about counterespionage. Starting with *The Pilot* (1823), Cooper wrote eleven sea stories. *The Pilot* gives an account of two love affairs and the schemes of a villain.

Cooper's greatness in American literature lies in the fact that he created a myth about the formative period of the American nation.

Selected Reading

The Last of the Mohicans

Cora and Alice Munro, daughters of Lieutenant Colonel Munro, are traveling with Major Duncan Heyward from Fort Edward to Fort William Henry, where Munro is in command. David Gamut, a naive singing teacher, accompanies them as well. They are guided through the forest by another native named Magua, who leads them through a shortcut. The party finally joins Natty Bumppo known as Hawk-eye, and his two Mohican friends, Chingachgook and his son Uncas. Heyward becomes suspicious that Magua is a Huron scout secretly allied with the French, which also troubles Hawk-eye and the Mohicans. On learning their doubts, Magua escapes. Thus Hawk-eye and the Mohicans lead their new companions to a hidden cave on an island in a river where they are attacked by the Hurons. Since ammunition is exhausted, Hawk-eye and the Mohicans escape with a promise to return for their companions, while Heyward, Gamut and the Munro sisters are captured by Magua and the Hurons. Magua offers to spare the party on condition that Cora becomes his wife, but is rejected. Enraged by the second refusal, he sentences the prisoners to death. Fortunately, Hawk-eye and the Mohicans rescue all four, and leads them to a dilapidated building that was involved with a battle between the Indians and the British some years ago. The Hurons decides to leave the area rather than disturb the graves of their own fellow-countrymen. The next day, Hawk-eye leads the party to Fort Henry, past a siege by the French army. Munro sends Hawk-eye to Fort Edward for reinforcements. However, Hawk-eye is captured by the French, who delivers him to Fort Henry without the letter. Heyward returns to Colonel Munro and announces his love for Alice, and Munro gives his permission for Heyward's courtship.

The French general, Montcalm, invites Munro to a parley, and shows him General Webb's letter, in which the British general refuses reinforcements. At this, Munro agrees to Montcalm's terms that the British soldiers must leave the fort and withdraw from the war for eighteen months. Outside the fort, the column of British prisoners is attacked by 2,000 Huron warriors, in which massacre Magua kidnaps Cora and Alice, and takes them to the Huron village. And David Gamut goes after them closely. Afterwards, Hawk-eye, the Mohicans, Heyward and Colonel Munro follow Magua, and cross a lake to intercept his trail. A canoe chase ensues, in which the rescuers eventually follow Magua to the Huron village. Here, they find Gamut (earlier spared by the Hurons as a harmless madman), who says that Alice is held in this village, and Cora in another belonging to the Lenape (Delaware). Disguised as a French medicine man, Heyward enters the Huron village with Gamut to rescue Alice. At the same time, Hawk-eye and Uncas set out to rescue Cora. After Alice is rescued, Uncas, Heyward, Alice and Hawk-eye travel to the Delaware village where Cora is held, also where Magua demands the return of his prisoners. Tamenund, the sage of the Delawares, frees the prisoners, except for Cora, whom he awards to Magua. To satisfy the laws of hospitality, Tamenund gives Magua a three-hour head start before pursuit. The Delawares vanquishes the Hurons, but Magua escapes with Cora and two other Hurons. Uncas, Hawk-eye and Heyward pursue them. In a fight at the edge of a cliff, Cora, Uncas and Magua are killed. The novel concludes with a lengthy account of the funerals of Uncas and Cora, and Hawk-eye renews his friendship with Chingachgook. Tamenund prophesies: "The pale-faces are masters of the earth, and the time of the red-men has not yet come again..."

An Excerpt from Chapter 12

But Uncas, denying his habits, we had almost said his nature, flew with instinctive delicacy, accompanied by Heyward, to the assistance of the females, and quickly releasing Alice, placed her in the arms of Cora. We shall not attempt to describe the gratitude to the Almighty Disposer of Events which glowed in the bosoms of the sisters, who were thus unexpectedly restored to life and to each other. Their thanksgivings were deep and silent; the offerings of their gentle spirits burning brightest and purest on the secret altars of their hearts; and their renovated and more earthly feelings exhibiting themselves in long and fervent though speechless caresses. As Alice rose from her knees, where she had sunk by the side of Cora, she threw herself on the bosom of the latter, and sobbed aloud the name of their aged father, while her soft, dove-like eyes, sparkled with the rays of hope.

"We are saved! We are saved!" she murmured, "to return to the arms of our dear, dear father, and his heart will not be broken with grief. And you, too, Cora, my sister, my more than sister, my mother; you, too, are spared. And Duncan," she added, looking round upon the youth with a smile of ineffable innocence, "even our own brave and noble Duncan has escaped without a hurt."

To these ardent and nearly innocent words Cora made no other answer than by straining the youthful speaker to her heart, as she bent over her in melting tenderness.

The manhood of Heyward felt no shame in dropping tears over this spectacle of affectionate rapture; and Uncas stood, fresh and blood-stained from the combat, a calm, and, apparently, an unmoved looker-on, it is true, but with eyes that had already lost their fierceness, and were beaming with a sympathy that elevated him far above the intelligence, and advanced him probably centuries before, the practices of his nation.

During this display of emotions so natural in their situation, Hawkeye, whose vigilant distrust had satisfied itself that the Hurons, who disfigured the heavenly scene, no longer possessed the power to interrupt its harmony, approached David[1], and liberated him from the bonds he had, until that moment, endured with the most exemplary patience.

William Cullen Bryant (1794–1878)

William Cullen Bryant was a Romantic poet in his passion for American wilderness and for a culturally independent America. But if Bryant was a Romantic in his attitude he was neoclassical in form.

William Cullen Bryant was born into the farming society in Cummington, Massachusetts. After one year at Williams College, he hoped to transfer to Yale, but a talk with his father made him realize that the family could not afford it. Instead, his father suggested a decent career as his best choice, so the disappointed poet began to study law and began to practice law in 1815 in nearby Plainfield, walking seven miles from Cummington every day. On one of these walks, he caught sight of a bird flying on the horizon and was inspired to write "To a Waterfowl" (1818).

Bryant was brought up in a family with two cultures and philosophies. On the one hand, there was his mother and her father. Bryant's maternal grandfather was a federalist in politics and an extreme Calvinist in religion. As head of the house and squire in the town, he was in the position to carry harsh justice. He believed thrift and industry to be main duties of man. And he would beat Bryant if Bryant was not speedy enough in the field. On the other hand, Bryant's father, Peter Bryant, was a doctor and a well-educated person. In addition to his medical practice and public service, Peter also wrote verse in the manner of Pope. His library included poems of the late-18th-century Romantic poets. The duality within the family explains in part why Bryant grew up a federalist and Calvinist but gradually became a Democrat and a Romanticist.

In addition to his poetic works, Bryant also established a reputation as an editor of journalism like the *New York Evening Post*. He promoted liberal causes such as free speech, free trade and the abolition of slavery. As one of the exponents of Abraham Lincoln, he introduced Lincoln at Cooper Union in 1860. In fact, it was the "Cooper Union speech" that lifted Lincoln to the nomination, and then the presidency. In his last decade, Bryant offered his translation of the

---

Note [1] David: David Gamut

Iliad and the *Odyssey* into English blank verse.

Among Bryant's works, "Thanatopsis"[1] (1817) exposes Bryant's talent to the public and "To a Waterfowl" is considered the finest. Bryant was an early advocate of American literary nationalism, and his own poetry focusing on nature as a metaphor for truth established a central pattern in the American literary tradition.

Bryant was also one of the early literary critics in America. He argued that ethical beauty should be emphasized in a poem. Nature can serve as a means of bodying forth idea. Diction should be selected to obtain suggestiveness and elevation.

Selected Reading

To a Waterfowl

In "To a Waterfowl," Bryant is convinced that just as God guides the waterfowl to its summer home, so too He guides the speaker of the poem through life to his ultimate destination, heaven. The poem is, in essence, a profession of faith in God.

To a Waterfowl

Whither[2], midst falling dew,
While glow the heavens with the last steps of day,
Far, through their rosy depths, dost thou pursue
Thy solitary way?

Vainly the fowler's[3] eye
Might mark thy distant flight to do thee wrong,
As, darkly seen against the crimson sky,
Thy figure floats along.

Seek'st thou the plashy[4] brink
Of weedy lake, or marge of river wide,
Or where the rocking billows rise and sink

Note [1] "Thanatopsis": Greek, meaning "view of death"
Note [2] Whither: Where
Note [3] fowler's: hunter's
Note [4] plashy: marshy, wet, having many puddles

On the chafed[1] ocean-side?

There is a Power[2] whose care
Teaches thy way along that pathless coast—
The desert and illimitable air—
Lone wandering, but not lost.

All day thy wings have fanned,
At that far height, the cold, thin atmosphere,
Yet stoop not, weary, to the welcome land,
Though the dark night is near.

And soon that toil shall end;
Soon shalt thou find a summer home, and rest,
And scream among thy fellows; reeds[3] shall bend,
Soon, o'er thy sheltered nest.

Thou'rt gone, the abyss of heaven
Hath swallowed up thy form; yet, on my heart
Deeply hath sunk the lesson thou hast given,
And shall not soon depart.

He[4] who, from zone to zone,
Guides through the boundless sky thy certain flight,
In the long way that I must tread alone,
Will lead my steps aright.

Summit of Romanticism—Transcendentalism

Transcendental Club In 1836 an informal group met in Concord, Massachusetts, to discuss theology, philosophy and literature. At first they called themselves the Symposium of Hedge Club, since it was Henry Hedge who helped initiate the meetings. But good-intentioned

Note [1] chafed: worn away by the sea
Note [2] Power: God
Note [3] reeds: tall grasses in marshland
Note [4] He: God

neighbors began to call the group members Transcendentalists since they were always engaged in lofty discourses. The group accepted the name and published a journal, *The Dial*. Emerson was ultimately the most representative transcendentalist, but William Channing was the one who had planted the seeds before him.

Channing was a Unitarian minister who proposed that human nature is potentially good, even godly. During a sermon delivered in Baltimore in 1819, Channing launched his ideas. At the heart of his belief is that human genius, if it is informed and unfettered, is the strongest moral and creative force. In other words, humans define God. This idea of Original Good seriously challenged the Puritan belief in Original Sin. Indeed, dissidents within the Puritans had already justified Original Good before Channing. It's more accurate to say that Channing voiced an idea that had already had a tradition. But it was he who made it so easily understandable. With this good news, Channing became one more voice in preserving and shaping the American mind.

Apart from the publication of *The Dial*, the transcendentalists established Brook Farm in 1841, a utopian community in which individuals were supposed to be better enabled towards self-realization. However, the experiment failed in 1847.

Transcendentalism   The phase of New England Transcendentalism is the summit of American Romanticism. It was a broad, philosophical movement in New England during the Romantic era peaking between 1835 and 1845. It stressed the role of divinity in nature and individual intuition, and exalted feelings over reason. It was, in essence, Romanticism on Puritan soil. Basically, transcendentalism has been defined philosophically as "the recognition in man of the capacity of knowing truth intuitively, or of attaining knowledge transcending the reach of the senses." Translated into literature, this belief became an emphasis on symbolic representation. Other concepts that accompanied transcendentalism include the idea that nature is ennobling and that the individual is divine and, therefore, self-reliant.

To have a full appreciation of American transcendentalism, it is necessary to identify its main sources. The Romantic idealism, as transcendentalism has come to be called, can be said to have begun with the introduction of idealistic philosophy from Germany and France. The idealistic concepts of Schelling and Fichte as well as of Kant have found their way to America. *Critique of Pure Reason* (1781) suggests that traditional metaphysics can be reformed through epistemology, as we can face metaphysical problems fruitfully by understanding the sources and limits of knowledge. Thus German Romanticism emphasized intuition as a means of piercing to the real essence of things. Neo-Platonism also contributed to the development of American transcendentalism. Neo-Platonism believes that spirit prevails over matter and that there is an ascending scale of spiritual values rising to absolute Good. In addition, Eastern mysticism, such as that by Confucius exerted great influence on the American Romanticism.

The transcendentalists placed emphasis on spirit, or the Oversoul, as the most important thing in the universe. The Oversoul, was an all-pervading power for goodness, omnipresent and omnipotent, from which all things came and of which all were a part. It existed in nature and man alike and constituted the chief element of the universe. Now this, obviously, represented a new way of looking at the world. It was apparently a reaction to the Newtonian concept of the universe. In the 18th century, it was generally held that the world was made up of matter. It was also a reaction against the direction that a mechanized, capitalist America was taking, against the popular tendency to get ahead in world affairs to the neglect of spiritual welfare.

Transcendentalism stressed the importance of the individual. To the transcendentalists the individual was the most important element of society. As the regeneration of society could only come about through the regeneration of the individual. So his perfection, his self-culture and self-improvement should become the first concern of his life. The ideal type of man was the self-reliant individual whom Emerson never stopped talking about all his life. To him, the individual soul communed with the Oversoul and was divine. Now this new notion of the individual and his importance represented, obviously, a new way of looking at man. It was a reaction against the Calvinist concept that man is totally depraved, sinful and can not hope to be saved except through the grace of God. It was also a reaction against the process of dehumanization which came in the wake of developing capitalism. The industrialization of New England was turning men into nonhumans. People were losing their individuality and were becoming uniform. The transcendentalists reasserted the importance of the individual and emphasized the significance of men regaining their lost personality.

The transcendentalists offered a fresh perception of nature as the symbol of the Spirit of God. Nature was, to them, not purely matter. It was alive, filled with God's overwhelming presence. It was the garment of the Oversoul. Therefore, it could exercise a healthy and restorative influence on the human mind. Besides, the physical world was a symbol of the spiritual. This in turn added to the tradition of literary symbolism in American literature.

Ralph Waldo Emerson (1803–1882)

Ralph Waldo Emerson, responsible for bringing transcendentalism to New England, was recognized throughout his life as the leader of the movement. Emersonian transcendentalism is actually a philosophical school which absorbed some ideological concerns of American Puritanism and European Romanticism, with its focus on the intuitive knowledge of human beings to grasp the absolute in the universe and the divinity of man.

Ralph Waldo Emerson was born in a family of a clergyman in Boston. He graduated from Harvard, where the liberal atmosphere of the college made him reconsider his Calvinist belief with which he was brought up. Rejecting the Calvinist tenets, he embraced the liberal Christianity of Unitarianism. Now Unitarianism was more rational and logical, occupying as it did a sort of middle ground between extremes. Its principles, on which most people agreed, included the fatherhood of God, the brotherhood of men, the leadership of Jesus, salvation by character, and continual progress of mankind. It was an obvious improvement on Calvinism which never accepted the prospect of man's perfectibility. After graduation, he became pastor of the Second Church of Boston in 1829. He resigned this position two years later when he found the rationality of Unitarianism intolerable. Then he traveled to Europe, spending most of his time in Italy and England, where he met many of the important writers of his time like Coleridge and Wordsworth. On his return to America, Emerson brought back with himself the influence of European Romanticism and retreated to a quiet study at Concord, Massachusetts, where he began to pursue his new path of "self-reliance." Then he formed a club with people like Henry Thoreau, which was later known as the Transcendental Club. And the unofficial manifesto for the Club was *Nature* (1836), his first little book. He also helped to found and edit for a time the transcendental journal, *The Dial*. Being active in spreading his ideas, Emerson later embarked on a series of lecture tours in England and America.

Emerson is generally known as an essayist with the publication of *Essays* (1841) and *Essays: Second Series* (1844). *Nature*, Emerson's first book, has been called "the Manifesto of American Transcendentalism" and is generally regarded as the Bible of New England transcendentalism. He is also famous for his other essays and lectures, such as "The American Scholar," "Divinity School Address" and "Self-Reliance." "The American Scholar" has been regarded as America's "intellectual Declaration of Independence." In the speech Emerson particularly warned that the past should be used to inspire and not to enslave the scholar. He argued that the age called to the Scholar for active participation and leadership, which further emphasized the importance of the individual. "Divinity School Address" was another speech delivered at the request of some graduates of the Harvard Divinity School and it caused what a scholar later called a "Tempest in a Boston Tea Cup." Emerson asserted the divinity of all men, thus treating Christ too as a human. As it was also conspicuous in an address for the Divinity School, Emerson did not quote or discuss the Bible, used no prayer, and denied the truth of miracles as taught by the church. What Emerson emphasized as being divine is the majesty of the individual soul, a theme consistent in all his writings. This address' insistence on the importance of Intuition also refutes the Church's authority in asserting or communicating "truth." In his essay "Self-Reliance," Emerson proposed the idea of "Trust thyself" and argued that every individual possesses a unique genius that can only be revealed when that individual has the courage to trust his own thoughts, attitudes and inclinations regardless of all public disapproval.

Philosophy

Oversoul   Emerson stated in *Nature*, "The universe is composed of Nature and the soul." He emphasized the need for idealism, for idealism sees the world in God. To him, there is a moment of "conversion" when one feels completely merged with the outside world, and when the soul has gone beyond the physical limits of the body to share the omniscience of the Oversoul. In a word, the soul has completely transcended the limits of individuality and become part of the Oversoul. He further argued that "there is one mind common to all individual men." That is to say, man is made in the image of God and is just a little less than Him. This is as much as to say that man is divine.

Individual Emerson believed in the infinite potential of the individual. To him, the individual is the most important of all. If man depends on himself, cultivates himself and brings out the divine in himself, he can hope to become better and even perfect. This is what he means by "the infinitude of man." In all his lectures, he tried to convince people that the possibilities for men to develop and improve himself are infinite. Men should and could be self-reliant. Each man should feel the world as his, and the world exists for him alone. He should determine his own existence. Everyone should understand that he makes himself by making his world, and that he makes the world by making himself. Consequently, the regeneration of the individual will lead to the regeneration of the society.

Nature Nature is, to him as to his Puritan forebears, emblematic of God. It meditates between man and God, and its voice leads to higher truth. In a word, "nature is the symbol of spirit." A natural implication of Emerson's view on nature is that the world around is symbolic. A flowing river indicates the ceaseless motion of the universe. The seasons correspond to the life span of man.

Emerson's philosophical discussion is sometimes difficult to understand, but he uses vivid comparisons and metaphors to make the general idea of his work clearly expressed.

Selected Reading

Nature

Nature, widely seen as a defining text of transcendentalism, consists of an introduction and eight brief chapters: Nature, Commodity, Beauty, Language, Discipline, Idealism, Spirit and Prospects. Each part takes a different perspective on the relationship between humans and nature.

In the book, Emerson employs the "transparent eye-ball" to describe the loss of individuation, where man feels "I am nothing; I see all." This immersion in nature provides the direct religious experience that Emerson was to call for all his life.

An Excerpt from Chapter 1

To speak truly, few adult persons can see nature. Most persons do not see the sun. At least they have a very superficial seeing. The sun illuminates only the eye of the man, but shines into the eye and the heart of the child. The lover of nature is he whose inward and outward senses are still truly adjusted to each other; who has retained the spirit of infancy even into the era of manhood. His intercourse with heaven and earth, becomes part of his daily food. In the presence of nature, a wild delight runs through the man, in spite of real sorrows. Nature says, —he is my creature, and maugre[1] all his impertinent griefs, he shall be glad with me. Not the sun or the summer alone, but every hour and season yields its tribute of delight; for every hour and change corresponds to and authorizes a different state of the mind, from breathless noon to grimmest midnight. Nature is a setting that fits equally well a comic or a mourning piece. In good health, the air is a cordial of incredible virtue. Crossing a bare common, in snow puddles, at twilight, under a clouded sky, without having in my thoughts any occurrence of special good fortune, I have enjoyed a perfect exhilaration. I am glad to the brink of fear. In the woods too, a man casts off his years, as the snake his slough, and at what period soever of life, is always a child. In the woods, is perpetual youth. Within these plantations of God, a decorum and sanctity reign, a perennial festival is dressed, and the guest sees not how he should tire of them in a thousand years. In the woods, we return to reason and faith. There I feel that nothing can befall me in life, —no disgrace, no calamity, (leaving me my eyes,) which nature cannot repair. Standing on the bare ground, —my head bathed by the blithe air, and uplifted into infinite space, —all mean egotism vanishes. I become a transparent eye-ball[2]; I am nothing; I see all; the currents of the Universal Being circulate through me; I am part or particle of God. The name of the nearest friend sounds then foreign and accidental: to be brothers, to be acquaintances, —master or servant, is then a trifle and a disturbance. I am the lover of uncontained and immortal beauty. In the wilderness, I find something more dear and connate[3] than in streets or villages. In the tranquil landscape, and especially in the distant line of the horizon, man beholds somewhat as beautiful as his own nature.

Note [1] maugre: in spite of

Note [2] I become a transparent eye-ball: This remarkable image, satirized in Emerson's time and learnedly explicated in ours, characterizes the paradoxical state of being in which one is merged into nature (or "Universal Being") even while retaining a unique perception of the experience.

Note [3] connate: related

Henry David Thoreau (1817–1862)

Henry David Thoreau, another renowned New England Transcendentalist, is Emerson's disciple and friend. He is known for putting transcendentalism into practice in person.

Henry David Thoreau was born in Concord, Massachusetts. His maternal grandfather was once involved in Harvard's 1766 student "Butter Rebellion." His father was an unsuccessful storekeeper and a maker of lead pencils, but his mother was an aspiring woman, determined to send her son to college. So she did. Thoreau went to Harvard, but did not like the life and the curriculum of the college. After graduation he stayed with his family, first helping his father to make pencils and then for a time running a private school. Thoreau made friends with Emerson, used his library, and embraced his ideas. In 1845 Thoreau built a cabin on some land belonging to Emerson by Walden Pond and moved in to live there in a very simple manner for a little over two years, which gave birth to a great transcendentalist work, *Walden* (1854).

During his stay in Walden, he went back occasionally to his village, and on one of these visits he was detained for a night in jail for refusing to pay a tax of two dollars only to protect against the Mexican War. The event was insignificant enough, since he was, in fact, soon set free after his aunt paid the sum for him. But it inspired him to write his famous essay, "Civil Disobedience" (1849), advocating passive resistance to unjust laws of society, which influenced people such as Mahatma Gandhi. In the 20th century, Gandhi based his doctrine of passive resistance chiefly on Thoreau's "Civil Disobedience." In return, the doctrine influenced Martin Luther King, who put forward the idea of non-violence protest.

Walden can be read on more than one level. But it is, first and foremost, a book on self-culture and human perfectibility. It is a book about man, what he is, and what he should be and must be. To achieve personal spiritual perfection, Thoreau thinks, the most important thing for man to do with his life is to be self-sufficient, so Thoreau sought to reduce his physical needs and material comforts to a minimum to get spiritual richness. It can also be observed in the book that Thoreau was very critical of modern civilization. It was in his opinion, degrading and enslaving man. "Civilized man is the slave of matter," he said on one occasion. He felt that humans should seek truth directly by themselves and not through imitation of others. And the best way to find truth is by leaving the life of hurry and bustle to get ahead in worldly affairs and sinking oneself in the wholesome atmosphere of nature. As he saw it, modern civilized life had dehumanized man and placed man in a spiritual quandary: By trying to amass material possessions, man is not really living; he is digging his own grave. Thoreau despised and pitied his fellow villagers and wished to be a chanticleer to wake them up from their spiritual slumbers and help make them into a new generation of men. Hence the book is full of people waking up: As a matter of fact, he woke up several times himself in the book. Therefore, the book not only fully demonstrates Emersonian ideas of self-reliance but also develops and tests Thoreau's own transcendental philosophy.

Thoreau's writing is full of heightened passion and living energy. But his enthusiasm is balanced by a sense of wit, humor and irony.

Selected Reading

Walden
An Excerpt from Where I lived, and What I Lived For

We must learn to reawaken and keep ourselves awake, not by mechanical aids, but by an infinite expectation of the dawn, which does not forsake us in our soundest sleep. I know of no more encouraging fact than the unquestionable ability of man to elevate his life by a conscious endeavor. It is something to be able to paint a particular picture, or to carve a statue, and so to make a few objects beautiful; but it is far more glorious to carve and paint the very atmosphere and medium through which we look, which morally we can do. To affect the quality of the day, that is the highest of arts. Every man is tasked to make his life, even in its details, worthy of the contemplation of his most elevated and critical hour. If we refused, or rather used up, such paltry information as we get, the oracles would distinctly inform us how this might be done.

I went to the woods because I wished to live deliberately, to front only the essential facts of life, and see if I could not learn what it had to teach, and not, when I came to die, discover that I had not lived. I did not wish to live what was not life, living is so dear; nor did I wish to practise resignation, unless it was quite necessary. I wanted to live deep and suck out all the marrow of life, to live so sturdily and Spartan-like as to put to rout all that was not life, to cut a broad swath and shave close, to drive life into a corner, and reduce it to its lowest terms, and, if it proved to be mean, why then to get the whole and genuine meanness of it, and publish its meanness to the world; or if it were sublime, to know it by experience, and be able to give a true account of it in my next excursion. For most men, it appears to me, are in a strange uncertainty about it, whether it is of the devil or of God, and have somewhat hastily concluded that it is the chief end of man here to "glorify God and enjoy him forever."[1]

Edgar Allan Poe (1809–1849)

Edgar Allan Poe was not associated with transcendentalism or any other noticeable-isms of his age, although his influence would be more recognized in Europe than that of any other

---

Note [1] "glorify God and enjoy him forever": from the Shorter Catechism in *The New England Primer*

American writer in his time. Poe, a critic, poet and short story writer, achieved a lot in these three aspects. His contribution to French symbolist poetry was made not primarily through his poetry but his stories and criticism.

Edgar Allan Poe was born in Boston, a child of struggling traveling actors. Both of his parents died within two years after his birth. Then Poe was taken into the home of John Allan, a rich merchant, whose name Poe later added to his own. Poe entered the University of Virginia, but left a short time later because he would not enter the profession of law as Allan wished. After a brief enlistment in the army, Poe accepted an appointment to West Point. Poe was dismissed because of misbehavior less than a year later. The episode marked the final break between Poe and the Allans.

For a time he lived in Baltimore with his father's sister and her daughter Virginia Clemm. He had published two volumes of poems, but had made no money and little reputation from them. He finally got a job as an editor. Confident of a secure position and steady income, Poe then married his young cousin, Virginia Clemm in 1935.

Later in his post on the *Messenger*, Poe showed his true talents as an editor, a poet, a literary critic and a writer of fiction. He remained for over two years, improving the magazine and building its circulation. Then he quit suddenly in 1837. With his family he set out to try his luck in New York and Philadelphia.

For several years he drifted and worked as an editor at various times of different magazines and newspapers. The years from 1837 to 1845 were hard, yet in spite of shifting jobs and chronic poverty, Poe managed to write some of his most famous stories during this period. His first collection of short stories, *Tales of the Grotesque and Arabesque*, came out in 1840. "The Raven" was published in 1845 as the title poem of a collection. Through his essays and reviews, Poe had also gained stature as literary critic. Yet none of his successes brought him security. Misfortune spoiled every opportunity and frustrated his dream of starting his own magazine.

Ironically, while Poe was struggling in America, his work was commanding more and more praise in Europe, where he was hailed as a pioneer in poetic and fictional techniques. His influence was especially strong on many French writers. In spite of his European fame, poverty remained his typical condition. After an agonizingly slow decline, his young wife Virginia died of tuberculosis in 1847. Two years later, at forty, Poe himself died.

Poems　In poetry, Poe is a master of moods. He conveys a mood through internal and external rhymes, regular rhythms, carefully chosen onomatopoeia and subtle suggestiveness. Poe's poetry seems to illustrate this belief: If the end of poetry is the contemplation of the beautiful, then the best manifestation of beauty is associated with sadness. Typically, the subject matter is the death of a beautiful woman. "To Helen" expresses Poe's grief at the death of Mrs. Jane Stanard. "Annabel Lee" is another poem about the loss of a beautiful woman. Love and death are the two major themes in Poe's poems and the two are often combined. In many cases the love in his poems is full of sorrow and melancholy, and is shadowed by death. "Annabel Lee" is a representative poem of this kind.

Poetic Principles   Poe's poetic theories are best elucidated in his "The Philosophy of Composition" (1846) and "The Poetic Principle" (1850). The poem, he says, should be short, readable at one sitting. Its chief aim is beauty, that is to say, to produce a feeling of beauty in the reader. Beauty aims at "an elevating excitement of the soul," and "beauty of whatever kind, in its supreme development, invariably excites the sensitive soul to tears. Thus, melancholy is the most legitimate of all the poetic tones." And he concludes that "the death of a beautiful woman is, unquestionably, the most poetical topic in the world." Poe is opposed to "the heresy of the didactic" and calls for "pure" poetry. What he seems to be is this: the artistry of the poem lies not in what is being said but in the way it is said. This emphasis on the poem's own integrity allows people to associate Poe with the school of "art for art's sake" and to regard him as a precursor to the school of New Criticism in the 20th-century America.

Short Stories   Poe, together with Hawthorne, modernized American short stories. Poe's stories are not just Gothic tales but they show, through carefully crafted symbols, complex characters in deep psychological states. The symbols are rays of light that Poe casts on those hidden, deep recessed of the human mind. Often, the stories gain added complexity and sophistication because of Poe's use of complex narrators. "The fall of the House of Usher" is narrated by someone who is likely to be dreaming since he tries to shake "of what must have been a dream." Due to his unique contribution to American literature, Poe is regarded as the father of detective short stories.

Selected Reading

To Helen[1]

Edgar Allan Poe wrote "To Helen" as a reflection on the beauty of Mrs. Jane Stanard, of Richmond, Va., who died in 1824. She was the mother of one of Poe's school classmates, Robert Stanard. When Robert invited Poe, then 14, to his home in 1823, Poe was greatly taken with the 27-year-old woman, who is said to have urged him to write poetry. He was later to write that she was his first real love.

In this poem, Beauty appears to refer to both soul and body. On the one hand, he represents her as Helen of Troy, the quintessence of physical beauty, at the beginning of the poem. On the other, he represents her as Psyche, the quintessence of soulful beauty, at the end of the poem. In Greek, *psyche* means *soul*.

Note [1] Helen: an allusion to Helen of Troy in Greek mythology

To Helen

Helen, thy beauty is to me
Like those Nicean[1] barks[2] of yore,
That gently, o'er a perfumed sea,
The weary, way-worn wanderer bore
To his own native shore.

On desperate seas long wont[3] to roam,
Thy hyacinth hair, thy classic face,
Thy Naiad[4] airs have brought me home
To the glory that was Greece.
And the grandeur that was Rome.

Lo! In yon brilliant window-niche
How statue-like I see thee stand!
The agate lamp within thy hand,
Ah! Psyche[5] from the regions which
Are Holy Land!

Annabel Lee

It is interpreted that "Annabel Lee" was written for Poe's wife Virginia Clemm, who had died two years prior. Virginia was the one he loved as a child, and the only one that had been his bride. In addition, Virginia and Poe never consummated their marriage, as "Annabel Lee" was a "maiden."

In the poem Annabel Lee was a very beautiful and innocent girl. Love was everything for her and her only wish was to love and to be loved. The boy and Lee loved each other so deeply even the angels in heaven were envying them. So a wind came out of the cloud

---

Note [1] Nicean: of or from Nicea (also spelled Nicaea), a city in ancient Bithynia (now part of present-day Turkey) near the site of the Trojan War

Note [2] barks: small sailing vessels

Note [3] wont: accustomed to

Note [4] Naiad: nymphlike, fairylike

Note [5] Psyche: goddess of soul. In Greek and Roman mythology, Psyche was a beautiful princess dear to the god of love, Eros (Cupid).

by night, chilling and killing her. She was buried in a tomb by the sea. The boy, full of sorrow and regret, missed her very much. Whenever he saw the moonlight, he thought of the beautiful face of Annabel Lee; whenever he saw the stars in the sky, he dreamt of the bright eyes of Annabel Lee. He believed their souls would remain together forever.

Annabel Lee

It was many and many a year ago,
In a kingdom by the sea,
That a maiden there lived whom you may know
By the name of ANNABEL LEE;
And this maiden she lived with no other thought
Than to love and be loved by me.

I was a child and she was a child,
In this kingdom by the sea;
But we loved with a love that was more than love—
I and my Annabel Lee—
With a love that the winged seraphs of heaven
Coveted her and me.

And this was the reason that, long ago,
In this kingdom by the sea,
A wind blew out of a cloud, chilling
My beautiful Annabel Lee;
So that her highborn kinsman came
And bore her away from me,
To shut her up in a sepulcher
In this kingdom by the sea.

The angels, not half so happy in heaven,
Went envying her and me—
Yes! —that was the reason (as all men know,
In this kingdom by the sea)
That the wind came out of the cloud by night,
Chilling and killing my Annabel Lee.

But our love it was stronger by far than the love

Of those who were older than we—

Of many far wiser than we—

And neither the angels in heaven above,

Nor the demons down under the sea,

Can ever dissever my soul from the soul

Of the beautiful ANNABEL LEE.

For the moon never beams without bringing me dreams

Of the beautiful Annabel Lee;

And the stars never rise but I feel the bright eyes

Of the beautiful ANNABEL LEE;

And so, all the night-tide, I lie down by the side

Of my darling—my darling—my life and my bride,

In the sepulcher there by the sea—

In her tomb by the sounding sea.

Nathaniel Hawthorne (1804–1864)

Nathaniel Hawthorne, an American novelist and short story writer, is known for his writings set in New England. His fiction works are considered part of the Romantic Movement and, more specifically, dark Romanticism.

Nathaniel Hawthorne was born in Salem, Massachusetts into a prominent Puritan family. His first American ancestor, William Hathorne, as a magistrate of the Bay Colony, was active in the persecution of the Quakers in the 1650s, while William's son, John Hathorne, served as one of the judges in the Salem Witchcraft Trials of 1692. To distinguish himself from his ancestors, Nathaniel added a "w" to make his name "Hawthorne." Anyway, the 17th-century prominence of his family declined during the century that followed. His father, Nathaniel Hathorne, Sr., was a sea captain and died of yellow fever when the young Nathaniel was four years old. Then his mother withdrew to a life of seclusion, which she maintained till her death. From Salem the family moved to Maine, where Hawthorne was educated at the Bowdoin College from 1821 to 1824, where he befriended Longfellow and Franklin Pierce. In the following years, Hawthorne lived in solitude and seclusion. He read widely, became further acquainted with local history and began to practice writing. His first attempt at novel writing, a book about his school life, proved to be a failure. The year of 1837 saw the publication of his *Twice-Told Tales*, a collection of short stories, which enjoyed critical attention.

After 1837, a series of salient events happened to Hawthorne, which mattered a lot to his literary imagination and creation. He met and married Sophia Peabody; he worked in the United

States Custom House in Boston and later in Salem, and joined Brook Farm, a transcendentalist community, which provided some authentic materials for his long works; he also stayed for some time at Concord and Lenox, where he met the principal literary figures of the time, Emerson and Thoreau and Melville. He was affected by the two transcendentalists and struck up a very intimate relationship with Melville, and all the three people had played an indispensable role in Hawthorne's literary career. During this period, Hawthorne wrote and published the best and the greatest of his works, including another collection of short stories *Mosses from an Old Manse* (1846) and his four major romances.

In 1853 Franklin Pierce became President and Hawthorne was appointed as a consul in Liverpool, England. Hawthorne died on a trip to the mountains with his friend Franklin Pierce. His son Julian was convicted of defrauding the public in 1912.

Hawthorne was predominantly a short story writer in his early career. Later, he proved to be good at novels. His four major romances[1] were written between the 1850s and the 1860s: *The Scarlet Letter* (1850), *The House of the Seven Gables* (1851), *The Blithedale Romance* (1852) and *The Marble Faun* (1860). Another novel-length romance, *Fanshawe*, was published anonymously in 1828. In *The Scarlet Letter*, Hawthorne does not intend to tell a love story nor a story of sin, but focuses his attention on the moral, emotional and psychological effects of consequences of sin on the people in general and those main characters in particular, so as to show the tension between society and individuals. The true value of the novel lies in the character of Hester and in its appealingness and truthfulness in reflecting and denouncing the world where Hester lived. The heroine embodies the original American dream of a new life in the wilderness of the new world, and of self-reliant action to realize that ideal.

Setting—Puritan New England   Hawthorne's view of man and human history originates, to a great extent, from Puritanism. He was not a Puritan himself, but he had Puritan ancestors who played an important role in his life and his works. He believed that "the wrong doing of one generation lives into the successive one," and often wondered if he might have inherited some of their guilt. This sensibility led to his understanding of evil being at the core of human life, which is typical of the Calvinistic belief that human beings are basically depraved and corrupted, hence, they should obey God to atone for their sins. In many of Hawthorne's stories and novels, the Puritan concept of life is condemned, or the Puritan past is shown in an almost totally negative light, especially in his *The House of the Seven Gables* and *The Scarlet Letter*.

Note [1] romances: Hawthorne defines a romance as being radically different from a novel by not being concerned with the possible or probable course of ordinary experience. In the preface to *The House of the Seven Gables*, his romance-writing is further described as using "atmospherical medium as to bring out or mellow the lights and deepen and enrich the shadows of the picture."

Themes—Evil and Sin, and Psychological Themes Hawthorne's works belong to dark Romanticism, cautionary tales that suggest that guilt, sin and evil are the most inherent natural qualities of humanity. Many of his works are inspired by Puritan New England, combining historical romance loaded with symbolism and deep psychological themes, bordering on surrealism. His depictions of the past are a version of historical fiction used only as a vehicle to express common themes of ancestral sin, guilt and retribution. His later writings also reflect his negative view of transcendentalism.

Hawthorne's literary world turns out to be the most disturbed, tormented and problematical. This has much to do with his "black" vision of life and human beings. According to Hawthorne, "There is evil in every human heart, which may remain latent, perhaps, through the whole life; but circumstances may rouse it to activity." So in almost every book he wrote, Hawthorne discusses sin and evil. In "Young Goodman Brown," he sets out to prove that everyone possesses some evil secret. "The Minister's Black Veil" goes further to suggest that everyone tries to hold the evil secret from one another in the way the minister tries to convince his people with his black veil. "The Birthmark" drives home symbolically Hawthorne's point that evil is man's birthmark, something he is born with.

One source of evil that Hawthorne is concerned most is overreaching intellect, which usually refers to someone who is too proud, too sure of himself. The tension between the head and the heart constitutes one of the dramatic moments, when the evil of "overreaching intellect" would be fully revealed. Hawthorne's intellectuals are usually dreadful villains, because they are devoid of warmth and feeling. What's more, they tend to go beyond and violate the natural order by doing something impossible and reaching the ultimate truth, without a sober mind about their own limitations as human beings.

Technique—Symbolism and Allegory Hawthorne is a great allegorist and almost every story can be read allegorically, as is the case in "Young Goodman Brown." Whereas allegory is used to hold fast against the crushing blows of reality, the symbol serves as a weapon to attack and penetrate it. Hawthorne is a master of symbolism, which he took from the Puritan tradition and bequeathed to American literature in a revivified form. The symbol can be found everywhere in his writing, and his masterpiece provides the most conclusive proof. By using Pearl as a thematic symbol, Hawthorne emphasizes the consequence that the sin of adultery has brought to the community and people living in that community. With the scarlet letter "A" as the biggest symbol of all, Hawthorne proves himself to be one of the best symbolists. As a key to the whole novel, the letter "A" takes on different layers of symbolic meanings as the plot develops, such as "Adultery," "Able" and even "Angel."

The ambiguity is one of the salient characteristics of Hawthorne's art. His ambiguity seems to be intentional. Many of his stories show the interplay of light and dark, good and evil, but do not offer easy explanations or resolutions. Hawthorne seems to imply that polarities of good and bad can not always be reconciled. Hawthorne does not make his characters completely good or admirably just and neither does he allow any neat interpretations. However, in some odd moments Hawthorne would instill an ironic laughter or a surprising comment.

Selected Reading

The Scarlet Letter

In June 1642 in the Puritan town of Boston a crowd gathers to witness the punishment of Hester Prynne, a young woman found guilty of adultery. Wearing a scarlet "A" which stands for adulteress, on her dress, she is required to stand on the scaffold for three hours to be exposed to public humiliation. When demanded by Arthur Dimmesdale, the minister of Hester's church, to name the father of her child, Hester refuses to say anything about it.

As Hester looks out over the crowd, she catches sight of a deformed man and recognizes him as her husband, who has been thought to be lost at sea. Learning the story of his wife's adultery, he is so angry that he makes up his mind to find out the child's father.

After Hester returns to her prison cell, the jailer brings in Roger Chillingworth, her husband who now acts as a physician to calm down Hester and her child. When Hester refuses to tell Chillingworth who her lover is, he threatens her to hide his real identity. And thus Hester agrees to Chillingworth's request and becomes worried.

Following her release from prison, Hester settles in a cottage at the edge of town and earns a meager living with her needlework. She lives a quiet life with her daughter, Pearl. Now and then she is troubled by her daughter's unusual fascination with her scarlet "A." As she grows older, Pearl becomes capricious and unruly. Her behavior sparks rumors and the church members suggest that Pearl be taken away from Hester. Hearing this, Hester goes to speak to Governor Bellingham. With him are ministers Wilson and Dimmesdale. Hester appeals to Dimmesdale in desperation and the minister persuades the governor to leave Pearl with Hester.

Because Dimmesdale's health has begun to fail, the townspeople are happy to have Chillingworth, the newly arrived physician, take up lodgings with their beloved minister. Being in such close contact with Dimmesdale, Chillingworth begin to suspect that the minister's illness results from some unconfessed guilt. He applies psychological pressure to the minister because he suspects Dimmesdale to be Pearl's father. One evening, pulling the sleeping Dimmesdale's vestment aside, Chillingworth sees a symbol that represents his shame on the minister's pale chest.

On night, tormented by his guilty conscience, Dimmesdale goes to the square where Hester was punished years earlier. After a while Hester comes by with little Pearl. Climbing the scaffold, he admits his guilt to them. As the three stand together, Chillingworth watch them from the shadows. Hester, shocked by Dimmesdale's deterioration, decides to plead with her husband to spare the sick minister.

Several days later, Hester meets Dimmesdale in the forest and tells him of her husband and his desire for revenge. She convinces Dimmesdale to leave Boston in secret on a ship for Europe where they can start life anew. Renewed by this plan, the minister seems to gain some energy. On Election Day, Dimmesdale gives what is declared to be one of his most inspired sermons. But as the procession leaves the church, Dimmesdale climbs upon the scaffold and confesses his sin, dying in Hester's arms. Later, most witnesses swear that they see a stigma in the form of a scarlet "A" upon his chest, although some denies this statement. Chillingworth, losing his will for revenge, dies shortly thereafter and leaves Pearl a substantial inheritance.

Several years later, Hester returns to her cottage and resumes wearing the scarlet letter. When she dies, she is buried near the grave of Dimmesdale, and they share a simple slate tombstone engraved with an escutcheon described as: "On a field, sable, the letter A, gules" ("On a field, black, the letter A, red").

An Excerpt from Chapter V: Hester at Her Needle

It may seem marvellous that, with the world before her—kept by no restrictive clause of her condemnation within the limits of the Puritan settlement, so remote and so obscure—free to return to her birth-place, or to any other European land, and there hide her character and identity under a new exterior, as completely as if emerging into another state of being—and having also the passes of the dark, inscrutable forest open to her, where the wildness of her nature might assimilate itself with a people whose customs and life were alien from the law that had condemned her—it may seem marvellous that this woman should still call that place her home, where, and where only, she must needs be the type of shame. But there is a fatality, a feeling so irresistible and inevitable that it has the force of doom, which almost invariably compels human beings to linger around and haunt, ghost-like, the spot where some great and marked event has given the color to their lifetime; and, still the more irresistibly, the darker the tinge that saddens it. Her sin, her ignominy, were the roots which she had struck into the soil. It was as if a new birth, with stronger assimilations than the first, had converted the forest-land, still so uncongenial to every other pilgrim and wanderer, into Hester Prynne's wild and dreary, but life-long home. All other scenes of earth—even that village of rural England, where happy infancy and stainless maidenhood seemed yet to be in her mother's keeping, like garments put off long ago—were foreign to her, in comparison. The chain that bound her here was of iron links, and galling to her inmost soul, but could never be broken.

It might be, too—doubtless it was so, although she hid the secret from herself, and grew pale whenever it struggled out of her heart, like a serpent from its hole—it might be that another feeling kept her within the scene and pathway that had been so fatal. There dwelt, there trode, the feet of one with whom she deemed herself connected in a union that, unrecognized on earth, would bring them together before the bar of final judgment, and make that their marriage-altar, for a joint futurity of endless retribution. Over and over again, the tempter of souls had thrust this idea upon Hester's contemplation, and laughed at the passionate desperate joy with which she seized, and then strove to cast it from her. She barely looked the idea in the face, and hastened to bar it in its dungeon. What she compelled herself to believe—what, finally, she reasoned upon as her motive for continuing a resident of New England—was half a truth, and half a self-delusion. Here, she said to herself had been the scene of her guilt, and here should be the scene of her earthly punishment; and so, perchance, the torture of her daily shame would at length purge her soul, and work out another purity than that which she had lost: more saint-like, because the result of martyrdom.

Herman Melville (1819–1891)

Herman Melville, an American novelist, is best known for his masterpiece, *Moby-Dick* (1851).

Herman Melville was born in New York into a family of substantial means. Ancestrally, the family had been the Calvinist Melvilles of Boston and his maternal grandfather had served in the American Revolution. When Melville was eleven, his father suffered heavy financial losses and soon died from worry and illness. The death came as a shock because Melville idolized his father. The family moved to Albany where Melville attended Albany Academy for a while. Then his restlessness and his tension with his mother brought an end to his education, although he continued on his own to read avidly from his father's library.

In the following years, Melville grew up a displaced person in a world of alienating and harsh reality, drifting into various occupations: a store clerk, a bank messenger, a country schoolteacher. Finally, in 1839 he signed on a British merchant ship, the *St. Lawrence*, bound to Liverpool and back. This would become material for his novel *Redburn* (1849). When he returned from Liverpool, Melville tried teaching again. Then, in 1841 he signed on the whaler *Acushnet* as a sailor. Now a common sailor was about the lowest of all workers at that time, but Melville was not even that. He was a whaler, about the lowest of all sailors. In that case, he saw life from the bottom of the society as Mark Twain did. He went to Liverpool, England, and the South Pacific, spending most of his young manhood undergoing one of the most brutalizing experiences for a man. His experiences and adventures on the sea furnished him with abundant materials for fiction.

The married life of Melville was more like that of Scott. Fitzgerald than that of Mark Twain. These men all married above them, but only Mark Twain enjoyed the understanding of his wife. The other two had to do hackwork for money so as to keep their wives in their extravagant style. Melville married Elizabeth Shaw, the daughter of a wealthy judge. To support her and his growing family, he had to write for money, which was especially difficult for a devoted literary artist like him.

During the summer of 1850, Melville and Hawthorne met and became good friends. Melville read Hawthorne's books and was deeply impressed. Actually Hawthorne's *Mosses from an Old Manse* brought about great changes in the younger writer's outlook on life and on the world. Against the background of New England transcendental optimism concerning man and his world, Melville found Hawthorne's understanding of evil at the core of American life, that blackness of vision, unusually fascinating. Under the influence of Hawthorne, Melville changed the original design of *Moby Dick* and rewrote it into a world classic. Apart from Hawthorne, Shakespearean tragic vision and Emersonian transcendentalism also produced some positive effects on his writing.

Melville's writings can be divided into two groups, each with something in common in the light of the thematic concern and imaginative focus. His early works were written after he was back from the sea, chiefly between 1846 and 1852, when he was considered to be at his best. Books poured forth like a torrent. Among them are *Typee* (1846), *Omoo* (1847) and *Mardi* (1849), which drew from his adventures among the people of the South Pacific islands; *Redburn* is a semi-autobiographical novel, concerning the suffering of a genteel youth among brutal sailors; in *White Jacket* (1850) Melville relates his life on a United States man-of-war. Of all these sea adventure stories, *Moby-Dick* proves to be the best. By writing such a book Melville reached the most flourishing stage of his literary creativity.

With the publication of *Pierre* (1852), a popular romance which provoked an outrageous repudiation, Melville's public fame was on the decline. Later he wrote *The Confidence-Man* (1857), which intends to explore the paradox of belief and hypocrisy, and *Billy Budd* (1924), which focuses on the sea and the conflict between innocence and corruption. There is a slight difference between these works and the early ones. In the early works, Melville is more enthusiastic about setting out on a quest for the meaning of the universe, hence they are more metaphysical and the main characters are ardent and self-dramatizing "I," defying God, as best reflected in Moby-Dick;

while in the late works, he admits, one must live by the rules. However, the purpose of Melville's fictional tales, exotic or philosophical, is to penetrate as deeply as possible into the metaphysical, theological, moral, psychological and social truths of human existence.

In his lifetime, Melville strongly held the Calvinistic doctrine: Man is evil-natured and human existence is a dark necessity that the man can not control. He also had a pessimistic view on man's quest for truth in the universe: This quest would invariably end in a terrifying nothingness.

One of the major themes in Melville is alienation, which he felt on different levels, between man and man, man and society, and man and nature. Captain Ahab seems to be the best illustration of it all. He cuts himself off from his wife and kid, and stays away most of the time from his crew, and he hates Moby Dick which is an embodiment of mature. He is angry because his pride is wounded. After the loss of his leg in his encounter with the white whale, he seems to hold God responsible for the presence of evil in the universe. Thus his anger assumes the proportions of a cosmic nature. He is bent on avenging himself. He hears of no objection.

A common theme with mid-19th-century authors like Cooper, Hawthorne and Melville is one of "rejection and quest," quest as a desire born out of the wish to reject. The heroes in Melville's works are forever found trying to escape from their corrupt world into a better place to live, or what he calls "another world." Ishmael, the narrator in *Moby-Dick*, resembles his namesake in the Bible in that he is a wanderer. He starts to feel bad, hoping to find a place where he can live a happy and ideal life. An escapist as he is, the voyage on *Pequod* proves to be a journey in quest of knowledge and values.

The theme of gender and sexuality appears to be fascinating, too, in Melville's works. Melville's male characters are the classic wanderers who struggle against odds and are caught in the harsh reality. Indeed, his world is the single-sex world, all males without females. But his male characters are androgynous, exhibiting both masculine and feminine qualities. The feminine in man, so to speak, is often shown as tenderness and compassion.

Moby-Dick is regarded as the first American prose epic. It turns out to be a symbolic voyage of the mind in quest of the truth and knowledge of the universe, a spiritual exploration into man's deep reality and psychology. Like Hawthorne, Melville is a master of allegory and symbolism, which is best exemplified in *Moby-Dick*. The *Pequod* is the microcosm of human society and the voyage becomes a search for truth. The white whale, Moby-Dick, stands for nature for Melville, for it is complex, unfathomable, malicious and beautiful as well. Moby-Dick is like a wall, hiding some unknown, mysterious things behind. Ahab wills the whole crew on the *Pequod* to join him in the pursuit of the big whale so as to pierce the wall, to root out the evil, but only to be destroyed by evil, in this case, by his own consuming desire, his madness. For the author, as well as for the reader and Ishmael, the narrator, Moby-Dick is still a mystery, an ultimate mystery of the universe, inscrutable and ambivalent and the voyage of the mind will forever remain a search, not a discovery, of the truth.

Symbolism is not the only way in which Melville has shaped and articulated the mighty theme of the book, others techniques are also employed to make *Moby-Dick* a world classic, such as the skillful use of Ishmael both as a character and a narrator. Moreover, his understanding of epic and tragedy is woven into it to present a great tragic epic, with Ahab as a tragic hero.

Selected Reading

Moby-Dick

Ishmael, the narrator of the story, feels like going to sea whenever depressed. At the Spouter Inn in New Bedford, he is first frightened but soon befriends Queequeg, who has been out selling shrunken heads. After a service at the Whaleman's Chapel, Queequeg and Ishmael set out for Nantucket, where they sign on a whaler *Pequod* the next day.

As the two friends are about to board the *Pequod*, they are accosted by the crazed Elijah, who utters vague warnings about Captain Ahab and the voyage. Anyway, the ship sets sail on Christmas day. The chief mate, Starbuck, chooses Queequeg for his harpooneer; the second mate, Stubb, chooses the Indian, Tashtego; and the third mate, Flask, chooses the African, Daggoo. Several days later, Ahab finally appears on deck. His appearance sends shivers through Ishmael, for he stands upon an artificial leg made of whale bone. After Ahab summons the crew, he hammers a gold doubloon to the mast and tells the men that the first to spot Moby-Dick, a white whale, will win the coin. It is revealed that it was Moby-Dick that took off his leg.

When the first whale is sighted and the boats are lowered, the sailors are surprised to see Ahab in his own boat with a mysterious crew who has been hidden below deck. The exotic Fedallah is his harpooner. A squall comes up during the chase. Ishmael's boat capsizes and is later nearly rammed by the *Pequod*.

After rounding the Cape of Good Hope, the ship has its first of many gams, or meetings with other ships. Ahab's sole purpose in communicating with these ships is to get news of Moby-Dick. Several of the ships have lost men to the whale. The *Rachel* has recently chased Moby-Dick and is now searching for a lost boat. The young son of the captain is in that boat, but Ahab refuses to join the search. Starbuck confronts Ahab and tries to convince him to abandon his mission to get his revenge on Moby-Dick, but in vain.

Stubb's boat is the first to kill a whale. While Stubb eats his whale steak, Fleece, the cook, delivers a sermon to the sharks. During the cleaning of another whale, Tashtego is rescued by Queequeg. Pip is temporarily abandoned in the sea during another whale chase which drives him to madness. Queequeg, stricken with fever and believing death is near, has the ship's carpenter build him a coffin.

Ahab has the blacksmith fashion a special harpoon, tempered in the blood of the heathen harpooners. During a storm, Ahab holds the harpoon above his head and it is struck by lightning. Later, Ahab has a dream, which is interpreted by Fedallah. The Parsee predicts that he will die before Ahab, that only hemp can kill Ahab, and that before he dies, Ahab will see two hearses upon the sea.

At last, Moby-Dick is sighted by Ahab. The chase lasts for three days. Fedallah dies, lashed by tangled lines to the body of the great beast. Ahab thrusts his harpoon into Moby-Dick, but his line runs afoul and catches him around the neck, and he is pulled down to the depths. Moby-Dick smashes into the bow of the *Pequod*, and Queequeg's coffin shoots out of the whirlpool created by the sinking ship. The only survivor, Ishmael, clings to this strange life buoy and is later rescued.

An Excerpt from Chapter 135: The Chase—Third Day

Diving beneath the settling ship, the whale ran quivering along its keel; but turning under water, swiftly shot to the surface again, far off the other bow, but within a few yards of Ahab's boat, where, for a time, he lay quiescent.

"I turn my body from the sun. What ho, Tashtego! Let me hear thy hammer. Oh! ye three unsurrendered spires of mine; thou uncracked keel; and only god-bullied hull; thou firm deck, and haughty helm, and Pole-pointed prow, —death-glorious ship! must ye then perish, and without me? Am I cut off from the last fond pride of meanest ship-wrecked captains? Oh, lonely death on lonely life! Oh, now I feel my topmost greatness lies in my topmost grief. Ho, ho! from all your furthest bounds, pour ye now in, ye bold billows of my whole foregone life, and top this one piled comber of my death! Towards thee I roll, thou all-destroying but unconquering whale; to the last I grapple with thee; from hell's heart I stab at thee; for hate's sake I spit my last breath at thee. Sink all coffins and all hearses to one common pool! and since neither can be mine, let me then tow to pieces, while still chasing thee, though tied to thee, thou damned whale! Thus, I give up the spear!"

The harpoon was darted; the stricken whale flew forward; with igniting velocity the line ran through the grooves; —ran foul. Ahab stooped to clear it; he did clear it; but the flying turn caught him round the neck, and voicelessly as Turkish mutes bowstring their victim, he was shot out of the boat, ere the crew knew he was gone. Next instant, the heavy eye-splice in the rope's final end flew out of the stark-empty tub, knocked down an oarsman, and smiting the sea, disappeared in its depths.

Henry Wadsworth Longfellow (1807–1882)

Henry Wadsworth Longfellow, the most popular American poet of his day, was so loved and honored by his fellows that his 75th birthday was celebrated across the United States.

Henry Wadsworth Longfellow was born into a Unitarian family in Portland, Maine, then still part of Massachusetts. His mother was the daughter of a Revolutionary War hero and his father was a prominent Portland lawyer and later a member of Congress. After graduating from Bowdoin College, Longfellow studied modern languages in Europe for three years, and then returned to Bowdoin to teach them.

Longfellow was a devoted husband and father, but his marriages ended in sadness and tragedy. In 1831 he married Mary Potter and soon published his first book, a description of his travels called *Outre-Mer* (1833–1835). But in 1835 during a second trip to Europe, Longfellow's life was greatly shaken when his wife died during a miscarriage. The young teacher spent a grief-stricken year in Germany and Switzerland.

Longfellow took a position at Harvard in 1836. Three years later, at the age of 32, he published his first collection of poems, *Voices of the Night* (1839), followed by *Ballads and Other Poems* (1841). Many of these poems like "A Psalm of Life" showed people triumphing over adversity, and in a struggling young nation that theme was inspiring. Both books were very popular, but Longfellow's growing duties as a professor left him little time to write more. In addition, Frances Appleton, the daughter of a wealthy Boston industrialist, had refused his proposal of marriage. However, Longfellow was determined to win Appleton's love. During the courtship, Longfellow frequently walked from Cambridge to the Appleton home by crossing the Boston Bridge. When the bridge was rebuilt in 1906, it was renamed the Longfellow Bridge. Frances finally accepted his proposal in 1843 and they two enjoyed their marriage life greatly. Content with his life, in 1847 Longfellow published *Evangeline*, a book-length poem about what would now be called "ethnic cleansing." The poem takes place as the British drive the French from Nova Scotia, and two lovers are parted, only to find each other years later when the man is about to die.

In 1854 Longfellow decided to quit teaching to devote all his time to poetry. He published *The Song of Hiawatha* (1855), a long poem about Native American life, and *The Courtship of Miles Standish and Other Poems* (1858). Both books were immensely successful, but Longfellow was now preoccupied with national events. With the country moving towards the Civil War, he wrote "Paul Revere's Ride," a call for courage in the coming conflict.

A few months after the war began in 1861, Frances Longfellow died, soon after her dress caught fire. Profoundly saddened, Longfellow published nothing for the next two years. He found comfort in his family and producing the first American translation of Dante's *Divine Comedy*.

When the Civil War ended in 1865, his fame kept growing. He not only brought European culture to the U.S., but popularized American folk themes abroad. His admirers included Lincoln,

Dickens, and Baudelaire. From 1866 to 1880 Longfellow published seven more books of poetry, and his 75th birthday was celebrated across the country. What's more, he was honored with degrees from Cambridge and Oxford and was given a private audience by Queen Victoria. After his death, he became the first American to have a bust in the Poet's Corner of Westminster Abbey[1].

In his works, Longfellow is mainly concerned with a spirit of optimism and faith in the goodness of life. His poetry is popular for its gentleness, sweetness, and purity. His writings also belong to the milder aspects of the Romantic Movement. Meanwhile, his work refuses to touch the religious and social struggles.

Selected Reading

A Psalm[2] of Life

Longfellow wrote "A Psalm of Life" shortly after completing lectures on German writer Johann Wolfgang von Goethe and was greatly inspired by him. He was also inspired by a heartfelt conversation he had with a friend and fellow professor at Harvard University.

The primary message of the poem is that life is beautiful. In the poem Longfellow advises that we are all here to live for today rather than waiting for death to take us. The message in it clearly illustrates that even in adversity we are to persevere and never give up. According to Longfellow, time is too swift to wait for death.

A Psalm of Life

—What the heart of the young man said to the psalmist

Tell me not, in mournful numbers,

Life is but[3] an empty dream!

Note [1] Westminster Abbey: a collegiate church governed by the Dean and Chapter of Westminster, as established by Royal Charter of Queen Elizabeth I in 1560, which created it as the Collegiate Church of St. Peter Westminster and a Royal Peculiar under the personal jurisdiction of the Sovereign. From the Middle Ages, aristocrats were buried inside chapels, while monks and other people associated with the Abbey were buried in the Cloisters and other areas. One of these was Geoffrey Chaucer, who was buried here as he had apartments in the Abbey where he was employed as master of the King's Works. Other poets, writers and musicians were buried or memorialized around Chaucer in what became known as Poets' Corner.

Note [2] Psalm: song that praises God

Note [3] but: only

For the soul is dead that slumbers[1],
And things are not what they seem.

Life is real! Life is earnest!
And the grave is not its goal;
Dust thou art, to dust returnest,
Was not spoken of the soul.

Not enjoyment, and not sorrow,
Is our destined end or way;
But to act, that each tomorrow
Find us farther than today.

Art is long, and Time is fleeting,[2]
And our hearts, though stout and brave,
Still, like muffled drums, are beating
Funeral marches to the grave.

In the world's broad field of battle,
In the bivouac[3] of Life,
Be not like dumb, driven cattle!
Be a hero in the strife!

Trust no future, howe'er pleasant!
Let the dead Past bury its dead!
Act, —act in the living present!
Heart within, and God o'erhead!

Lives of great men all remind us
We can make our lives sublime,
And departing, leave behind us
Footprints on the sands of time;

Note [1] slumber: sleep

Note [2] Art is long, and Time is fleeting: an allusion to a line from Seneca's work *De Brevitate Vitae*, which
states "*vita brevis est, ars longa*," or "Life is brief, art long."

Note [3] bivouac: camp

Footprints, that perhaps another,

Sailing o'er life's solemn main,

A forlorn[1] and shipwrecked brother,

Seeing, shall take heart again.

Let us, then, be up and doing,

With a heart for any fate;

Still achieving, still pursuing,

Learn to labor[2] and to wait.

＼ Walt Whitman (1819–1892)

Walt Whitman, one of the most influential poets in the 19th century, is mainly known for his *Leaves of Grass* (1855), which has been considered a monumental work because of its uniquely poetic embodiment of American democratic ideals.

Walt Whitman was born in the family of a carpenter on Long Island, New York. When he was four years old, the family moved to Brooklyn. After some years of education in public schools, Whitman began to drift from one occupation to another—office boy, printer and wandering school-teacher. However, he had already shown his strong love for literature, reading a great deal, especially the works of Shakespeare and Milton. He was also fond of music. In addition, he was a contributor to and editor of various magazines and newspapers.

In 1848 he gave up all regular employment and started off on "a leisurely journey and working expedition." He stayed awhile in New Orleans, and then turned back northward, up the Mississippi to the Great Lakes, and finally returned to Brooklyn. The sights and the life that he absorbed greatly affected his views. It was during these years that Whitman began to show his democratic partisanship. And the ideas governing Whitman's poetry-writing gradually took shape. Feeling compelled to speak up for something new and vital he found in the air of the nation, Whitman turned to the manual work of carpentry, as an experiment to familiarize himself with the reality and essence of the life. At the same time, he widened his reading to a new scale and made it more systematic. After enriching himself simultaneously by these two very different approaches, Whitman was able to put forward his own set of aesthetic principles and devoted himself to the composition of his *Leaves of Grass*.

During the Civil War, in 1863, Whitman went to attend on wounded soldiers in Washington, D.C. until the end of the War. In 1873 Whitman had paralytic stroke. During his last nineteen

---

Note [1] forlorn: lonely and unhappy

Note [2] labor: work

years, he continued to work on his revision of *Leaves of Grass* along with his creation of new works.

Though he was attacked in his lifetime for his offensive subject matter of sexuality and for his unconventional style, Walt Whitman has proved a great figure in the literary history of the United States because he embodies a new ideal, a new world and a new life style.

Walt Whitman is a poet with a strong sense of mission, having devoted all his life to the creation of the "single" poem, *Leaves of Grass*. The work has nine editions and the first edition was published in 1855. In this giant work, openness, freedom, and above all, individualism are all that concerned him. His aim was nothing less than to express some new poetical feelings and to initiate a poetic tradition in which difference should be recognized. The genuine participation of a poet in a common cultural effort was, according to Whitman, to behave as a supreme individualist; however, the poet's essential purpose was to identify his ego with the world, and more specifically with the democratic "en-masse" of America, which is established in the opening lines of "Song of Myself."

As Whitman saw it, poetry could play a vital part in the process of creating a new nation. It could enable Americans to celebrate their release from the Old World and help them to define themselves in the new world of happiness. Hence, his poetry is full of fresh themes. He shows concern for the whole hard-working people and the burgeoning life of cities. To Whitman, the fast growth of industry and wealth in cities indicated a lively future of the nation, despite the crowded, noisy, and squalid conditions and the slackness in morality.

The realization of the individual value also found a tough position in Whitman's poems in a particular way. Most of the poems in *Leaves of Grass* sing of the "en-masse" and the self as well. In celebrating the self, Whitman gives emphasis to the physical dimension of the self and openly celebrates sexuality. Pursuit of love and happiness is approved of repeatedly and affectionately in his lines.

Some of Whitman's poems are politically committed. Before and during the Civil War, Whitman firmly stood on the side of the North and wrote a series of poems which were gathered as a collection under the title of *Drum Taps* (1865). Not a lover of violence and blood-shed, Whitman expressed much mourning for the suffering of the young lives in the battlefield and showed a determination to carry on the fighting dauntlessly until the final victory, as we may find in poems like "Cavalry Crossing a Ford." To the death of Lincoln, many poems are dedicated, among which the most famous is "When Lilacs Last in the Dooryard Bloom'd."

Whitman's poetic style is marked, first of all, by the use of the poetic "I," with which Whitman creates a triangular relationship: "I" the poet, the subject in the poem, and "you" the reader. In such manner, Whitman invites the reader to participate in the process of sympathetic identification. Whitman is also innovative in the form of his poetry. What he prefers for his new subject and new poetic feelings is "free verse," that is, poetry without a fixed beat or regular thyme scheme. By means of "free verse," he believed, he has turned the poem into an open field, an area of vital possibility where the reader can allow his own imagination to play. Parallelism and phonetic recurrence, the repetition of words and phrases at the beginning of the line, in the middle or at the end, also contribute to the musicality of his poems.

Whitman's rhetoric is relatively simple, and rather crude. Another method employed by him is to make colors and images fleet past the mind's eye of the reader. He also shows strong tendency to use oral English.

Selected Reading

Song of Myself

As Walt Whitman, the specific individual, melts away into the abstract "Myself," the poem explores the possibilities for communion between individuals. Starting from the premise that "what I assume you shall assume" Whitman tries to prove that he both encompasses and is indistinguishable from the universe.

An Excerpt

I celebrate myself, and sing myself,
And what I assume you shall assume,
For every atom belonging to me as good belongs to you.

I loafe and invite my soul,
I lean and loafe at my ease observing a spear of summer grass.

My tongue, every atom of my blood, form'd from this soil, this air,
Born here of parents born here from parents the same, and their parents the same,
I, now thirty-seven years old in perfect health begin,
Hoping to cease not till death.

Creeds and schools in abeyance,
Retiring back a while sufficed at what they are, but never forgotten,
I harbor for good or bad, I permit to speak at every hazard,
Nature without check with original energy.

Part Four

American Realism

Debates over Slavery

Up until the Civil War, half of the United States were slave states and the other half were free states. As Abraham Lincoln said, the nation was "a house divided against itself." Over the question of slavery, the United States was filled with high emotions and fierce debates. Indeed, the system of slavery was a monstrous contradiction at the heart of a country that made claims to freedom, democracy and equality. The Founding Fathers had hoped that slavery would shrivel away in the course of time. Since the Constitution prohibited importing additional slaves, slaveholders would eventually turn to free sources of labor. But the invention of the cotton gin and the expanding cotton markets in the U.K. and in New England increased the demand for cotton grown in much of the South. Slaves were cheap labor for a profitable cotton industry. When slaves could not be imported, they were bred. Thus slave-breeding, the purpose of which was to reproduce new salves, became a profitable business.

The arguments made by defenders of slavery were various and changed over time. Some argued that slavery was an institution as old as human history and it was sanctified by the Bible. Some others claimed that slavery helped Christianize people who were less than civilized. The most racist would hold that blacks were less than human and were not capable of developing into free beings. All these arguments were in fact based on the perception of African Americans as not being the equal of whites. With these and other arguments, many white Southerners insisted that they should have the right to define and keep their own form of social organization. In national politics, pressures from the South led to the Missouri Compromise[1] of 1820 and the Fugitive Slave Act of 1850, which made it illegal to assist an escaped slave.

Abolishing slavery was not the only reason why the Civil War was fought. When the southern states claimed the rights of secession, President Lincoln's primary concern was to keep the Union; abolishing slavery was secondary to him. But in the North abolitionist sentiment had been rising. There was an ever more vigorous protest against the possibility of slavery spreading into the West. Abolitionism then became a noble cause. By 1862 Lincoln had drafted the *Emancipation Proclamation* that would free the slaves and change once again the character of the Untied States.

Abolitionism gained momentum among writers after 1850. For the earlier generation of writers, the question of slavery was not so central an issue. But the Fugitive Slave Act of 1850 enraged many writers, as the law imposed upon the Northerners the legal obligation to help slave

---

Note [1] the Missouri Compromise: an agreement passed in 1820 between the pro-slavery and anti-slavery factions in the United States Congress, involving primarily the regulation of slavery in the western territories. It prohibited slavery in the former Louisiana Territory north of the parallel 36°30′ north except within the boundaries of the proposed state of Missouri.

owners protect their "property." After the 1857 decision[1] that blacks were not considered citizens by law, it was increasingly difficult for public personalities to avoid the question. It is in this context that we should understand the intents and implications of anti-slavery writing by writers of different backgrounds.

＼ Harriet Beecher Stowe (1811–1896)

Harriet Beecher Stowe, an American writer and reformer, is best known for the anti-slavery novel *Uncle Tom's Cabin* (1852). The novel played a significant role in engendering moral opposition to slavery prior to the outbreak of the Civil War.

Harriet Beecher Stowe was born in Litchfield, Connecticut and raised primarily in Hartford into a family with deep religious convictions and a social conscience, which would leave a historical legacy in educational reform, the revision of Calvinist theology, abolition, literature and women's suffrage. Harriet enrolled in the Hartford Female Seminary run by her older sister Catharine, where she received a traditional academic education usually reserved for males. In 1832 the family moved to Cincinnati, Ohio, where her father became the President of Lane Theological Seminary. Cincinnati was a hotbed of the abolitionist movement and was where she gained first-hand knowledge of slavery and the Underground Railroad. At that time, Cincinnati's trade and shipping business on the Ohio River was booming, attracting numerous migrants including many free blacks and Irish immigrants who worked on the state's canals and railroads. The city had been wracked in the Cincinnati riots of 1829, when ethnic Irish attacked blacks, trying to drive them out of the city. Beecher met a number of African Americans who had suffered in those attacks, and their experience contributed to her later writing about slavery.

It was in the literary club that she met Calvin Ellis Stowe and they got married in 1836. He was an ardent critic of slavery, and the Stowes supported the Underground Railroad, temporarily housing several fugitive slaves in their home. Most slaves continued north to secure freedom in Canada.

Stowe wrote *Uncle Tom's Cabin* in reaction to the Fugitive Slave Act of 1850. In the book she expresses her moral outrage at the institution of slavery and its destructive effects on both races and especially on maternal bonds. *Uncle Tom's Cabin* is dominated by Stowe's outrage over the evil of slavery. While Stowe weaves other subthemes throughout her text, such as the moral authority of motherhood and the redemptive role of the Christian faith. She emphasizes the immorality of slavery and its incompatibility with true Christianity.

Note [1] the 1857 decision: referring to the Dred Scott Decision, a ruling by the U.S. Supreme Court that people of African descent brought into the United States and held as slaves (or their descendants, whether or not they were slaves) were not protected by the Constitution and could never be U.S. citizens

In addition to novels, she wrote non-fiction books on a wide range of subjects including homemaking, the raising of children and religion. She wrote in an informal conversational style and presented herself as an average wife and mother. Her style and her narrative use of local dialect predated works like Mark Twain's by 30 years.

Selected Reading

Uncle Tom's Cabin

To pay off his debts, Mr. Shelby, a plantation owner in Kentucky, intends to sell two of his slaves to Mr. Haley, a slave trader. The slaves to be turned over are Uncle Tom, a faithful and honest worker of middle age, and Harry, a bright boy about five years old. Mrs. Shelby is appalled at the prospect that both Uncle Tom and little Harry will be separated from their families. Once she promised her maid, Eliza, that her child, Harry, would never be sold. Young George Shelby also hates to see Uncle Tom go because he regards the man as his friend.

When overhearing the news, Eliza decides to run away with her son and departs that night. On the contrary, Tom resigns himself to the sale. However, Eliza's husband, George Harris, has also decided to escape and hopes to meet Eliza in Canada.

The next day Haley hires two slave-catchers to track down Eliza, as she and Harry have fled all the way to the Ohio River. When the pursuers catch up and spot her, Eliza has no choice but to cross the river by jumping from one floating ice to another, holding young Harry in her arms. Later, Eliza is lucky enough to be assisted by Senator Bird and his wife. Touched by Eliza's story, Senator Bird decides to take Eliza and Harry to the home of John Van Trompe, located deep in woods seven miles away. Trompe once owned blacks, but freed them after realizing the evils of slavery. Afterwards Eliza and Harry move to a Quaker settlement, where they meet George Harris and leave for Canada together.

Meanwhile, Tom says sad goodbye to his friends and family, and is shackled. Young George Shelby promises to bring him back one day. On the boat bound for New Orleans, Tom saves and befriends a young white girl, Eva. Deeply grateful to Tom, Eva's father, Augustine St. Clare, buys Tom and takes him to their home in New Orleans.

Since St. Clare's wife is sick, St. Clare has brought his cousin, Miss Ophelia to attend to the household. Miss Ophelia is opposed to slavery but dislikes blacks. Anyway, Tom and Eva begin to relate to one another because of the deep Christian faith they both share. When she reads to him from the Bible, Tom explains the passages. Over the next two years, life is easy to Tom. What is more, St. Clare also comes to understand the evils of slavery, and Miss Ophelia begins to overcome her prejudice against blacks. The changes result in part from the influence of Eva and Tom, who see the goodness in everyone. One day St. Clare is convinced that a man so worthy as Tom should not be deprived of freedom.

Unfortunately, Eva becomes sicker and dies soon. Before her death, Eva has asked her father to free his slaves and St. Clare has promised to do so. Shortly afterward, St. Clare is stabbed to death while attempting to break up a fight. Consequently, the legal work required to free Tom is never completed and Tom's easy life comes to an end. Mrs. Clare, against the wishes of her husband and daughter, sells Tom to a brutal slave owner, Simon Legree, who runs a cotton plantation.

In Legree's house, Tom maintains his kind character despite Legree's maltreatment. When Legree orders Tom to whip a woman, Tom disobeys him. Although flogged for it, Tom tells Legree that he can take his body but he can never take his soul, for it belongs to God. Tom's godliness somehow pierces Legree's ungodliness, wondering whether he has offended divine powers. A heavy drinker, he begins to hallucinate, hearing strange noises and seeing ghosts. Two slave women, Cassy and Emmeline, conspire to play "supernatural" tricks on him. One night, Cassy comes to Tom and tries to persuade him to kill Legree with an axe. Refusing to commit the crime, Tom, instead, urges Cassy to escape with Emmeline and chooses to stay on his part, for he believes God wants him to stay and to comfort other slaves. Subsequently, Cassy and Emmeline run off into the surrounding wilderness to misguide Legree to think that they have escaped. Then, they retrace their steps and hide in the attic of Legree's mansion. There, they plan to wear him down until it is the right time for them to flee. Legree searches swamps and forests with bloodhounds, but in vain. In frustration, he beats Tom severely when Tom refuses to confess the whereabouts of Cassy and Emmeline.

Finally George Shelby comes to free Tom, but it is too late. Before Tom dies, he even hopes that Legree will repent his sins so that he can enter heaven. George Shelby buries him on a knoll outside the boundary of the plantation and leaves.

In the following days, Cassy and Emmeline continue to "haunt" the house until Legree is gravely ill after drinking heavily and sleeping fitfully. Then they escape and come across Emily de Thoux who turns out to be the sister of George Harris while aboard. The ensuing conversations reveal that Cassy is Eliza's mother.

After George Shelby arrives in Kentucky, he frees his slaves and tells them to remember Tom's sacrifice and his belief in Christianity. Eventually Emily, Cassy and Emmeline reach Canada, where they reunite with George Harris and Eliza.

An Excerpt from Chapter VII: The Mother's Struggle

It is impossible to conceive of a human creature more wholly desolate and forlorn than Eliza, when she turned her footsteps from Uncle Tom's cabin.

Her husband's suffering and dangers, and the danger of her child, all blended in her mind, with a confused and stunning sense of the risk she was running, in leaving the only home she had ever known, and cutting loose from the protection of a friend whom she loved and revered. Then there was the parting from every familiar object, —the place where she had grown up, the trees under which she had played, the groves where she had walked many an evening in happier days, by the side of her young husband, —everything, as it lay in the clear, frosty starlight, seemed to speak reproachfully to her, and ask her whither could she go from a home like that?

But stronger than all was maternal love, wrought into a paroxysm of frenzy by the near approach of a fearful danger. Her boy was old enough to have walked by her side, and, in an indifferent case, she would only have led him by the hand; but now the bare thought of putting him out of her arms made her shudder, and she strained him to her bosom with a convulsive grasp, as she went rapidly forward.

The frosty ground creaked beneath her feet, and she trembled at the sound; every quaking leaf and fluttering shadow sent the blood backward to her heart, and quickened her footsteps. She wondered within herself at the strength that seemed to be come upon her; for she felt the weight of her boy as if it had been a feather, and every flutter of fear seemed to increase the supernatural power that bore her on, while from her pale lips burst forth, in frequent ejaculations, the prayer to a Friend above—"Lord, help! Lord, save me!"

If it were *your* Harry, mother, or your Willie, that were going to be torn from you by a brutal trader, tomorrow morning, —if you had seen the man, and heard that the papers were signed and delivered, and you had only from twelve o'clock till morning to make good your escape, —how fast could you walk? How many miles could you make in those few brief hours, with the darling at your bosom, —the little sleepy head on your shoulder, —the small, soft arms trustingly holding on to your neck?

For the child slept. At first, the novelty and alarm kept him waking; but his mother so hurriedly repressed every breath or sound, and so assured him that if he were only still she would certainly save him, that he clung quietly round her neck, only asking, as he found himself sinking to sleep,

"Mother, I don't need to keep awake, do I?"

"No, my darling; sleep, if you want to."

"But, mother, if I do get asleep, you won't let him get me?"

"No! so may God help me!" said his mother, with a paler cheek, and a brighter light in her large dark eyes.

"You're sure, an't you, mother?"

"Yes, sure!" said the mother, in a voice that startled herself; for it seemed to her to come from a spirit within, that was no part of her; and the boy dropped his little weary head on her shoulder, and was soon asleep. How the touch of those warm arms, the gentle breathings that came in her neck, seemed to add fire and spirit to her movements! It seemed to her as if strength poured into her in electric streams, from every gentle touch and movement of the sleeping, confiding child. Sublime is the dominion of the mind over the body, that, for a time, can make flesh and nerve impregnable, and string the sinews like steel, so that the weak become so mighty.

Historical Background after the Civil War

The period ranging from 1865 to 1914 has been referred to as the Age of Realism in the literary history of the United States, which is actually a movement or tendency that dominated the spirit of American literature, especially American fiction, from the 1850s onwards. Realism was a reaction against Romanticism or a move away from the bias towards romance and self-creating fictions, and paved the way to modernism.

The American society after the Civil War provided rich soil for the rise and development of realism. The fifty years between the end of the Civil War and the outbreak of the First World War is one of the periods in American history characterized with changes, in relation to every aspect of American life, politically, economically, culturally and religiously. The scale of the change was so vast that it indicated a fundamental redirection in the nature and ideology of the American society. First of all, the Civil War affected both the social and the value system of the country. America had transformed itself from a Jeffersonian agrarian community into an industrialized and commercialized society. Wilderness was challenged by civilization. The dominance of New England as the center of cultural life of the United States began to give way to New York. The war also brought some noticeable changes to American economy. It had stimulated the technological development, and new methods of organization and management were tested to adapt to industrial modernization on a large scale. Railway, electricity and wireless telephone rendered everyday life more convenient. The burgeoning economy and industry stepped up urbanization. American cities grew fast, with one half of the American population concentrated in about a dozen cities by the end of the First World War.

However, the changes were not all for the better. The industrialization and urbanization were accompanied by the incalculable suffering of the laboring people. In the countryside, increasing numbers of farmers were squeezed off the land to become city job-seekers, causing an oversupply of labor, which kept wages down and allowed the industrialists to maintain working conditions of notorious danger and discomfort for men, women and children. Therefore, polarization of the well-being started to show up, with the poor poorer and the rich richer. The concentration of power and wealth gave birth to buccaneers, tycoons and slums, and ghettos as well. As far as the ideology was concerned, people were on a shaking ground. They became dubious about the human nature and the benevolence of God, which the transcendentalists cared most. It taught men that life was not so good, man was not and God was not. In fact, the war also marked a change in the quality of American life, a deterioration of American moral values.

Gone were the frontier and the spirit of the frontiersman, which is the spirit of freedom and human connection, and gone was a place to escape for the American Dream. The frontier had been a factor of great importance in American life. As long as the frontier was there, people could always hope to escape troubles over the nest hill and have a better life ahead. Now that the frontier was about to close and the safety value was ceasing to operate, a reexamination of life began. The worth of the American Dream, the idealized, romantic view of man and his life in the New World, began to lose its hold on the imagination of the people. Beneath the glittering surface of prosperity there lay suffering and unhappiness. Disillusionment and frustration were widely felt. What had been expected to be a "Golden Age" turned out to be a "Gilded" one.

The literary scene after the Civil War proved to be quite different a picture. The harsh realities of life as well as the disillusion of heroism resulting from the dark memories of the Civil War had set the nation against the romance. The Americans began to be tired of the sentimental feelings of Romanticism. A new generation of writers, dissatisfied with the Romantic ideas in the older generation, came up with a new inspiration. This new attitude was characterized by a great interest in the realities of life. It aimed at the truthful representation of common life. This literary interest in the so-called "reality" of life started a new period in the American literary writings known as the Age of Realism.

＼ Emily Dickinson (1830–1886)

Emily Dickinson, almost unknown in her lifetime, has come to be regarded as one of the great American poets of the 19th century.

Emily Dickinson was born in Amherst, Massachusetts, where her father was a prominent lawyer and politician. She attended Amherst Academy from 1840 to 1847. Her family was very closely knit. Both she and her sister remained at home and did not marry. Emily seldom left Amherst, and later made one trip as far as Washington and two or three trips to Boston. After 1852 she became a total recluse, not leaving her house nor seeing even close friends. Her early letters and descriptions of herself in her youth reveal an attractive girl with a lively wit. Her later retirement from the world, though perhaps affected by an unhappy love affair, seems mainly to have resulted from her own personality, from a desire to separate herself from the world. The range of her poetry suggests not her limited experiences but the power of her creativity and imagination. Nevertheless, she read intensively—Shakespeare, classic myths, the Bible, Keats, the Bronte sisters, the Brownings, Emerson, Thoreau and Hawthorne.

Dickinson's poetry writing began in the early 1850s. Altogether, she wrote 1,775 poems, of which only seven had been published during her lifetime. As her poetry continues to be issued after its first appearance in 1890, her fame has kept rising.

Dickinson's poems are usually based on her own experiences, her sorrows and joys. Dickinson called this stream of poems a continuous fragmented "letter to the world." But within her little lyrics Dickinson addresses those issues that concern the whole human beings, which include religion, death, immortality, love and nature. In some of her poems she wrote about her doubt and belief about religious subjects. While she desired salvation and immortality, she denied the orthodox view of paradise. Although she believed in God, she sometimes doubted His benevolence. Her poems concerning death and immortality range over the physical as well as the psychological and emotional aspects of death. Love is another common subject. One group of her love poems treat the suffering and frustration love can cause. Many of them are striking and original depictions of the longing for shared moments, the pain of separation and the futility of finding happiness. The other group of love poems focuses on the physical aspect of desire, in which Dickinson deals with the influence of the male power over the female. More than five hundred poems Dickinson wrote are about nature, in which her general skepticism about the relationship between man and nature is well-expressed. On one hand, she shared with her romantic and transcendental predecessors who believed that a mythical bond between man and nature existed, that nature revealed to man things about mankind and universe. On the other hand, she felt about nature's inscrutability and indifference to the life and interests of human beings.

Dickinson's poetry is unique and unconventional in its own way. Her poems have no title, hence are always quoted by their first line. The form of her poetry is often irregular, and her irregular or sometimes inverted sentence structure also confuses readers. Her poems are usually short, concise, simple and direct, and many of them are centered on a single image or symbol and focused on subject matter. But, Dickinson's poetry, despite its ostensible formal simplicity, is remarkable for its variety, subtlety and richness.

Selected Reading

In her poems about death, Dickinson looked at death from the point of view of both the living and the dying. She even imagined her own death, the loss of her own body, and the journey of her soul to the unknown world. This poem is a description of the moment of death, a poem universally considered one of her masterpieces. She was imagining: When she died, a fly buzz—the symbol of death; her relatives and friends had cried too much; the god of death came into the room. She made her last will and gave everything away to her relative and friends. Her sight became dim, but she could hear the fly; she felt as if the buzz was blue, then she could not see the windows, she could not see anything— darkness covered all.

I Heard a Fly Buzz—When I Died—

I heard a Fly buzz—when I died—
The Stillness in the Room
Was like the Stillness in the Air
Between the Heaves of Storm.

The Eyes around—had wrung them dry,[1]
And Breaths were gathering firm
For that last Onset, when the King[2]
Be witnessed—in the Room—

I willed my Keepsakes—Signed away
What portion of me be
Assignable—and then it was
There interposed a Fly—

With Blue[3]—uncertain, stumbling Buzz,
Between the light—and me—
And then the Windows failed—and then
I could not see to see—

Note [1] The Eyes around—had wrung them dry: The relatives and friends cried and cried so that there were no tears any more.
Note [2] the King: the God of death
Note [3] With Blue—uncertain stumbling Buzz: The sight of the dying became dim, but her listening was sensitive.

Because I Could Not Stop for Death—

Because I could not stop for Death—
He kindly stopped for me—
The Carriage held but just Ourselves—
And Immortality.

We slowly drove—He knew no haste,
And I had put away
My labor, and my leisure too,
For his Civility.

We passed the School, where children strove
At Recess—in the Ring—
We passed the Fields of Gazing Grain—
We passed the Setting Sun—
Or rather—He passed Us—
The Dews drew quivering and chill—
For only Gossamer, my Gown—
My Tippet[1]—only Tulle—

We paused before a House that seemed
A Swelling of the Ground—
The Roof was scarcely visible—
The Cornice—in the Ground—

Since then—'tis centuries—and yet
Feels shorter than the Day
I first surmised the Horses' Heads
Were toward Eternity—

Note [1] Tippet: shoulder cape

Mark Twain (1835–1910)

Mark Twain, the pseudonym of Samuel Langhorne Clemens, is a giant in American literature and has been invariably associated with local colorism[1].

Mark Twain was born in Florida, Missouri. When Twain was four, his family moved to Hannibal, Missouri, a port town on the Mississippi River, which later served as the inspiration for the fictional town of St. Petersburg in *The Adventures of Tom Sawyer* (1876) and *The Adventures of Huckleberry Finn* (1885). Missouri had been admitted as a slave state in 1821 as part of the Missouri Compromise, and from an early age Twain was exposed to the institution of slavery, a theme which he was to explore in his work. The family was poor and Twain's father failed repeatedly in his business attempts. In 1847, when Twain was eleven, his father died. So he went to work at various occupations: a typesetter, a printer and a riverboat pilot. He once remarked that riverboat piloting was the best time in his life and his river experiences, simple and carefree, was best shown in his *Life on the Mississippi* (1883).

When the Civil War broke out, Twain headed west to join his brother in Nevada. After he failed at mining, he turned to journalism. In 1865 his humorous story, "The Celebrated Jumping Frog of Calaveras County" was published, based on a story he heard in Angels Camp, California, where he had spent some time as a miner. The short story brought international attention and soon his humor and satire earned praise from critics and peers.

In 1867 Twain set sail on the pleasure cruiser *Quaker City* for five months, which resulted in *The Innocents Abroad* (1869). In 1872 Twain published a second piece of travel literature, *Roughing It* (1872), a semi-autobiographical account of Twain's journey from Missouri to Nevada, his subsequent life in the American West and his visit to Hawaii. The book lampoons American and Western society in the same way that *The Innocents Abroad* critiques the various countries of Europe and the Middle East. *The Gilded Age* (1873) is also notable, written in collaboration with his neighbor, Charles Dudley Warner. Twain's next two works drew on his experiences on the Mississippi River. *Old Times on the Mississippi* (1875), a series of sketches featured Twain's disillusionment with Romanticism. It eventually became the starting point for *Life on the Mississippi*. However, it was *The Adventure of Tom Sawyer* and *The Adventures of Huckleberry Finn* that firmly established Twain's position in the literary scene.

As a sequel to *The Adventures of Tom Sawyer*, *The Adventures of Huckleberry Finn* marks the climax of Twain's literary creativity. Hemingway once described the novel as the book from which "all modern American literature comes." The theme of slavery is perhaps the most well

---

Note [1] local colorism: In literature, regionalism or local color refers to fiction or poetry that focuses on specific features of a particular region, including characters, dialects, customs, history and landscape. Famous local colorists are Mark Twain, Harriet Beecher Stowe, John Steinbeck, William Faulkner, etc.

known aspect of this novel, which provides an allegory to explain how and why slavery is wrong. Twain uses Jim, a main character and a slave, to demonstrate the humanity of slaves. Jim expresses the complicated human emotions and struggles with the path of his life. To prevent being sold and forced to separate from his family, Jim runs away from his owner, Miss Watson, and works towards obtaining freedom so he can buy his family's freedom. All along their journey downriver, Jim cares for and protects Huck, not as a servant, but as a friend. The profound portrait of Huck is another great contribution of the book to the legacy of American literature. The climax arises with Huck's inner struggle between his heart and his head, between his affection for Jim and the laws of the society. As he makes final decision, to follow his own good-hearted moral impulse rather than conventional morality, Huck grows.

Twain is known as a local colorist, who preferred to present social life through portraits of the local characters of his regions, including people living in that area, the landscape and other peculiarities like the customs, dialects, costumes and so on. Consequently, the rich material became the endless resources for his fiction, and the Mississippi valley and the West became his major theme. Unlike James and Howells, Mark Twain wrote about the lower-class people, because they were the people he knew so well and their life was the one he himself had lived.

Another fact that makes Twain unique is his magic power with language, his use of vernacular. His words are colloquial, concrete and direct in effect, and his sentence structures are simple, even ungrammatical, which is typical of the spoken language. And Twain skillfully used the colloquialism to cast his protagonists in their everyday life. What's more, his characters, confined to a particular region and to a particular historical moment, speak with a strong accent, which is true of his local colorism.

Mark Twain's humor is remarkable. A great deal of his humor is characterized by puns, straight-faced exaggeration, repetition and anti-climax, let alone tricks of travesty and invective. However, his humor is a kind of artistic style used to criticize the social injustice and satirize the decayed romanticism.

Selected Reading

The Adventures of Huckleberry Finn

To keep young Huckleberry Finn away from his drunken and abusive father, the Widow Douglas takes him into her home in St. Petersburg, Missouri. With the help of her sister, Miss Watson, she attempts to civilize the boy, making him wash, attend church, read and write, and go to school. However, Huck still yearns for freedom, so one night he sneaks out with Tom Sawyer. With some other boys, they form a band of robbers known as Tom Sawyer's Gang, which eventually breaks up.

Gradually Huck gets used to his life at the Widow Douglas' house, until his drunken father, Pap, reappears to demand Huck's money. Huck turns to Judge Thatcher for help and asks him to keep the money. To protect Huck, the Widow Douglas and the judge attempt to legalize the widow's adoption of Huck. But another judge believes in the rights of Huck's natural father. Finally, outraged when the Widow Douglas warns him to stay away from her house, Pap kidnaps Huck and holds him in an isolated cabin across the river from St. Petersburg. When Pap gets drunk, he beats Huck now and then. Tired of his confinement and hating the beatings, Huck escapes from Pap by faking his own death, killing a pig and spreading its blood all over the cabin.

Eventually, Huck escapes to Jackson's Island in the Mississippi and encounters Jim, one of Miss Watson's slaves. Jim has run away after overhearing Miss Watson's talk about selling him. Then Huck and Jim team up despite Huck's uncertainty about the morality of helping a runaway slave. After heavy flooding on the river caused by a storm, the two catch a raft and a house floating on the river. Unexpectedly, in the house Jim discovers the naked body of a dead man and prevents Huck from seeing the corpse.

Meanwhile, Huck decides to go back to St. Petersburg to find out what people are saying about him and Jim. He disguises himself as a girl and paddles the canoe across the river to the lower part of town after sunset. Mrs. Loftus, a newcomer to St. Petersburg, tells him about the murder of a boy named Huck Finn. She also says that Pap Finn is a suspect and that a reward is offered for the capture of Jim. Before Huck leaves, Mrs. Loftus discovers that he is a boy in disguise, but promises not to say anything about it. Huck returns to Jim and tells him that a search party is coming to Jackson's Island that very night. Jim and Huck immediately set out down the river on their raft and intends to take a steamship into the states where slavery is prohibited. Along the way, the adventurers encounter robbers and slave hunters. Despite the fact that he is morally obliged to turn Jim in, Huck decides to protect him when the slave hunters ask questions. After a thick fog descends on the river, Huck and Jim unknowingly pass Cairo. Traveling onward, their raft is hit by a steamboat and Huck and Jim are separated for a while.

Huck ends up in the home of the kind Grangerfords, a family of Southern aristocrats locked in a bitter and silly feud with a neighboring clan, the Shepherdsons. The elopement of a Grangerford daughter with a Shepherdson son leads to a gun battle in which many in the families are killed. While Huck is caught up in the feud, Jim shows up with the repaired raft. Huck hurries to Jim's hiding place, and they take off down the river.

A few days later, Huck and Jim rescue two con artists, the "duke" —a displaced English duke and the "king" —the long-lost heir to the French throne. Unable to get rid of them, Huck and Jim continue down the river with the two frauds, who work their swindles along the way. In a town on the shore Huck witnesses the lynching and murder of a harmless drunkard by an Arkansas aristocrat. Meanwhile, the duke and the king cheat the townspeople of their money by performing a play called the *Royal Nonesuch*. What's worse, they two pretend to be brothers of the recently deceased Peter Wilks and intend to claim his legacy. Growing to admire the Wilks sisters' kindness, Huck steals the dead Peter Wilks' gold from the duke and the king but is forced to hide it in Wilks' coffin. As Huck is about to expose the scheme, the arrival of two new men who seem to be the real brothers throws everything into confusion. While Huck leaves for the raft, the two villains manage to barely escape from the angry people. Later, to Huck's dismay, they sell Jim to Silas and Sally Phelps, who happen to be Tom Sawyer's uncle and aunt.

Resolving to free Jim, Huck comes to the plantation of the Phelps, where Jim is held. The Phelps mistake Huck for Tom, who is due to arrive for a visit, and Huck goes along with their mistake. When he intercepts the real Tom Sawyer on the road and tells him everything, Tom decides to pretend to be his own younger brother, Sid. In the meantime, Jim has told the family that the townspeople capture the duke and king, who are then tarred and feathered and ridden out of town on a rail. During the following rescue, Tom is shot in the leg and Jim remains by his side, risking recapture rather than completing his escape alone. Finally, all are returned to the Phelps' house, where Tom receives treatment from a doctor and Jim ends up back in chains. Then Tom's aunt Polly arrives and reveals Huck and Tom's true identities to the Phelps family. Jim is revealed to be a free man: Miss Watson died two months earlier and freed Jim in her will, but Tom chooses not to reveal this information to Huck so that he can come up with an artful rescue plan for Jim. Jim tells Huck that the dead body they have found on the floating house off Jackson's Island is Pap's, so Huck may now return safely to St. Petersburg. Aunt Sally then steps in and offers to adopt Huck, but Huck, who has had enough "civilizing," announces his plan to set out for the West.

An Excerpt from Chapter 31

Once I said to myself it would be a thousand times better for Jim to be a slave at home where his family was, as long as he'd *got* to be a slave, and so I'd better write a letter to Tom Sawyer and tell him to tell Miss Watson where he was. But I soon give up that notion for two things: She'd be mad and disgusted at his rascality and ungratefulness for leaving her, and so she'd sell him straight down the river again; and if she didn't, everybody naturally despises an ungrateful nigger, and they'd make Jim feel it all the time, and so he'd feel ornery and disgraced. And then think of *me*! It would get all around that Huck Finn helped a nigger to get his freedom; and if I was ever to see anybody from that town again I'd be ready to get down and lick his boots for shame. That's just the way: A person does a low-down thing, and then he don't want to take no consequences of it. Thinks as long as he can hide it, it ain't no disgrace. That was my fix[1] exactly. The more I studied about this, the more my conscience went to grinding me, and the more wicked and low-down and ornery I got to feeling. And at last, when it hit me all of a sudden that here was the plain hand of Providence[2] slapping me in the face and letting me know my wickedness was being watched all the time from up there in heaven, whilst I was stealing a poor old woman's nigger that hadn't ever done me no harm, and now was showing me there's One that's always on the lookout, and ain't agoing to allow no such miserable doings to go only just so fur and no further, I most dropped in my tracks I was so scared. Well, I tried the best I could to kinder soften it up somehow for myself, by saying I was brung up wicked, and so I warn't so much to blame; but something inside of me kept saying, "There was the Sunday-school, you could a gone to it; and if you'd a done it they'd a learnt you, there, that people that acts as I'd been acting about that nigger goes to everlasting fire."

It made me shiver. And I about made up my mind to pray; and see if I couldn't try to quit being the kind of a boy I was, and be better. So I kneeled down. But the words wouldn't come. Why wouldn't they? It wasn't no use to try and hide it from Him. Nor from *me*, neither. I knowed very well why they wouldn't come. It was because my heart warn't right; it was because I warn't square; it was because I was playing double. I was letting *on* to give up sin, but away inside of me I was holding on to the biggest one of all. I was trying to make my mouth *say* I would do the right thing and the clean thing, and go and write to that nigger's owner and tell where he was; but deep down in me I knowed it was a lie—and He knowed it. You can't pray a lie—I found that out.

So I was full of trouble, full as I could be; and didn't know what to do. At last I had an idea; and I says, I'll go and write the letter—and *then* see if I can pray. Why, it was astonishing, the way I felt as light as a feather right straight off, and my troubles all gone. So I got a piece of paper and a pencil, all glad and excited, and set down and wrote:

Miss Watson, your runaway nigger Jim is down here two mile below Pikesville, and Mr. Phelps has got him and he will give him up for the reward if you send.

HUCK FINN

Note [1] fix: difficult situation

Note [2] Providence: God

I felt good and all washed clean of sin for the first time I had ever felt so in my life, and I knowed I could pray now. But I didn't do it straight off, but laid the paper down and set there thinking—thinking how good it was all this happened so, and how near I come to being lost and going to hell. And went on thinking. And got to thinking over our trip down the river; and I see Jim before me, all the time, in the day and in the night-time, sometimes moonlight, sometimes storms, and we a floating along, talking and singing and laughing. But somehow I couldn't seem to strike no places to harden me against him, but only the other kind. I'd see him standing my watch on top of his'n, 'stead of calling me, so I could go on sleeping; and see him how glad he was when I come back out of the fog; and when I come to him again in the swamp, up there where the feud was; and such-like times; and would always call me honey, and pet me and do everything he could think of for me, and how good he always was; and at last I struck the time I saved him by telling the men we had small-pox aboard, and he was so grateful, and said I was the best friend old Jim ever had in the world, and the *only* one he's got now; and then I happened to look around and see that paper.

It was a close place. I took it up, and held it in my hand. I was a trembling, because I'd got to decide, forever, betwixt two things, and I knowed it. I studied a minute, sort of holding my breath, and then says to myself:

"All right, then, I'll go to hell" —and tore it up.

It was awful thoughts, and awful words, but they was said. And I let them stay said; and never thought no more about reforming. I shoved the whole thing out of my head; and said I would take up wickedness again, which was in my line, being brung up to it, and the other warn't. And for a starter I would go to work and steal Jim out of slavery again; and if I could think up anything worse, I would do that, too; because as long as I was in, and in for good, I might as well go the whole hog[1].

Henry James (1843–1916)

Henry James, the first American writer to conceive his career in international terms, is also regarded as the founder of psychological realism and the forerunner of the 20th-century stream-of-consciousness novels.

Henry James was born in New York into a wealthy family, the son of the theological writer Henry James, Sr. and the younger brother of the distinguished philosopher and psychologist William James, who made a great contribution to the theory of the stream-of-consciousness technique. The James family was one of the most productive intellectual families in the history

---

Note [1] go the whole hog: do it thoroughly

of the United States, and Henry James was its most gifted literary stylist and innovator. James was one of the few authors in the American literary history who was not obliged to work for a living. When he was very young, James was taken back and forth across the Atlantic, and the European education he received exposed him early to an international society. In 1862, James entered Harvard Law School, where he met William Dean Howells and developed a lifelong friendship with him. During his study at Harvard, James read intensively Balzac, George Eliot and Hawthorne. Later he toured England, France and Italy, and met Flaubert, Maupassant, Zola and Turgenev, who exerted a great influence on James. While Mark Twain and William Dean Howells satirized European manners at times, Henry James was an admirer of ancient European civilization. The materialistic bent on American life and its lack of culture and sophistication, he believed, could not provide him with enough materials for great literary works, so he settled down in London in 1876. In 1915 he became a naturalized British citizen, largely in protest against America's failure to join England in the First World War. The following year James died in London shortly after receiving the Order of Merit[1].

Despite his achievement in various kinds of literary works, it is his novels and his literary essays that make James a fascinating case in the American literary history. The literary career of Henry James is generally divided into three periods. In the first period (1865–1882) James took great interest in international themes. In almost all the stories and novels, James treated the clashes between two different cultures and the emotional and moral problems of Americans in Europe, or Europeans in America. *The American* (1877) tells a story about a young and innocent American confronting the complexity of the European life. *Daisy Miller* (1878), a novella about a young American girl who gets "killed" by the winter in Rome, brought James international fame for the first time. In *The Europeans* (1878) the scene is shifted back to America, where some Europeans, who are actually expatriated Americans, learn with difficult to adapt themselves to the American life. The first period of James' fiction, usually considered to have culminated in *The Portrait of a Lady* (1881), concentrated on the contrast between Europe and America. The style of these novels is generally straightforward and, though personally characteristic, well within the norms of the 19th-century fiction.

James experimented with different themes and forms in his middle period. In particular, he began writing on explicitly political themes. *The Bostonians* (1886) is a bittersweet tragicomedy, which satirizes the women liberation movement that took place in Boston. The political theme turns darker in *The Princess Casamassima* (1886), which exposes the anarchist conspiracy in the

Note [1] the Order of Merit: a dynastic order recognizing distinguished service in the armed forces, science, art, literature, or for the promotion of culture, from King George V for his services to the British nation

slum of London. He also tried writing for the theater, but gave it up soon because neither of the plays he produced made a hit. However, James did have a significant try in writing some short fictions during this period.

In his last and major period, James returned to his international theme. From 1895 to 1900 he wrote some novellas and stories dealing with childhood and adolescence, the most famous of which is *What Maisie Knows* (1897). After that, he successively created the following great books: *The Wings of the Dove* (1902), *The Ambassadors* (1903) and *The Golden Bowl* (1904). These demanding novels are widely considered to be James' most influential contribution to literature. The treatment of the international theme in this period is characterized by the richness of syntax and characterization and the originality in point of view, symbolism, metaphoric texture and organizing rhythm. James is now more mature as an artist, more at home in the craft of fiction.

James' fame generally rests upon his novels and stories with the international theme. These novels are always set against a larger international background and centered on the conflict between the innocence of American culture and the sophistication of European culture. The typical pattern of the conflict between the two cultures seems to be that of a young American man or an American girl who goes to Europe and affronts his or her destiny. The unsophisticated boy or girl would be beguiled, betrayed, cruelly wronged at the hands of those who pretend to stand for the highest possible civilization. Marriage and love are used by James as the focal point of the confrontation between the two value systems. And the protagonist usually goes through a painful process of a spiritual growth, gaining knowledge of good and evil from the conflict.

Henry James' literary criticism, an indispensable part of his contribution to literature, is both concerned with form and devoted to human values. The theme of his essay "The Art of Fiction" clearly indicates that the aim of the novel is to present life, so it is not surprising to find in his writings human experiences explored in every possible form: illusion, despair, reward, torment, inspiration, delight, etc. He also advocates the freedom of the artist to write about anything that concerns him, even the disagreeable, the ugly and the commonplace. The artist should be able to "feel" the life, to understand human nature, and then to record them in his own art form.

Moreover, James' realism is characterized by his psychological approach to his subject matter. His fictional world is concerned more with the inner life of human beings than with overt human actions. His best and most mature works will render the drama of individual consciousness and convey the moment-to-moment sense of human experience as bewilderment and discovery. As a result, readers observe people and events filtering through the individual consciousness and participate in his experience. This emphasis on psychology and on the human consciousness proves to be a big breakthrough in novel writing and has great influence on the coming generations. That is why James is generally regarded as the forerunner of the 20th-century stream-of-consciousness novels and the founder of psychological realism.

One of James' literary techniques innovated to cater for this psychological emphasis is his narrative "point of view." As the author, James avoids the authorial omniscience as much as possible and makes his characters reveal themselves with his minimal intervention. So it is often the case that in his novels the main story is presented through one or several minds and their different perspectives. This narrative method proves to be successful in bringing out his themes.

As to his language, James is not so easy to understand. He is often highly refined and insightful. With a large vocabulary, he is always accurate in word selection, trying to find the best expression for his literary imagination. Therefore James is not only one of the most important realists of the period before the First World War, but also the most expert stylist of his time.

Selected Reading

Daisy Miller

Frederick Winterbourne, a young American, has come from Geneva to visit his aunt. Winterbourne is wealthy and Europeanized, having been educated in Switzerland. Daisy Miller, another fascinating young American, is also traveling with her mother and her nine-year-old brother Randolph. Her father is a wealthy businessman in New York, who has sent his family overseas to get some culture.

When Daisy and Winterbourne first meet in a garden of the grand hotel in Vevery, Switzerland, Winterbourne is greatly taken by her beauty. Although startled by Daisy's audacity and innocence, Winterbourne believes that the Millers are simply ignorant of the social norms. Unlike Winterbourne, his aunt, Mrs. Costello, considers the Millers to be vulgar, for they treat their courier, Eugenio, as an equal. She also thinks Daisy is a shameless girl for agreeing to visit the Château de Chillon, a medieval castle, with Winterbourne after they have known each other for only half an hour. However, it never occurs to Daisy that her flirtatious American ways are out of place in Europe. Her mother, Mrs. Miller, is also oblivious to the impropriety of her daughter's behavior. Nonetheless, Winterbourne and Daisy have a good time together at the old castle. When Winterbourne tells her that he has to return to Geneva the next day, Daisy becomes disappointed and even angry. Finally he promises to visit the Millers in Rome, which both of them plan to visit.

In Rome, Winterbourne learns of Daisy's increasing intimacy with a young Italian, Giovanelli, which makes her socially exceptionable. Then he comes across Daisy in the parlor of Mrs. Walker, an American expatriate, whose moral values have adapted to those of Italian society. To others' great shock, Daisy mentions to bring Mr. Giovanelli to an upcoming party, which upsets Mrs. Walker a lot. When Daisy announces she is about to go out for a walk in the Pincio, a public park, with this Mr. Giovanelli, Mrs. Walker warns her not to go. She reminds her both that there is a dangerous "Roman Fever" going around, and that being seen in public with lower-class Italian men will ruin Daisy's reputation. However, Daisy refuses to be dissuaded. Afterwards, Winterbourne walks with her to the park and meets Mr. Giovanelli, a handsome, clever man, but not a gentleman. Worrying about Daisy, Winterbourne insists on sticking with Daisy and Giovanelli as they take their walk. Suddenly, Mrs. Walker appears and begs Daisy to get into her carriage in order to save her reputation. But Daisy steadfastly refuses, turning away to continue her walk with Giovanelli. Then Mrs. Walker leaves with Winterbourne, looking at the pair with tears in her eyes.

Later that week, Daisy comes to Mrs. Walker's party, and brings Mr. Giovanelli with her. Deeply angry with Daisy, Mrs. Walker decides not to speak with her. For the first time, Daisy seems to understand the consequences of her apparently innocent actions. After this, Winterbourne never sees Daisy at parties any more, since the Americans in Rome have stopped inviting her. Every time he sees her at home, Giovanelli is also there. Winterbourne cannot figure out if the two are engaged, nor is it clear what Daisy's feelings are toward Winterbourne. As for himself, Winterbourne cannot decide whether to go on believing Daisy is a "nice girl" or stop worrying about her.

One spring day, Winterbourne runs into Daisy and Giovanelli in a flowering ruin. When Winterbourne tries to tell her that the other Americans now all scorn her for her actions, she tells Winterbourne that she's engaged to Giovanelli.

Very late one evening, while walking home from a dinner party past the Colosseum, Winterbourne decides to indulge himself in the huge ruin by moonlight. Seeing Daisy and Giovanelli again, Winterbourne scolds Giovanelli for allowing Daisy to stay out so late, reminding them of the danger of catching the Roman Fever. When he implies that Daisy has lost his esteem, she seems hurt so much that she says she does not care. As it turns out, Daisy does catch the fever, and a week later she dies. Mrs. Miller, her mother, tells Winterbourne that Daisy asks her to tell him that she is never engaged to Giovanelli. At Daisy's funeral, Giovanelli comes up to Winterbourne, saying that Daisy is the most beautiful girl he has ever met, and the most innocent.

Later, Winterbourne goes back to Geneva to resume his studies. But the next time he sees his aunt, he tells her she was right in a comment she made the spring before: Winterbourne, who had lived too long in Europe, was on track to make some large mistake. Now he feels she has finally made it.

An Excerpt from Part 3

Winterbourne—suddenly and rather oddly rubbed the wrong way by this—raised his eyebrows. "I think it's a pity to make too much fuss about it."

"It's a pity to let the girl ruin herself!"

"She is very innocent," he reasoned in his own troubled interest.

"She's very reckless!" cried Mrs. Walker. "And goodness knows how far—left to itself—it may go. Did you ever," she proceeded to enquire, "see anything so blatantly as the mother? After you had all left me just now I couldn't sit still for thinking of it. It seemed too pitiful not even to attempt to save her. I ordered the carriage and put on my bonnet and came here as quickly as possible. Thank Heaven I have found you!"

"What do you propose to do with us?" asked Winterbourne, uncomfortably smiling.

"To ask her to get in, to drive her about here for half an hour—so that the world may see she's not running absolutely wild—and then to take her safely home."

"I don't think it's a very happy thought," he said after reflexion, "but you're at liberty to try."

Mrs. Walker accordingly tried. The young man went in pursuit of their young lady who had simply nodded and smiled, from her distance, at her recent patroness in the carriage and then had gone her way with her companion. On learning, in the event, that Mrs. Walker had followed her, she retraced her steps, however, with a perfect good grace and with Mr. Giovanelli at her side. She professed herself "enchanted" to have a chance to present this gentleman to her good friend. She immediately achieved the introduction; declaring with it, and as if it were of as little importance, that she had never in her life seen anything so lovely as that lady's carriage rug.

"I am glad you admire it," said her poor pursuer, smiling sweetly. "Will you get in and let me put it over you?"

"Oh, no, thank you," —Daisy knew her mind. "I shall admire it much more as I see you driving round with it."

"Do get in and drive *with* me!" Mrs. Walker pleaded.

"That would be charming, but it's so fascinating just as I am!" —with which the girl radiantly took in the gentlemen on either side of her.

"It may be fascinating, dear child, but it's not the custom here," urged the lady of the victoria, leaning forward in her vehicle with her hands devoutly clasped.

"Well, it ought to be, then!" Daisy imperturbably laughed. "If I didn't walk I should expire."

"You should walk with your mother, dear," cried Mrs. Walker with a loss of patience.

"With my mother dear?" the girl amusedly echoed. Winterbourne saw that she scented interference. "My mother never walked ten steps in her life. And then, you know," she blandly added, "I am more than five years old."

"You are old enough to be more reasonable. You are old enough, dear Miss Miller, to be talked about."

Daisy wondered to extravagance. "Talked about? What do you mean?"

"Come into my carriage, and I will tell you."

Daisy turned shining eyes again from one of the gentlemen beside her to the other. Mr. Giovanelli was bowing to and fro, rubbing down his gloves and laughing very irresponsibly; Winterbourne thought the scene the most unpleasant possible. "I don't think I want to know what you mean," the girl presently said. "I don't think I should like it."

Winterbourne only wished that Mrs. Walker would tuck up her carriage rug and drive away, but this lady, as she afterward told him, did not feel she could "rest there." "Should you prefer being thought a very reckless girl?" she accordingly asked.

"Gracious me!" exclaimed Daisy. She looked again at Mr. Giovanelli, then she turned to her other companion. There was a little pink flush in her cheek; she was tremendously pretty. "Does Mr. Winterbourne think," she put to him with a wonderful bright intensity of appeal, "that—to save my reputation—I ought to get into the carriage?"

It really embarrassed him; for an instant he cast about—so strange was it to hear her speak that way of her "reputation." But he himself in fact had to speak in accordance with gallantry. The finest gallantry here was surely just to tell her the truth; and the truth, for our young man, as the few indications I have been able to give have made him known to the reader, was that his charming friend should listen to the voice for civilized society. He took in again exquisite prettiness and then said the more distinctly: "I think you should get into the carriage."

Daisy gave the rein to her amusement. "I never heard anything so stiff! If this is improper, Mrs. Walker," she pursued, "then I am all improper, and you had better give me right up. Goodbye; I hope you'll have a lovely ride!" —and with Mr. Giovanelli, who made a triumphantly obsequious salute, she turned away.

Mrs. Walker sat looking after her, and there were tears in Mrs. Walker's eyes. "Get in here, sir," she said to Winterbourne, indicating the place beside her. The young man answered that he felt bound to accompany Miss Miller; whereupon the lady of the victoria declared that if he refused her this favor she would never speak to him again. She was evidently wound up. He accordingly hastened to overtake Daisy and her more faithful ally, and, offering her his hand, told her that Mrs. Walker had made a stringent claim on his presence. He had expected her to answer with something rather free, something still more significant of the perversity from which the voice of society, through the lips of their distressed friend, had so endeavored to dissuade her. But she only let her hand slip, as she scarce looked at him, through his lightly awkward grasp; while Mr. Giovanelli, to make it worse, bade him farewell with too emphatic a flourish of the hat.

Naturalism

Naturalism is an outgrowth of realism, which begins after Romanticism, in part as a reaction to it. Unlike the Romantic ideal, which focuses on the inner life of the individual, realism is devoted to the description of the details of everyday existence as an expression of the social milieu of the characters. In naturalist literature, the general direction of realism is taken further and the subjects changes to primarily people of lower birth. And writers concentrate on the filth of society and see the travails of the lower classes as the focal point of their writing. Unlike realism, which focuses on literary technique, naturalism implies a philosophical position. For naturalistic writers, since human beings are, in Emile Zola's phrase, "human beasts," characters can be studied through their relationships to their surroundings.

Naturalistic writers are influenced by the evolution theory of Charles Darwin (1809–1882). His "natural selection," for which Herbert Spencer (1820–1903) later substituted "survival of the fittest," justifies the fierce competition and the subsequent immorality. Man does everything only in order to survive in the struggle for existence. It is also believed that one's heredity and social environment decide one's character.

Whereas realism seeks only to describe subjects as they really are, naturalism also attempts to determine "scientifically" the underlying forces, like the environment or heredity, influencing these subjects' actions. For example, Émile Zola's works has a sexual frankness along with a pervasive pessimism. In addition, naturalistic works never fail to expose the dark harshness of life, including poverty, racism, prejudice, disease, prostitution, filth, etc. They are often very pessimistic and frequently criticized for being too blunt.

In the United States, the genre is associated with writers such as Jack London, and most prominently Stephen Crane, Frank Norris, and Theodore Dreiser. The term naturalism operates primarily in counter distinction to realism, particularly the mode of realism associated with William Dean Howells and Henry James. In philosophical and generic terms, American naturalism must be defined rather more loosely, as a reaction against the realist fiction of the 1870s and 1880s, whose scope is limited to middle-class or "local color" topics, with taboos on sexuality and violence.

The naturalist often describes his characters as though they are conditioned and controlled by environment, heredity, instinct, or chance. But he also suggests a compensating humanistic value in his characters or their fates, which affirms the significance of the individual and of his life. The tension here is between the naturalist's desire to represent in fiction the new, discomfiting truths which he has found in the ideas and life of his late-19th-century world, and also his desire to find some meaning in experience which reasserts the validity of the human enterprise.

Theodore Dreiser (1871–1945)

Theodore Dreiser, an American journalist and novelist, was one of the leading literary figures to employ naturalism in his writings. While his writings often focused on the commonplace and sordid in human existence, they also challenged contemporary perspectives on the ideal American family.

Theodore Dreiser was born in Terre Hanta, Indiana into a German immigrant family. Living in a poor and intensely religious family, Dreiser had a very unhappy childhood. After quitting school at the age of fifteen, he went in 1887 to Chicago, where he earned meager support from a variety of menial jobs. With the help of a high-school teacher he spent a year at Indiana University. In 1892 he began his career as a reporter, first with the Chicago *Globe* and then with several other newspapers. Slowly he groped his way to an authorship.

His first novel *Sister Carrie* was published in 1900. In the following years Dreiser turned to writing novels as a full-time career. His second novel *Jenni Gerhardt* (1911) was more successful than *Sister Carrie*. After that he published *The Financier* (1912) and *The Titan* (1914), with *The Stoic* (1947), called his "Trilogy of Desire." While Dreiser was giving full play to his talent in his novel-writing, *The Genius* (1915) was again, like *Sister Carrie*, subjected to a "moral" siege. All the novels he produced during this period directed their target of attack at the corrosive influence of the American society and the evil way toward wealth. For ten years he was engaged in writing travel accounts, plays and short stories. In 1925 he published his greatest and most successful novel *An American Tragedy*. In most of his works, he makes a point of exploring the role played by heredity and environment in shaping a character's fate. This motif is all prominent in *An American Tragedy*, *Jennie Gerhardt* and *The Bulwark* (1946).

In his own life, Dreiser proved that he was just as controlled by his sexual appetite as were his characters. Separating permanently from his wife Sara White without a divorce in 1909, Dreiser carried on several affairs at once. In 1919, he met Helen Patges Richardson, a young and beautiful actress. They had a relationship for about twenty-five years that survived periods of separation, estrangement and his affairs. Dreiser and Richardson finally got married in 1944, two years after Sara died.

In his lifetime Dreiser was controversial as a man and as a writer. As time passes, however, Dreiser has become recognized as both a profound and prescient critic of debased American values and a powerful novelist of critical realism. Dreiser has a unique style characterized by his excessively long sentences that appear to be awkward in structure and disorganized in voice. He tends to present life in a very realistic way with no comment and no judgment. His stunning character development and his portrayal of rural and urban American life has an enormous influence on the generations to follow.

Selected Reading

Sister Carrie

Dissatisfied with life in her rural Wisconsin home, 18-year-old Carrie Meeber takes the train to Chicago, where her older sister and her husband have agreed to take her in. On the train, Carrie meets Charles Drouet, a traveling salesman, who is attracted by her simple beauty and unspoiled manner. They exchange addresses and promise to keep in touch.

To her great disappointment, Carrie finds that her life under her sister's roof is far from happy. Both Minnie Hanson and Sven Hanson are hard-working with no enjoyment for life. Consequently, they disapprove of Carrie's interest in Chicago's recreational opportunities, particularly the theater. So Carrie writes to Drouet and discourages him from calling her.

Supposed to pay rent to the Hansons, she takes a job in a shoe factory. Before long, she is shocked by the coarse manners of the factory workers, the physical demands of the job, as well as the squalid factory conditions. One day, after an illness that costs her job, she encounters Drouet on a downtown street. Still taken by her beauty, he persuades her to dine with him and buys her some clothes. Smothered by the coldness in her sister's house, Carrie moves to live with Drouet a few days later.

Carrie now lives in a large apartment and acquires some sophisticated mannerisms, even though she struggles with the moral implications of being a kept woman. By the time Drouet introduces Carrie to George Hurstwood, the manager of a respectable salon, her material appearance has improved considerably. Hurstwood, unhappy with and distant from his wife and children, instantly becomes fascinated with Carrie's beauty. Before long they start an affair, meeting secretly. Later Drouet asks Carrie to play a role in a theatrical presentation. Both Drouet and Hurstwood are moved deeply by Carrie's stunning performance due to her natural aptitude for play.

The next day everything is uncovered: Drouet discovers that he has been cheated, Carrie learns that Hurstwood is married, and Hurstwood's wife learns about Hurstwood's love affair. Faced with his wife's financial demands and Carrie's rejection, Hurstwood is so hopeless that he takes a large sum of money from his employer's unlocked safe. Claiming that Drouet is hurt, he forces Carrie to escapes with him to Montreal. Once they arrive in Montreal, Hurstword is tracked down by a private detective, who urges him to return most of the stolen funds.

Then the couple get married hastily and move to New York, where Hurstwood rent a flat where they live as George and Carrie Wheeler. Then Hurstwood invests his money in a second-rate saloon. As he and Carrie settle down to a routine existence in New York, they grow more and more distant from each other. After only a few years, Hurstwood's business partner terminates the partnership and Hurstwood loses all his money. Too arrogant to accept most of the job opportunities available to him, Hurstwood begin to stay at home all day. In the end, Carrie sets out to look for job and gets one as a chorus girl. Once again, her aptitude for theater serves her well. As Hurstwood declines into obscurity, Carrie rises to fame day by day. She leaves Hurstwood and moves to live with a new friend.

Hurstwood ultimately joins the homeless of New York, taking odd jobs, falling ill with pneumonia, and even becoming a beggar. Reduced to standing in line for bread and charity, he finally commits suicide. Meanwhile, Carrie becomes a famous actress, but finds that money and fame fails to satisfy her longings or bring her happiness and that nothing will.

An Excerpt from Chapter 47: The Way of the Beaten: A Harp in the Wind

And now Carrie had attained that which in the beginning seemed life's object, or at least, such fraction of it as human beings ever attain of their original desires. She could look about on her gowns and carriage, her furniture and bank account. Friends there were, as the world takes it—those who would bow and smile in acknowledgment of her success. For these she had once craved. Applause there was, and publicity—once far off, essential things, but now grown trivial and indifferent. Beauty also—her type of loveliness—and yet she was lonely. In her rocking-chair she sat, when not otherwise engaged—singing and dreaming.[1]

Thus in life there is ever the intellectual and the emotional nature—the mind that reasons, and the mind that feels. Of one come the men of action—generals and statesmen; of the other, the poets and dreamers—artists all.

As harps in the wind, the latter respond to every breath of fancy voicing in their

Note [1] In her rocking-chair she sat, when not otherwise engaged—singing and dreaming: She was dreaming of the bright future. Although she was often disillusioned, she was not in despair.

moods all the ebb and flow of the ideal.

Man has not yet comprehended the dreamer any more than he has the ideal. For him the laws and morals of the world are unduly severe. Ever hearkening[1] to the sound of beauty, straining for the flash of its distant wings, he watches to follow, wearying his feet in traveling. So watched Carrie, so followed, rocking and singing.

And it must be remembered that reason had little part in this. Chicago dawning, she saw the city offering more of loveliness than she had ever known, and instinctively, by force of her moods alone, clung to it. In fine raiment and elegant surroundings, men seemed to be contented. Hence, she drew near these things. Chicago, New York; Drouet, Hurstwood; the world of fashion and the world of stage—these were but incidents. Not them, but that which they represented, she longed for. Time proved the representation false.

Oh, the tangle of human life! How dimly as yet we see. Here was Carrie, in the beginning poor, unsophisticated, emotional; responding with desire to everything most lovely in life, yet finding herself turned as by a wall. Laws to say: "Be allured, if you will, by everything lovely, but draw not nigh[2] unless by righteousness." Convention to say: "You shall not better your situation save by honest labor." If honest labor be unremunerative and difficult to endure; if it be the long, long road which never reaches beauty, but wearies the feet and the heart; if the drag to follow beauty be such that one abandons the admired way, taking rather the despised path leading to her dreams quickly, who shall cast the first stone[3]? Not evil, but longing for that which is better, more often directs the steps of the erring. Not evil, but goodness more often allures the feeling mind unused to reason.

Amid the tinsel and shine of her state walked Carrie, unhappy. As when Drouet took her, she had thought: "Now am I lifted into that which is best;" as when Hurstwood seemingly offered her the better way: "Now am I happy." But since the world goes its way past all who will not partake of its folly, she now found herself alone[4]. Her purse was open

---

Note [1] hearkening: listening (to)

Note [2] nigh: near

Note [3] who shall cast the first stone: who shall begin first? "Throw the first stone" is from the Bible. People bring a woman who commits adultery to Jesus, "Teacher," they said to Jesus, "this woman was caught in the very act of committing adultery. In our Law Moses commanded that such a woman must be stoned to death. Now, what do you say?" They said this to trap Jesus, so that they could accuse him. But he bent over and wrote on the ground with his finger. As they stood there asking him questions, he straightly ended up and said to them, "whichever one of you has committed no sin may throw the first stone at her." Then he bent over again and wrote on the ground. When they heard this, they all left, one by one, the older ones first.

Note [4] But since the world goes its way…, she now found herself alone: Because Carrie didn't want to go with the tide, she felt lonely.

to him whose need was greatest. In her walks on Broadway, she no longer thought of the elegance of the creatures who passed her. Had they more of that peace and beauty which glimmered afar off, then were they to be envied.

Drouet abandoned his claim and was seen no more. Of Hurstwood's death she was not even aware. A slow, black boat setting out from the pier at Twenty-seventh Street upon its weekly errand bore, with many others, his nameless body to the Potter's Field[1].

Thus passed all that was of interest concerning these twain in their relation to her. Their influence upon her life is explicable alone by the nature of her longings. Time was when both represented for her all that was most potent in earthly success. They were the personal representatives of a state most blessed to attain—the titled ambassadors of comfort and peace, aglow with their credentials. It is but natural that when the world which they represented no longer allured her, its ambassadors should be discredited. Even had Hurstwood returned in his original beauty and glory, he could not now have allured her. She had learned that in his world, as in her own present state, was not happiness.

Sitting alone, she was now an illustration of the devious ways by which one who feels, rather than reasons, may be led in the pursuit of beauty. Though often disillusioned, she was still waiting for that halcyon day when she should be led forth among dreams become real. Ames had pointed out a farther step, but on and on beyond that, if accomplished, would lie others for her. It was forever to be the pursuit of that radiance of delight which tints the distant hilltops of the world.

Oh, Carrie, Carrie! Oh, blind strivings of the human heart! Onward, onward, it saith[2], and where beauty leads, there it follows. Whether it be the tinkle of a lone sheep bell o'er some quiet landscape, or the glimmer of beauty in sylvan places, or the show of soul in some passing eye, the heart knows and makes answer, following. It is when the feet weary and hope seems vain that the heartaches and the longings arise. Know, then, that for you is neither surfeit nor content. In your rocking-chair, by your window dreaming, shall you long, alone. In your rocking-chair, by your window, shall you dream such happiness as you may never feel.

Jack London (1876–1916)

Jack London, a pioneer in the then-burgeoning world of commercial magazine fiction, is one of the first Americans to make a lucrative career exclusively from writing.

Jack London, born near Third and Brannan Streets in San Francisco, was deserted by his

---

Note [1] Potter's Field: public graveyard in the suburbs of New York City
Note [2] it saith: it says

father. He was raised in Oakland through infancy by an ex-slave, Virginia Prentiss, because his mother was ill. London was essentially self-educated. He taught himself in the public library, mainly just by reading books. In 1885 he was inspired by Ouida's long Victorian novel *Signa*, which describes an unschooled Italian peasant child who achieves fame as an opera composer.

Seeking a way out of his hard work, London borrowed money from his black foster-mother Virginia Prentiss, and became an oyster pirate himself. In 1893, he signed on to the sealing schooner *Sophie Sutherland*, bound for the coast of Japan. When he returned, the country was in the grip of the panic and Oakland was swept by labor unrest. He joined Kelly's industrial army and began his career as a tramp. After many experiences as a hobo and a sailor, he returned to Oakland and attended Oakland High School, where he contributed a number of articles to the high school's magazine, *The Aegis*. His first published work was "Typhoon off the Coast of Japan" (1893), an account of his sailing experiences. Jack London desperately wanted to attend the University of California and in 1896 did so. But financial circumstances forced him to leave in 1897.

In later life London indulged his very wide-ranging interests with a personal library of 15,000 volumes. In 1897, London and his brother-in-law sailed to join the Klondike Gold Rush where he would later set his first successful stories. London survived the hardships of the Klondike, and these struggles inspired what is often called his best short story, "To Build a Fire" (1902).

On returning to Oakland in 1898, he began struggling seriously to break into print, a struggle memorably described in his novel, *Martin Eden* (1900).

London started his writing career, just as new printing technologies enabled lower-cost production of magazines, which resulted in a boom in popular magazines aiming at a wide public, and a strong market for short fiction. Jack London's most famous novels included *The Call of the Wild* (1903), *White Fang* (1906), *The Sea-Wolf* (1904), *The Iron Heel* (1908) and *Martin Eden*. Although he was accused of plagiarism many times during his career, his stories on man and nature has been quite popular all over the world. In them, London stripes everything down to the symbolic starkness of dream, to a primordial simplicity that has the strange and compelling power of ancient myth.

O. Henry (1862–1910)

O. Henry, the pseudonym of American writer William Sydney Porter, is famous for his short stories with twist endings.

O. Henry was born in Greensboro, North Carolina. When he was three, O. Henry's mother died, and he and his father moved into the home of his paternal grandmother. As a child, O. Henry was always reading and his favorite reading was *One Thousand and One Nights*. After receiving some education early in his life, he was licensed as a pharmacist at the age of 19. At the drugstore, he also showed off his natural artistic talents by sketching the townsfolk.

O. Henry traveled to Texas in 1882, hoping that a change of air would help alleviate a persistent cough he had developed. While on the ranch, he learned bits of Spanish and German from the mix of immigrant ranch hands. He also spent time reading classic literature. O. Henry's health did improve and he traveled to Austin in 1884. Apart from his various occupations: pharmacist, draftsman, bank teller and journalist, he began writing as a sideline to employment. Then O. Henry met and began courting Athol Estes from a wealthy family. Her mother objected to the match because Athol was suffering from tuberculosis. In 1887 O. Henry eloped with Athol to the home of Reverend R. K. Smoot, where they were married. The couple continued to participate in musical and theater groups, and Athol encouraged her husband to pursue his writing.

In the following years, he continued his contributions to magazines and newspapers, and finally worked full time on his humorous weekly called *The Rolling Stone*, which featured satire on life, people and politics. After *The Rolling Stone* failed in 1895, O. Henry started writing for the *Houston Post* in Houston.

O. Henry's most prolific writing period started in 1902, when he moved to New York, where he wrote a story a week for the *New York World Sunday Magazine*. His wit, characterization and plot twists were adored by his readers, but panned by the critics. Yet, he went on to gain international recognition and was credited with defining the short story as a literary art form. Due to his contribution to short stories, The O. Henry Award is established to be given to short stories of exceptional merit.

O. Henry's stories are famous for their surprise endings, often referred to as an "O. Henry ending." He is called the American answer to Guy de Maupassant. Both authors write twist endings, but O. Henry's stories are much more playful and optimistic.

Among his more popular offerings, "The Gift of the Magi," is recited countless times every Christmas to demonstrate the power of giving, echoing the words of Jesus that "it is more blessed to give than to receive." It is about a young couple who are short of money but desperately wants to buy each other Christmas gifts. Unbeknownst to Jim, Della sells her most valuable possession, her beautiful hair, in order to buy a platinum fob chain for Jim's watch; while unbeknownst to Della, Jim sells his own most valuable possession, his watch, to buy jeweled combs for Della's hair. The essential premise of this story has been copied, reworked, parodied and otherwise retold since it was written.

Part Five

American Modernism

Philosophical and Historical Background

Marxism and Darwinism   Marxism is an indispensable paradigm for modernism because it defines "modernity" as a historical stage in which capitalism, profit-oriented and technology-driven, seriously changes the world we live in and our "humanity." Marxist idea of "class" remains basic and relevant in social understanding. In the American context, "class" increasing informs discussions of "race" and "gender." Through these categories Americans become better able to analyze social injustice and oppression. The idea of "alienation," basic to Marxism, is also basic to modern literature. For instance, Marxism can offer powerful insights into the alienation theme in Kafka.

Darwinism also continues to exert a great influence on man's mind in the modern period. People used to believe in God partly because they were told that they were created by God, based on the Bible. But now Charles Darwin shatters the world by declaring that we, human beings, have evolved from lower animals, which has nothing to do with God. Their sufferings make them become dubious about the benevolence of God. The long established belief is further challenged by the two world wars in the 20th century, which echoes Nietzsche's words, "God is Dead!"

Sigmund Freud (1856–1939)—the "father" of psychoanalysis   Freud is best known for his theories of the unconscious mind. Crucial to the operation of the unconscious is "repression." According to Freud, people often experience thoughts and feelings, esp. childhood experiences that are so painful that they can not bear them. Such thoughts and feelings—and associated memories—could not, Freud argued, be banished from the mind, but could be banished from consciousness. Thus they come to constitute the unconscious. Although we do not recall them consciously, they continue to influence our behavior and life in the future.

Eventually, Freud abandoned the idea of the unconscious and proposed that the psyche could be divided into three parts: ego, superego and id. The id is concerned with instinctual drives and human desires. Ego is the rational, realistic personality process. Superego is the idealized image that a person builds of himself in response to authority and social pressures. The id and the superego often come into conflict with each other. It is the task of the ego, according to Freud, to try to fine a realistic way to resolve the conflict.

Oedipus complex is a Freudian term originating from a Greek tragedy, in which King Oedipus unknowingly killed his father and married his mother. Freud developed the notion of the Oedipus complex to explain the child's unconscious desire for the exclusive love of the parent of the opposite sex, occurring around the age of five and a half years (a period known as the phallic stage in Freudian theory). This desire includes jealousy toward the parent of the same sex and the unconscious wish for that parent's death.

Friedrich Wilhelm Nietzsche (1844–1900)   The German philosopher Nietzsche is known as one of the main representatives of atheistic philosophy. Nietzsche was prophetic in the sense that he raised fundamental questions about the two key traditions of the West—Christianity and philosophy. He is famous for the phrase, "God is dead." However, he is often characterized as the most religious atheist. In this contradictory tension lies the enigmatic thinker, Nietzsche, who raised a number of fundamental questions that challenge the root of the philosophical tradition of the West. Among the most poignant are his criticisms of Christianity and the Western trust in rationality. Nietzsche's sincere and uncompromising quest for truth and his tragic life have touched the hearts of a wide range of people. Nietzsche believes that the higher values of Western culture, a combination of Christianity and Platonism, have devaluated themselves and that it is time to reevaluate all existing values.

Nietzsche made a sharp distinction between Jesus and Christianity. While he severely criticized Christianity, he had a high esteem for Jesus. For Nietzsche, Jesus is the only "authentic Christian" who lived according to what he taught. Christianity promises everything, but fulfills nothing.

As Husserl and Kierkegaard realized, one may hold certain beliefs underneath rational thinking. Nietzsche and Schopenhauer pointed out that, underneath rational discourse, human reason has unnoticed irrational drives.

Albert Einstein (1879–1955)   The beginning of the 20th century saw the rapid development in all fields of technology at a speed the world had never seen. The summit of this was represented by Einstein, who revolutionized science with his theory of relativity. Einstein was a German-born theoretical physicist. He is best known for his theory of relativity and specifically the equation $E=mc^2$, which indicates the relationship between mass and energy (or mass-energy equivalence). Einstein received the 1921 Nobel Prize in Physics "for his services to Theoretical Physics, and especially for his discovery of the law of the photoelectric effect."

World War I and World War II   With the wars the whole world had undergone a dramatic social change, a transformation from order to disorder. And so had the United States. On one hand, the United States' participation in World War I marked a crucial stage in the nation's evolution to a world power. Since the wars were not fought on the American soil, by the second decade of the 20th century, the United States had become the most powerful industrialized nation in the world, outstripping Britain and Germany in terms of industrial production. Despite its booming industry and material prosperity, there was a widespread moral decay and spiritual crisis. Young people who joined the war found that the war was not as glorious and heroic as it was claimed to be. Disillusioned and disgusted by the reality in America, they became careless about their life so much so that some began to indulge in drugs. Girls wore short skirts and boys took drugs. In a word, the first few decades of the 20th century was best described as a spiritual wasteland.

Modernism can be regarded as an advanced form of realism, but more complex and more diversified than realism. While realism is concerned with what is the reality, modernism cares more about how the reality is narrated. Besides, language is not just a transparent medium of reality, but it is constitutive of reality. It is characterized by some new experimentation on the form of literature and new interpretations, such as psychoanalysis, open-endedness and perspectivism.

Ezra Pound (1885–1972)

Ezra Pound, an American expatriate and critic, was a major figure of the modernist movement in the early-20th-century poetry and a leading spokesman of the Imagist Movement.

Ezra Pound was born in Hailey, Idaho, United States. He studied for two years at the University of Pennsylvania and later received his B.A. from Hamilton College in 1905. During his studies at Penn, he met and befriended William Carlos Williams, and H.D. (Hilda Doolittle), to whom he was engaged for a time. He taught at Wabash College in Crawfordsville, Indiana for less than a year, and left as the result of a minor scandal. In 1908 Pound traveled to Europe. He finally settled in London where he met William Butler Yeats, after spending several months in Venice.

In the years before World War I, Pound was largely responsible for the appearance of imagism and vorticism, philosophies and poetics deeply rooted in the ideogrammatic method he had developed through his study of Eastern culture. These two movements helped bring to notice the work of new poets and artists like James Joyce, William Carlos Williams and H.D. Pound also edited his friend T.S. Eliot's *The Waste Land*, the poem that was to force the new poetic sensibility into broader public attention.

World War I, however, shattered Pound's belief in modern Western civilization and he abandoned London soon for Europe, but not before he published "Homage to Sextus Propertius" (1919) and "Hugh Selwyn Mauberley" (1920). If these poems together form a farewell to Pound's London career, *The Cantos*, which he began in 1915, pointed his way forward. The years from 1920 to 1924 Pound spent in Paris, where he was involved in a popular literary salon run by American woman writer Gertrude Stein and began to devote himself to the experimentations on poetry. During World War II, he turned to support the Italian government, engaged in some radio broadcasts of anti-Semitism and pro-Fascism. As a result, he was arrested in 1945 on charges of treason. Declared insane, he was confined in a hospital in Washington, D.C., for over 12 years. During these years, he produced *The Pisan Cantos* (1948), for which he was awarded the Bollingen Prize in 1949. He was released in 1958, thanks to a campaign by his fellow writers, and returned to live in Italy until his death.

Despite the fact he was politically controversial, Pound's literary achievement can not be ignored. He composed poems, wrote criticisms and did translations. His poetic works include *Collected Early Poems of Ezra Pound* (1982), *Personae* (1909) and his lifelong work *The Cantos* published between 1916 and 1969. *The Cantos* consist of a long, incomplete poem in 120 sections.

Each of these sections is referred to as a *canto*, Italian for *song*. Most of the cantos were written between 1915 and 1962, although much of the early work was abandoned and the early cantos, as finally published, date from 1922 onwards. It is a book-length work, and is widely considered to be one of the most formidable poems in the English language and among the most significant works of poetry in the 20th century. The poem is dense and abstract, with no single narrative or narrator, resembling more a collage of disparate but thematically related fragments. In particular, the themes of economics, governance and culture, and their relation to the creative activity of the poet are all constants throughout the piece.

In addition, Pound wrote some critical essays, such as *Make It New* (1934), *Literary Essays* (1954), *The ABC of Reading* (1934) and *Polite Essays* (1937).These essays illustrate his evaluation of literary traditions and modern writing. He also published several volumes of translation, including *The Translations of Ezra Pound* (1953), *Confucius* (1969) and *Shih-Ching* (1954). These works provide a deep understanding of Pound's association with Oriental literature.

The Imagist Movement, which flourished from 1909 to 1917, involved quite a number of British and American writers and poets. This is a movement that advanced modernism in arts which concentrated on reforming the medium of poetry as opposed to Romanism. As one of the leaders of the imagism, Pound endorsed three main principles, which include direct treatment of poetic subjects, elimination of merely ornamental or superfluous words and rhythmical composition in the sequence of the musical phrase rather than in the sequence of a metronome.

By means of myth and personae, Pound argues that the poet must "screen himself" and speak indirectly through an impersonal and objective story. His poetry is also dense with allusions at the expense of syntax and summary statements. In spite of all this, Pound's reputation as a forerunner of the 20th-century American poetry has never been depreciated.

Selected Reading

In the Station of the Metro[1]

By linking human faces, a synecdoche for people themselves, with petals on a damp bough, the poet calls attention to both the elegance of human life, and its transience. A dark, wet bough implies that it has just rained, and the petals stuck to the bough were shortly before attached to flowers from the tree. They may still be living, but they will not be for long. In this way, Pound calls attention to human mortality as a whole—we are all dying. This is the essence of the poem.

Note [1] Metro: Paris subway

In a Station of the Metro

The apparition[1] of these faces in the crowd;

Petals on a wet, black bough.

❧ Robert Frost (1874–1963)

Robert Frost, one of the most popular American poets of the 20th century, was honored with Pulitzer Prizes four times. Frost was invited to read his poem "The Gift Outright" at the inauguration of President John F. Kennedy in 1961.

Robert Frost was born in San Francisco, California, where he spent his childhood. In 1885 after his father died of tuberculosis, the Frosts moved to Massachusetts. Frost attended Dartmouth College and Harvard, worked farms and taught school. In his spare time, he wrote poetry. Disappointed with the little attention his poems received, he moved to Great Britain to present his work to readers there. As he had expected, *A Boy's Will* (1913) and *North of Boston* (1914) including "Mending Wall" were published one after another.

Having established his reputation, Frost returned to the United States in 1915 and bought a farm in New Hampshire, where he launched a career of writing, teaching and lecturing. In the following years, he published more books of poetry: *Mountain Interval* (1916) including "The Road Not Taken"; *New Hampshire* (1923) including "Stopping by Woods on a Snowy Evening," which won him the first Pulitzer Prize; Collected *Poems* (1930) and *A Further Range* (1935) winning him another two Pulitzer Prizes; *A Witness Tree* (1942) including "The Gift Outright," which won him the fourth Pulitzer Prize. Due to his remarkable achievement, Frost received honorary degrees from Princeton, Oxford and Cambridge universities and was the first one to receive two honorary degrees from Dartmouth College.

Frost is generally considered a regional poet whose subject matters mainly focus on the landscape and people in New England. The rural life in New England was frequently employed to illustrate complex social and philosophical themes, such as the basic themes of man's life: the individual's relationships to himself, to his fellow-man, to his world and to his God.

Robert Frost has long been well known as a poet who can hardly be classified with the old or the new. Unlike his contemporaries in the early 20th century, he does not break up with the poetic tradition nor made any experiment on form. Instead, he learns from the tradition, especially the familiar conventions of nature poetry and of classical pastoral poetry, and makes the colloquial New England speech into a poetic expression. However, profound ideas are delivered under the disguise

---

Note [1] apparition: a visible appearance of something not present, and especially of a dead person

of the plain language and simple form, for what Frost does is to take symbols from the limited human world and the pastoral landscape to refer to the great world beyond the rustic scene.

Selected Reading

The Road Not Taken

Two roads diverged in a yellow wood,
And sorry I could not travel both
And be one traveler, long I stood
And looked down one as far as I could
To where it bent in the undergrowth;

Then took the other, as just as fair,
And having perhaps the better claim[1],
Because it was grassy and wanted[2] wear;
Though as for that the passing there
Had worn them really about the same,

And both that morning equally lay,
In leaves no step had trodden black.
Oh, I kept the first for another day!
Yet knowing how way leads on to way,
I doubted if I should ever come back.

I shall be telling this with a sigh[3]
Somewhere ages and ages hence:
Two roads diverged in a wood, and I—
I took the one less traveled by,
And that has made all the difference.

Note [1] claim: reason

Note [2] wanted: desired

Note [3] sigh: indicating relief or happiness, or regret or sorrow. The interpretation of its meaning is up to the reader.

Stopping by Woods on a Snowy Evening

Whose woods these are I think I know.
His house is in the village though;
He will not see me stopping here
To watch his woods fill up with snow.

My little horse must think it queer
To stop without a farmhouse near
Between the woods and frozen lake
The darkest evening of the year.

He gives his harness bells a shake
To ask if there is some mistake.
The only other sound's the sweep
Of easy wind and downy flake.

The woods are lovely, dark and deep,
But I have promises to keep,
And miles to go before I sleep,
And miles to go before I sleep.

The Jazz Age　The Jazz Age was a movement that took place during the 1920s, or the Roaring Twenties, from which jazz music and dance emerged with the introduction of mainstream radio and the end of the war. The 1920s was a decade of profound social changes. The most obvious signs of change were the rise of a consumer-oriented economy and of mass entertainment, which helped to bring about a "revolution in morals and manners." Sexual mores, gender roles, hair styles and dress all changed profoundly during the 1920s. Many Americans regarded these changes as liberation from the country's past. But for others, morals seemed to be decaying, and the United States seemed to be changing in undesirable ways. The result was a thinly veiled "cultural civil war." The young set themselves free, especially the young women. They shocked the older generation with their new hair style (a short bob) and the clothes that they wore were often much shorter than had been seen and tended to expose their legs and knees. The wearing of what were considered skimpy beach wear in public could get the Flappers, as they were known, arrested for indecent exposure. They wore silk stockings rolled just above the knee and they got their hair cut at male barbers. Consequently, the Jazz Age was characterized by individualism and a great emphasis on the pursuit of pleasure and enjoyment.

F. Scott Fitzgerald (1896–1940)

Francis Scott Key Fitzgerald, one of the greatest American novelists and short story writers of the 1920s, is generally regarded as the leading spokesman of the Jazz Age and a representative of the Lost Generation.

F. Scott Fitzgerald was born into an upper-middle class family in St. Paul, Minnesota. Early in his life, he admired his gentlemanly father for his upper-class manners, but was a little sensitive to the poor Irish beginnings of his mother. After receiving education in private schools, he entered Princeton University in 1913. However, he dropped out in 1917 to enlist in the army in Alabama, when America entered World War I.

The 1920s proved the most influential decade of Fitzgerald's literary career. His first novel *This Side of Paradise* was published in 1920 and became one of the most popular books of the year, defining the flapper generation. It won him not only wealth and fame, but also the expensive gift Zelda Sayre, a beautiful woman from a prominent family. She became the prototype of the rich, beautiful women whom Fitzgerald characterized vividly in his works. His second novel *The Beautiful and Damned* published in 1922 further increased his fame. *The Great Gatsby* considered his masterpiece was published in 1925. *Tender is the Night* (1934) was another important novel. Meanwhile, Fitzgerald made several excursions to Europe and became friends with many members of the American expatriate community in Paris, notably Ernest Hemingway.

In the 1930s, a series of misfortunes happened to Fitzgerald: His reputation declined; his health fell; Zelda was confined to a sanitarium for the rest of her life due to some mental breakdowns. In the end, he died of a heart attack, with his last novel *The Last Tycoon* unfinished.

In addition to novels, Fitzgerald produced some popular short stories, such as *Flappers and Philosophers* (1921), *Tales of the Jazz Age* (1922), *All the Sad Young Men* (1926), *Taps at Reveille* (1935).

In both his novels and short stories, Fitzgerald never spares an intimate touch to deal with the bankruptcy of the American dream, which is highlighted by the disillusionment of the protagonists' personal dreams due to the clash between their romantic vision of life and the sordid reality. A great number of his stories start with the basic situation in which a rising young man of the middle class is in love with the daughter of a very rich family. The young man is not attracted by the fortune in itself; he is not seeking money so much as what money can bring to him; and he loves the girl not so much as he loves what the girl symbolizes. Money is only a convenient and inadequate symbol for what he dreams of earning, and love merely a vehicle that can transport him to a magic world of eternal happiness. The man's real dream is that of achieving a new status and a new essence, of rising to a loftier place in the mysterious hierarchy of human worth. That is why Daisy seems so charming to Gatsby and that is why Gatsby has directed his whole life to winning back her love. Although the protagonist's pursuit of his dream only proves to be futile since what he seeks is nothing but an illusion, and even a nightmare in some cases, Fitzgerald does not negate the affirmative role the "magic moments" plays, which attend the hope and expectations of eternal happiness.

The Great Gatsby chronicles an era that Fitzgerald himself dubbed the "Jazz Age." Following the shock and chaos of World War I, American society enjoyed unprecedented levels of prosperity during the 1920s as the economy soared. At the same time, Prohibition, the ban on the sale and consumption of alcohol mandated by the Eighteenth Amendment, made millionaires out of bootleggers and gave rise to organized crime. Although Fitzgerald, like Nick Carraway in his novel, idolized the riches and glamor of the age, he was uncomfortable with the unrestrained materialism and lack of morality that went with it. Nick Carraway tells the story in first-person point of view. In describing and analyzing the characters, he sometimes relies on second-hand information, or hearsay, that he is unable to verify. His account, his commentary and his interaction with the characters make him resemble the chorus in an ancient Greek tragedy.

Fitzgerald is a great stylist in American literature. His style, closely related to his themes, is explicit and chilly. His accurate dialogues, his careful observation of mannerism, styles, models and attitudes provide the reader with a vivid sense of reality. He follows the Jamesian tradition in using the scenic method in his chapters, each one of which consists of one or more dramatic scenes. He also skillfully employs the device of having events observed by a "central consciousness" to his great advantage. The accurate details, the completely original diction and metaphors, the bold impressionistic and colorful quality have all proved his consummate artistry.

Selected Reading

The Great Gatsby

Nick Carraway, the narrator of the story, takes a job in New York as a bond salesman. He rents a small house in West Egg, Long Island, next to the lavish mansion of Jay Gatsby, a mysterious millionaire who holds extravagant parties. West Egg is home to nouveaux riches families unwelcome in the inner circles of old-money aristocrats in nearby East Egg, located across a narrow bay separating the two Eggs. Unlike other residents in West Egg, Nick can move into East Egg society, for his cousin, Daisy Fay Buchanan, resides in East Egg with her husband, Tom. There they introduce Nick to Jordan Baker, an attractive, cynical young golfer with whom Nick begins a romantic relationship. She reveals to Nick that Tom has a mistress, Myrtle Wilson. Not long after this revelation, Nick travels to

New York with Tom and Myrtle to an apartment where they keep for their affair. At the apartment, a vulgar and bizarre party takes place.

As the summer progresses, Nick eventually receives an invitation to one of Gatsby's parties, to which few people are invited and Gatsby entertain his guests extravagantly. At the party Nick encounters Jordan Baker and they meet Gatsby himself, an aloof and surprisingly young man. Through Jordan, Nick later learns that Gatsby came across Daisy in 1917 and has been deeply in love with her. Gatsby's extravagant lifestyle and wild parties intend to impress Daisy in the hope of winning back her love. Gatsby now wants Nick to arrange a reunion with Daisy. So Nick invites Daisy to have tea at his house, without telling her that Gatsby will also be there. After an initial awkwardness, Gatsby and Daisy, as Gatsby has expected, reestablish their connection. They begin an affair and after a short time, Tom grows increasingly suspicious of his wife's relationship with Gatsby. At a luncheon at the Buchanans' house, Daisy speaks to Gatsby with such undisguised intimacy that Tom realizes she is in love with Gatsby. Despite his own extramarital affair, he is outraged by his wife's infidelity. He forces the group to drive into New York City and confronts Gatsby at the Plaza Hotel, asserting that he and Daisy have a history that Gatsby could never understand. In addition to that, he announces to his wife that Gatsby is a criminal whose fortune comes from bootlegging alcohol and other illegal activities. Daisy realizes that her allegiance is to Tom, and Tom contemptuously sends her back to East Egg with Gatsby, attempting to prove that Gatsby can not hurt him.

When Nick, Jordan and Tom drive through the valley of ashes on their way home, they find out that Gatsby's car has struck and has killed Tom's mistress, Myrtle. Nick learns from Gatsby that Daisy, not Gatsby himself, has driven the car, but Gatsby intends to take the blame anyway. Myrtle's husband, George, thinks that the driver of the yellow car is the secret lover of his wife and sets out to track down its owner. After finding out the yellow car is Gatsby's, he arrives at Gatsby's mansion where he fatally shoots both Gatsby and himself. Nick later discovers that it is Tom who tells Wilson that Gatsby is the driver of the car. Daisy never does anything to expose the lie. Nick stages an unsettlingly small funeral for Gatsby, which no one attends except Gatsby's father who considers his son to be great. Then Nick moves back to the Midwest, disillusioned with the Eastern lifestyle.

An Excerpt from Chapter III

I believe that on the first night I went to Gatsby's house I was one of the few guests who had actually been invited. People were not invited—they went there. They got into automobiles which bore them out to Long Island and somehow they ended up at Gatsby's door. Once there they were introduced by somebody who knew Gatsby and after that they conducted themselves according to the rules of behavior associated with amusement parks. Sometimes they came and went without having met Gatsby at all, came for the party with a simplicity of heart that was its own ticket of admission.

I had been actually invited. A chauffeur in a uniform of robin's egg blue crossed my lawn early that Saturday morning with a surprisingly formal note from his employer: The honor would be entirely Gatsby's, it said, if I would attend his "little party" that night. He had seen me several times and had intended to call on me long before but a peculiar combination of circumstances had prevented it—signed Jay Gatsby, in a majestic hand[1].

Dressed up in white flannels, I went over to his lawn a little after seven and wandered around rather ill at ease among swirls and eddies of people I didn't know—though here and there was a face I had noticed on the commuting train. I was immediately struck by the number of young Englishmen dotted about; all well dressed, all looking a little hungry and all talking in low earnest voices to solid and prosperous Americans. I was sure that they were selling something: bonds or insurance or automobiles. They were at least agonizingly aware of the easy money in the vicinity[2] and convinced that it was theirs for a few words in the right key[3].

As soon as I arrived I made an attempt to find my host, but the two or three people of whom I asked his whereabouts stared at me in such an amazed way, and denied so vehemently any knowledge of his movements, that I slunk off in the direction of the cocktail table—the only place in the garden where a single man could linger without looking purposeless and alone.

I was on my way to get roaring drunk from sheer embarrassment when Jordan Baker came out of the house and stood at the head of the marble steps, leaning a little backward and looking with contemptuous interest down into the garden.

Welcome or not, I found it necessary to attach myself to someone before I should begin to address cordial remarks to the passers-by.

"Hello!" I roared, advancing toward her. My voice seemed unnaturally loud across the garden.

"I thought you might be here," she responded absently as I came up. "I remembered you lived next door to—"

She held my hand impersonally, as a promise that she'd take care of me in a minute,

---

Note [1] majestic hand: bold handwriting

Note [2] They were at least... in the vicinity: The Englishman realized that they could make money easily from the rich Americans at the party.

Note [3] in the right key: in a proper way

and gave ear to two girls in twin yellow dresses, who stopped at the foot of the steps.

"Hello!" they cried together. "Sorry you didn't win."

That was for the golf tournament. She had lost in the finals the week before.

"You don't know who we are," said one of the girls in yellow, "but we met you here about a month ago."

"You've dyed your hair since then," remarked Jordan, and I started but the girls had moved casually on and her remark was addressed to the premature moon, produced like the supper, no doubt, out of a caterer's basket. With Jordan's slender golden arm resting in mine, we descended the steps and sauntered about the garden. A tray of cocktails floated at us through the twilight, and we sat down at a table with the two girls in yellow and three men, each one introduced to us as Mr. Mumble.

"Do you come to these parties often?" inquired Jordan of the girl beside her.

"The last one was the one I met you at," answered the girl, in an alert confident voice. She turned to her companion: "Wasn't it for you, Lucille?"

It was for Lucille, too.

"I like to come," Lucille said. "I never care what I do, so I always have a good time. When I was here last I tore my gown on a chair, and he asked me my name and address— inside of a week[1] I got a package from Croirier's with a new evening gown in it."

"Did you keep it?" asked Jordan.

"Sure I did. I was going to wear it tonight, but it was too big in the bust and had to be altered. It was gas blue with lavender beads. Two hundred and sixty-five dollars."

"There's something funny about a fellow that'll do a thing like that," said the other girl eagerly. "He doesn't want any trouble with *anybody*."

"Who doesn't?" I inquired.

"Gatsby. Somebody told me—"

The two girls and Jordan leaned together confidentially.

"Somebody told me they thought he killed a man once."

A thrill passed over all of us. The three Mr. Mumbles bent forward and listened eagerly.

"I don't think it's so much *that*," argued Lucille skeptically, "it's more that he was a German spy during the war."

One of the men nodded in confirmation.

"I heard that from a man who knew all about him, grew up with him in Germany," he assured us positively.

Note [1] inside of a week: within a week

"Oh, no," said the first girl, "it couldn't be that, because he was in the American army during the war." As our credulity switched back to her she leaned forward with enthusiasm. "You look at him sometimes when he thinks nobody's looking at him. I'll bet he killed a man."

She narrowed her eyes and shivered. Lucille shivered. We all turned and looked around for Gatsby. It was testimony to the romantic speculation he inspired that there were whispers about him from those who found little that it was necessary to whisper about in this world.

The "Lost Generation"　The "Lost Generation" is a term used to refer to the generation, actually a group of young people who lived through World War I. Disillusioned with the way of life in America, they began to write and they wrote from their own experiences in the war. They were basically expatriates who left America and formed a community of writers and artists in Paris, involved with other European novelists and poets in their experimentation on new modes of thought and expression. These writers were later named by an American writer, Gertrude Stein, also an expatriate, "The Lost Generation." The term was popularized by Ernest Hemingway who used it as one of two contrasting epigraphs for his novel, *The Sun Also Rises*. This generation included distinguished artists such as F. Scott Fitzgerald, T. S. Eliot and Earnest Hemingway.

＼ Ernest Hemingway (1899–1961)

Ernest Hemingway, an American novelist and short story writer, is generally regarded as the leading spokesman of the Lost Generation. For his powerful style, he was awarded the Nobel Prize for literature in 1954.

Ernest Hemingway was born in Oak Park, Illinois. As a child, Hemingway lived up to his parents' expectations, behaving himself very well both in study and in life. He also went hunting and fishing with his father in the woods and lakes of northern Michigan, which provided him with first-hand materials to draw on in his later writing. After high school, he began his writing career as a reporter for the *Kansas City Star*. Based on his experience in World War I, the Spanish Civil War and World War II, he wrote many novels and short stories. Depressed, Hemingway shot himself with a gun in the end.

When World War I broke out, Hemingway left his reporting job to serve the war, joining the American Red Cross Ambulance Corps. At the Italian front in 1918, Hemingway was wounded and receiving treatment in a Milan hospital where he was to meet a nurse. Afterwards, Hemingway left for Paris, where he was introduced to Gertrude Stein and got involved in the American expatriate circle that became known as the "Lost Generation." Then he went to serve the Spanish Civil War as a reporter. As the United States entered World War II in 1941, for the first time in his life Hemingway took an active part in a war. Aboard the *Pilar*, Hemingway and his crew were charged with sinking Nazi submarines off the coasts of Cuba and the United States.

Hemingway made his debut in American literature with the publication of the short story collection *In Our Time* (1925). The story is about Nick Adams, who goes out camping along a river to fish, while at the same time suffering flashbacks to traumatic, wartime memories. Adams struggles with his grim experiences of death until he finds peace through the act of partaking in nature by coming to the river to fish. During his time in Montparnasse, Paris, Hemingway wrote his second novel, *The Sun Also Rises* (1926). The semi-autobiographical novel, following a group of expatriate Americans in Europe, was successful and won much critical acclaim. Inspired by his war experiences, he created some more novels, such as *A Farewell to Arms* (1929) and *For Whom the Bell Tolls* (1940). After World War II, Hemingway started work on *The Garden of Eden*, which was never finished and would be published posthumously in a much abridged form in 1986. In 1952 Hemingway published *The Old Man and the Sea*. Considered as his greatest work, the novella's enormous success fulfilled Hemingway probably for the last time in his life. It earned him both the Pulitzer Prize and the Nobel Prize for Literature, and restored his international reputation, which had suffered after the disastrous publication of his over-the-top novel *Across the River and into the Trees* (1950).

A Farewell to Arms is considered one of his greatest novels, based on Hemingway's experience in World War I. It details the tragically doomed romance between Frederic Henry, an American soldier in convalescence, and Catherine Barkley, a British nurse. After recovering sufficiently from his wounds, Henry invites Barkley to run away with him, away from the war, to Switzerland and a life of peace, but their hopes are smashed: After a tumultuous escape across Lake Geneva, Barkley, heavily pregnant, collapses and dies during labor. The novel closes with Henry's dark ruminations on his lost honor and love.

For Whom the Bell Tolls draws extensively from Hemingway's experience during the Spanish Civil War. Based on real events, the novel follows three days in the life of Robert Jordan, an American dynamiter fighting with Spanish guerillas on the side of the Republicans. Jordan is one of Hemingway's Code Heroes: a drifter with no sense of belonging, who finds himself fighting in Spain more out of boredom than out of any allegiance to ideology. The novel begins with Jordan setting out on another mission to dynamite a bridge to prevent the Nationalist Army from taking the city of Madrid. When he encounters the Spanish rebels, he is supposed to assist. However, a change occurs within him. Befriending the old man Anselmo and the boisterous matriarch Pilar, and falling in love with the beautiful young Maria, Jordan at last finds a sense of place and purpose amongst the doomed rebels. It is one of Hemingway's most notable accomplishments, and one of his most life-affirming works.

The Old Man and the Sea tells the story of an aging Cuban fisherman Santiago, who sets out to fish for one last time despite his past vain attempts. Santiago fails to catch any fish after spending

84 days at sea. Obviously, he is another loser as a fisherman, but he is persistent and happens to catches a big marlin this time. The fish drags Santiago's boat for three days at sea. When it becomes exhausted, Santiago manages to kill it and lashes it to the boat. Although continuously attacked by sharks on the way back, the old man exhausts all means to fight back. Finally he gets back to the destination successfully with only a skeleton of the marlin.

In his world, Hemingway deals with a limited range of characters in quite similar circumstances and measures them against an unvarying code, known as "grace under pressure." It is actually an attitude towards life that Hemingway has been trying to demonstrate in his works. Those who survive in the process of seeking to master the code with honesty, discipline and restraint are Hemingway Code Heroes. In the general situation of his novels, life is full of tension and battles; the world is in chaos; man is always fighting desperately a losing battle. However, though life is but a losing battle, it is a struggle man who can dominate in such a way that loss becomes dignity. Man can be physically destroyed but never defeated spiritually.

"The dignity of movement of an iceberg is due to only one-eighth of it being above water." Typical of this "iceberg" analogy is Hemingway's style. According to Hemingway, good literary writing should be able to make readers feel the emotion of the characters directly and the best way to produce the effect is to set down exactly every particular kind of feeling without any authorial comments, without conventionally emotive language, and with a bare minimum of adjectives and adverbs. For example, *The Old Man and the Sea* can also be seen as a meditation upon youth and age, even though the protagonist spends little or no time thinking on those terms.

In addition, Hemingway develops the style of colloquialism initiated by Mark Twain. The accents and mannerisms of human speech are so well presented that the characters are full of flesh and blood. The use of short, simple and conventional words and sentences has an effect of clearness, terseness and great care. In other words, "Less is more." No wonder Hemingway was highly praised by the Nobel Prize Committee for "his powerful style-forming mastery of the art" of creating modern fictions.

Selected Reading

A Farewell to Arms

Lieutenant Frederic Henry is a young American ambulance driver serving in the Italian army during World War I. At the beginning, upon his return to the front from leave, Henry learns that a British hospital is set up. Soon he is introduced to Catherine Barkley, an English nurse, by his friend Rinaldi.

When Henry is wounded on the battlefield, he is brought to a hospital in Milan to recover. Several doctors recommend that he stay in bed for six months and then undergo a necessary operation on his knee. Unable to accept such a long period of recovery, Henry finds Dr. Valentini who agrees to operate immediately. Henry learns happily that Catherine has been transferred to Milan and begins his recuperation under her care. During the following months, his relationship with Catherine intensifies, even though he does not take it seriously at first.

Once Henry's damaged leg has healed, the army grants him three weeks convalescence leave, after which he is scheduled to return to the front. He tries to plan a trip with Catherine, who reveals to him that she is pregnant. The following day, Henry is diagnosed with jaundice, and Miss Van Campen, the superintendent of the hospital, accuses him of bringing the disease on himself through excessive drinking. Believing Henry's illness to be an attempt to avoid his duty as a serviceman, Miss Van Campen has Henry's leave revoked, and he is sent to the front once the jaundice has cleared. As they part, Catherine and Henry pledge their mutual devotion.

Henry travels to the front, where Italian forces are losing ground and manpower daily. Soon after Henry's arrival, a bombardment begins. When word comes that German troops are breaking through the Italian lines, the Allied forces prepare to retreat. Henry leads his team of ambulance drivers into the great column of evacuating troops. The men pick up two engineering sergeants and two frightened young girls on their way. Henry and his drivers then decide to leave the column and take secondary roads, which they assume will be faster. When one of their vehicles stalls in the mud, Henry orders the two engineers to help in the effort to free the vehicle. When they refuse, he shoots one of them. The drivers continue in the other trucks until they get stuck again. They send off the young girls and continue on foot toward Udine. As they move on, one of the drivers is shot dead by the easily frightened rear guard of the Italian army. Another driver marches off to surrender himself, while Henry and the remaining driver seek refuge at a farmhouse. When they rejoin the retreat the following day, the soldiers, enraged by the Italian defeat, pull commanding officers from the melee and execute them on sight. The battle police seize Henry, who, at a crucial moment, breaks away and dives into the river. After swimming a safe distance downstream, Henry boards a train bound for Milan. He hides beneath a tarp that covers stockpiled artillery, thinking that his obligations to the war effort are over and dreaming of his return to Catherine.

Henry reunites with Catherine in the town of Stresa. From there, the two escape to safety in Switzerland, rowing all night in a tiny borrowed boat. They settle happily in a lovely town called Montreux and agree to put aside the war forever. Although Henry is sometimes plagued by guilt for abandoning the men on the front, the two are happy to live a peaceful life. When spring arrives, the couple moves to Lausanne so that they can be closer to the hospital. Early one morning, Unfortunately, Catherine goes into labor. The delivery is exceptionally painful and complicated. Catherine delivers a dead baby and, later that night, dies of a hemorrhage. Henry stays at her side until she is gone. He attempts to say goodbye but can not. He walks back to his hotel in the rain.

An Excerpt from Chapter XLI

Finally a new doctor came in with two nurses and they lifted Catherine onto a wheeled stretcher and we started down the hall. The stretcher went rapidly down the hall and into the elevator where every one had to crowd against the wall to make room; then up, then an open door and out of the elevator and down the hall on rubber wheels to the operating room. I did not recognize the doctor with his cap and mask on. There was another doctor and more nurses.

"*They've got to give me something,*" Catherine said. "*They've got to give me something.* Oh please, doctor, give me enough to do some good!"

One of the doctors put a mask over her face and I looked through the door and saw the bright small amphitheatre of the operating room.

"You can go in the other door and sit up there," a nurse said to me. There were benches behind a rail that looked down on the white table and the lights. I looked at Catherine. The mask was over her face and she was quiet now. They wheeled the stretcher forward. I turned away and walked down the hall. Two nurses were hurrying toward the entrance to the gallery.

"It's a Caesarean[1]," one said. "They're going to do a Caesarean."

The other one laughed, "We're just in time. Aren't we lucky?" They went in the door that led to the gallery.

Another nurse came along. She was hurrying too.

"You go right in there. Go right in," she said.

"I'm staying outside."

She hurried in. I walked up and down the hall. I was afraid to go in. I looked out the window. It was dark but in the light from the window I could see it was raining. I went into a room at the far end of the hall and looked at the labels on bottles in a glass case. Then I came out and stood in the empty hall and watched the door of the operating room.

Note [1] Caesarean: operation by which a baby is removed from the uterus by cutting through the abdominal wall

A doctor came out followed by a nurse. He held something in his two hands that looked like a freshly skinned rabbit and hurried across the corridor with it and in through another door. I went down to the door he had gone into and found them in the room doing things to a new-born child. The doctor held him up for me to see. He held him by the heels and slapped him.

"Is he all right?"

"He's magnificent. He'll weigh five kilos."

I had no feeling for him. He did not seem to have anything to do with me. I felt no feeling of fatherhood.

"Aren't you proud of your son?" the nurse asked. They were washing him and wrapping him in something. I saw the little dark face and dark hand, but I did not see him move or hear him cry. The doctor was doing something to him again. He looked upset.

"No," I said. "He nearly killed his mother."

"It isn't the little darling's fault. Didn't you want a boy?"

"No," I said. The doctor was busy with him. He held him up by the feet and slapped him. I did not wait to see it. I went out in the hail. I could go in now and see. I went in the door and a little way down the gallery. The nurses who were sitting at the rail motioned for me to come down where they were. I shook my head. I could see enough where I was.

I thought Catherine was dead. She looked dead. Her face was gray, the part of it that I could see. Down below, under the light, the doctor was sewing up the great long, forceps-spread, thick-edged, wound. Another doctor in a mask gave the unaesthetic. Two nurses in masks handed things. It looked like a drawing of the Inquisition[1]. I knew as I watched I could have watched it all, but I was glad I hadn't. I do not think I could have watched them cut, but I watched the wound closed into a high welted ridge with quick skilful-looking stitches like a cobbler's, and was glad. When the wound was closed I went out into the hall and walked up and down again. After a while the doctor came out.

"How is she?"

"She is all right. Did you watch?"

He looked tired.

"I saw you sew up. The incision looked very long."

"You thought so?"

"Yes. Will that scar flatten out?"

"Oh, yes."

Note [1] the Inquisition: court appointed by the Roman Catholic Church to discover and suppress heresy and to punish heretics in medieval and early modern times

After a while they brought out the wheeled stretcher and took it very rapidly down the hallway to the elevator. I went along beside it. Catherine was moaning. Downstairs they put her in the bed in her room. I sat in a chair at the foot of the bed. There was a nurse in the room. I got up and stood by the bed. It was dark in the room. Catherine put out her hand. "Hello, darling," she said. Her voice was very weak and tired.

"Hello, you sweet."

"What sort of baby was it?"

"Sh—don't talk," the nurse said.

"A boy. He's long and wide and dark."

"Is he all right?"

"Yes," I said. "He's fine."

I saw the nurse look at me strangely.

"I'm awfully tired," Catherine said. "And I hurt like hell. Are you all right, darling?"

"I'm fine. Don't talk."

"You were lovely to me. Oh, darling, I hurt dreadfully. What does he look like?"

"He looks like a skinned rabbit with a puckered-up old-man's face."

"You must go out," the nurse said. "Madame Henry must not talk."

"I'll be outside."

"Go and get something to eat."

"No. I'll be outside." I kissed Catherine. She was very gray and weak and tired.

"May I speak to you?" I said to the nurse. She came out in the hall with me. I walked a little way down the hall.

"What's the matter with the baby?" I asked.

"Didn't you know?"

"No."

"He wasn't alive."

"He was dead?"

"They couldn't start him breathing. The cord was caught around his neck or something."

"So he's dead."

"Yes. It's such a shame. He was such a fine big boy. I thought you knew."

"No," I said. "You better go back in with Madame."

I sat down on the chair in front of a table where there were nurses' reports hung on clips at the side and looked out of the window. I could see nothing but the dark and the rain falling across the light from the window. So that was it. The baby was dead. That was why the doctor looked so tired. But why had they acted the way they did in the room with him?

They supposed he would come around and start breathing probably. I had no religion but I knew he ought to have been baptized. But what if he never breathed at all. He hadn't. He had never been alive. Except in Catherine. I'd felt him kick there often enough. But I hadn't for a week. Maybe he was choked all the time. Poor little kid. I wished the hell I'd been choked like that. No I didn't. Still there would not be all this dying to go through. Now Catherine would die. That was what you did. You died. You did not know what it was about. You never had time to learn. They threw you in and told you the rules and the first time they caught you off base[1] they killed you. Or they killed you gratuitously like Aymo[2]. Or gave you the syphilis like Rinaldi[3]. But they killed you in the end. You could count on that. Stay around and they would kill you.

William Faulkner (1897–1962)

William Faulkner, along with Mark Twain and Tennessee Williams, was considered a representative writer of Southern literature. Known for his novels and short stories, Faulkner was awarded the 1949 Nobel Prize for Literature in 1950.

William Faulkner, born in New Albany, Mississippi, was raised in Oxford. His great-grandfather served as a colonel in the Confederate Army, founded a railroad, and gave his name to the town of Falkner, Mississippi. Perhaps most importantly, Colonel Falkner wrote several novels and other works, establishing a literary tradition in the family. During World War I, Falkner joined the Canadian and later the British Royal Air Force, yet he did not see combat. Faulkner began to change the spelling of his name around this time. He then studied for a while at the University of Mississippi, and temporarily worked for a New York bookstore and a New Orleans newspaper. In 1926 his vision was further widened on a trip to Europe, where he was exposed to the experimental writing of James Joyce and of the ideas of Sigmund Freud. Later in his life, except for some trips to Europe and Asia, and a few brief stays in Hollywood as a scriptwriter, he worked on his novels and short stories on a farm in Oxford.

Faulkner's most celebrated novels include *The Sound and the Fury* (1929), *As I Lay Dying* (1930), *Light in August* (1932), *The Unvanquished* (1938) and *Absalom, Absalom!* (1936). In 1931 in an effort to make money, Faulkner crafted *Sanctuary* (1931), a sensationalist "pulp fiction"-styled novel. Its themes of evil and corruption resonate to this day. A sequel to the book, *Requiem for a Nun* (1951), is the only play that Faulkner published. It includes an introduction that is actually one sentence spanning more than a page. He received a Pulitzer Prize for *Intruder in the*

Note [1] off base: a technical term in baseball; here in an unprepared state
Note [2] Aymo: a truck driver in the Italian army
Note [3] Rinaldi: a doctor in the Italian army

Dust (1948) and won National Book Awards for his *Collected Stories* (1951) and *A Fable* (1955). Faulkner also wrote two volumes of poetry, *The Marble Faun* (1924) and *A Green Bough* (1933), neither of which was well received.

Faulkner set many of his short stories and novels in his fictional Yoknapatawpha County, based on Lafayette County, Mississippi. Their common theme is the decay of the old South represented by the Sartoris and Compson families, and the emergence of ruthless and brash newcomers represented by the Snopeses. The novel *Sanctuary* is about the degeneration of Temple Drake, a young girl from a distinguished southern family. Often considered Faulkner's masterpiece, *The Sound and the Fury* takes place in the Yoknapatawpha County and focuses on the downfall of the Compson family, a once proud dynasty that has fallen into ruin after the divisiveness of the American Civil War. The distortion of time through the use of the inner monologue is fused particularly successfully in *The Sound and the Fury*, the downfall of the Compson family seen through the minds of several characters.

In most of his works, Faulker is also concerned with racial discrimination. *Requiem for a Nun*, written partly as a drama, centers on the courtroom trial of a Negro woman who has once been a party to Temple Drake's debauchery. In *Light in August*, prejudice is shown to be most destructive when it is internalized, as in Joe Christmas, who believes, though there is no proof of it, that one of his parents was a Negro. The theme of racial prejudice is brought up again in *Absalom, Absalom!* in which a young man is rejected by his father and brother because of his mixed blood. Faulkner's most outspoken moral evaluation of the relationship and the problems between Negroes and whites is to be found in the anti-racist *Intruder in the Dust*.

Faulkner proves to be a master of his own particular style of writing. The most characteristic way of structuring his stories is to fragment the chronological time. He deliberately breaks up the chronology of his narrative by juxtaposing the past with the present. The modern stream-of-consciousness technique is also employed by Faulkner to emphasize the reactions and inner musings of the narrator. Moreover, Faulkner is good at presenting multiple points of view so as to reach a high degree of truth. Symbolism and allusions are also used to construct his stories.

Selected Reading

A Rose for Emily

The story is divided into five sections. In section I, Emily Grierson's death is presented and the entire town attend her funeral in her home, which no stranger has entered for more than ten years, Emily's house is regarded as the last vestige of the grandeur of a lost era in the neighborhood. Colonel Sartoris, the town's previous mayor, suspended Emily's tax responsibilities to the town after her father's death. As new town leaders take over, they make unsuccessful attempts to get Emily to resume payments. When members of the Board of Aldermen pay her a visit, in the dusty and antiquated parlor, Emily reasserts the fact that she is not required to pay taxes in Jefferson and that the officials should talk to Colonel Sartoris, who has been dead for almost a decade, about the matter. Finally she asks her servant to show the men out.

In section II, it is revealed that thirty years earlier, the townspeople detected a powerful odor emanating from her house. Her father had just died, and Emily had been abandoned by the man whom the townsfolk believed Emily was to marry. As complaints mounted, Judge Stevens, the mayor at the time, decided to have lime sprinkled along the foundation of the Grierson home in the middle of the night. Within a couple of weeks, the odor subsided, but the townspeople began to pity the increasingly reclusive Emily. The townspeople had always believed that the Griersons thought too highly of themselves, with Emily's father driving off the many suitors deemed not good enough for his daughter.

The day after Mr. Grierson's death, the women of the town called on Emily to offer their condolences. Meeting them at the door, Emily stated that her father was not dead, a charade that she kept up for three days. She finally turned her father's body over for burial.

In section III, Emily suffered a long illness after this incident. The summer after her father's death, the town contracted workers to pave the sidewalks. A construction company, under the direction of northerner Homer Barron, was offered the job. Homer soon was seen taking Emily on buggy rides on Sunday afternoons, which scandalized the town and increased the condescension and pity they had for Emily. They felt that she was forgetting her family pride and becoming involved with a man below her. Somehow she went to the drug store to purchase arsenic, offering no reason for it.

In section IV, some of the townspeople were worried that Emily would use the poison to kill herself. Her potential marriage to Homer seemed increasingly unlikely, despite their continued Sunday ritual. The more outraged women of the town insisted that the Baptist minister talk with Emily, but in vain. So the minister's wife wrote to Emily's two cousins in Alabama, who arrived for an extended stay. Because Emily ordered a silver toilet set monogrammed with Homer's initials, talk of the couple's marriage resumed. Homer, absent from town, was believed to be preparing for Emily's move to the North or avoiding Emily's intrusive relatives.

After the cousins' departure, Homer entered the Grierson home one evening and then was never seen again. Despite the occasional lesson she gave in china painting, her door remained closed to outsiders. Except for the occasional glimpse of her in the window, nothing has been heard from her until her death.

In section V, after Emily dies, Emily's body is laid out in the parlor and the women, town elders, and two cousins attend the service. The door to a sealed upstairs room that has not been opened in forty years is broken down by the townspeople. The room is frozen in time, with the items for an upcoming wedding and a man's suit laid out. Homer Barron's body is stretched on the bed as well, in an advanced state of decay. The onlookers then notice the indentation of a head in the pillow beside Homer's body and a long strand of Emily's gray hair on the pillow.

An Excerpt from Section I

When Miss Emily Grierson died, our whole town went to her funeral: the men through a sort of respectful affection for a fallen monument, the women mostly out of curiosity to see the inside of her house, which no one save an old man-servant—a combined gardener and cook—had seen in at least ten years.

It was a big, squarish frame house that had once been white, decorated with cupolas and spires and scrolled balconies in the heavily lightsome style of the seventies, set on what had once been our most select street. But garages and cotton gins had encroached and obliterated even the august names of that neighborhood; only Miss Emily's house was left, lifting its stubborn and coquettish decay above the cotton wagons and the gasoline pumps—an eyesore among eyesores. And now Miss Emily had gone to join the representatives of those august names where they lay in the cedar-bemused cemetery among the ranked and anonymous graves of Union and Confederate soldiers who fell at the battle of Jefferson.

Alive, Miss Emily had been a tradition, a duty and a care; a sort of hereditary obligation upon the town, dating from that day in 1894 when Colonel Sartoris, the mayor—he who fathered the edict that no Negro woman should appear on the streets without an apron—remitted her taxes, the dispensation dating from the death of her father on into perpetuity. Not that Miss Emily would have accepted charity. Colonel Sartoris invented an involved tale to the effect that Miss Emily's father had loaned money to the town, which the town, as a matter of Business, preferred this way of repaying. Only a man of Colonel Sartoris' generation and thought could have invented it, and only a woman could have believed it.

When the next generation, with its more modern ideas, became mayors and aldermen, this arrangement created some little dissatisfaction. On the first of the year they mailed her a tax notice. February came, and there was no reply. They wrote her a formal letter, asking her to call at the sheriff's office at her convenience. A week later the mayor wrote her himself, offering to call or to send his car for her, and received in reply a note on paper of an archaic shape, in a thin, flowing calligraphy in faded ink, to the effect that she no longer went out at all. The tax notice was also enclosed, without comment.

They called a special meeting of the Board of Aldermen. A deputation waited upon her, knocked at the door through which no visitor had passed since she ceased giving china-painting lessons eight or ten years earlier. They were admitted by the old Negro into a dim hall from which a stairway mounted into still more shadow. It smelled of dust and disuse—a close, dank smell. The Negro led them into the parlor. It was furnished in heavy, leather-covered furniture. When the Negro opened the blinds of one window, they could see that the leather was cracked; and when they sat down, a faint dust rose sluggishly about their thighs, spinning with slow motes in the single sun-ray. On a tarnished gilt easel before the fireplace stood a crayon portrait of Miss Emily's father.

They rose when she entered—a small, fat woman in black, with a thin gold chain descending to her waist and vanishing into her belt, leaning on an ebony cane with a tarnished gold head. Her skeleton was small and spare; perhaps that was why what would have been merely plumpness in another was obesity in her. She looked bloated, like a body long submerged in motionless water, and of that pallid hue. Her eyes, lost in the fatty ridges of her face, looked like two small pieces of coal pressed into a lump of dough as they moved from one face to another while the visitors stated their errand.

She did not ask them to sit. She just stood in the door and listened quietly until the spokesman came to a stumbling halt. Then they could hear the invisible watch ticking at the end of the gold chain.

Her voice was dry and cold. "I have no taxes in Jefferson. Colonel Sartoris explained it to me. Perhaps one of you can gain access to the city records and satisfy yourselves."

"But we have. We are the city authorities, Miss Emily. Didn't you get a notice from the sheriff, signed by him?"

"I received a paper, yes," Miss Emily said. "Perhaps he considers himself the sheriff... I have no taxes in Jefferson."

"But there is nothing on the books to show that, you see We must go by the—"

"See Colonel Sartoris. I have no taxes in Jefferson."

"But, Miss Emily—"

"See Colonel Sartoris. (Colonel Sartoris had been dead almost ten years.) I have no taxes in Jefferson. Tobe!" The Negro appeared. "Show these gentlemen out."

❧ T. S. Eliot (1888–1965)

Thomas Stearns Eliot, an American-born poet, dramatist and literary critic, is considered a prominent figure who best presents the world of disillusionment and frustration in the 20th century. He was naturalized as a British citizen in 1927 and was awarded the Nobel Prize for Literature and the Order of Merit in 1948.

Thomas Stearns Eliot was born into a prominent family at St. Louis, Missouri. After educated at St. Louis' Smith Academy and Milton Academy, he studied philosophy at Harvard. He then studied literature and philosophy in Sorbonne, Marburg and Oxford. Eliot got married with Vivienne Haigh-Wood in 1915. After a short visit to the U.S. to meet his family, he took a few teaching jobs. During Eliot's university career, he studied with a number of world-famous philosophers including George Santayana, Henri Bergson and Bertrand Russell.

After World War I, in the 1920s, he spent time with other great artists in the Montparnasse Quarter in Paris, where he was associated with Picasso, Ezra Pound, James Joyce, Marcel Proust, William Carlos Williams and Marcel Duchamp. French poetry was a particularly strong influence on Eliot's work, in particular Charles Baudelaire.

In 1927 Eliot took British citizenship and converted to Anglicanism. Eliot separated from his wife in 1933 and Vivienne was committed to a mental hospital in 1938. Eliot's second marriage with Esmé Valerie Fletcher in 1957 was happy but short. He was awarded the Nobel Prize in Literature and the Order of Merit in 1948. Eliot died of emphysema in London. On the second anniversary of his death a large stone placed on the floor of Poets' Corner in Westminster Abbey was dedicated to Eliot.

The poem that made his name, "The Love Song of J. Alfred Prufrock" in the form of dramatic monologue[1] published in 1915, is seen as a masterpiece of the Modernist Movement. It was followed by some of the best-known poems in the English language, including *Gerontion* (1920), *The Waste Land* (1922), *The Hollow Men* (1925), *Ash Wednesday* (1930) and *Four Quartets* (1945).

After *The Waste Land*, Eliot set out to write plays as well. The play featured "Sweeney," a character who had appeared in a number of his poems. Although Eliot did not finish the play, he did publish two scenes from the piece. These scenes, titled *Fragment of a Prologue* (1926) and *Fragment of an Agon* (1927), were published together in 1932 as *Sweeney Agonistes*. A pageant play by Eliot called *The Rock*, a collaborative effort, was performed in 1934. *Murder in the Cathedral* (1935), concerning the death of the martyr, was more successful. After this, he worked on commercial plays for more general audiences: *The Family Reunion* (1939), *The Cocktail Party*

Note [1] dramatic monologue: literary, usually verse composition in which a speaker reveals his or her character, often in relation to a critical situation or event, in a monologue addressed to the reader or to a presumed listener

(1949), *The Confidential Clerk* (1953) and *The Elder Statesman* (1958). The Broadway production in New York of *The Cocktail Party* received the 1950 Tony Award for Best Play.

Eliot also made significant contributions to the field of literary criticism, strongly influencing the school of New Criticism. In his critical essay "Tradition and the Individual Talent," Eliot argues that art must be understood not in a vacuum, but in the context of previous pieces of art. This essay was an important influence over the New Criticism by introducing the idea that the value of a work of art must be viewed in the context of the artist's previous works, a "simultaneous order" of works (i.e., "tradition"). Eliot himself employed this concept in many of his works, especially in his long-poem *The Waste Land*.

In 1922 Eliot published *The Waste Land* in *The Criterion*, which was composed during a period of personal difficulty for Eliot—his marriage was floundering, and both he and Vivienne suffered from disordered nerves. Regarded as a typical representation of the post-war generation, it makes use of sexual failure to indicate spiritual crisis in the modern world. Thus modern civilization, characterized by disorder and disillusionment, has lost its purpose, meaning and significance.

Eliot's works are difficult to read, for they are full of disconnected images and symbols. His learned quotations and allusions contribute much to the theme of futility, frustration and fragmentization. What adds more power to his style is the interaction between the past, the present and the future.

Selected Reading

The Waste Land

The poem is 433 lines long and is divided into five sections, which are not logically constructed or connected. Section I, "The Burial of the Dead," deals chiefly with the theme of death in life. Section II, "A Game of Chess," gives a rather concrete illustration of the sterile situation. A picture of spiritual emptiness is presented with the reproduction of a contemporary pub conversation between two cockney women. Section III, "The Fire Sermon," expresses a painfully elegiac feeling by juxtaposing the vulgarity and shallowness of the modern with the beauty and simplicity of the past. In Section IV, "Death by Water," the drowned Phoenician Sailor is an emblem of futile worries over profit and loss, youth and age. The title of Section V, "What the Thunder Said," appears to be derived from an Indian myth, in which the supreme lord of the Creation speaks through the thunder. As the drought breaks and the thunder speaks, various elusive suggestions of hope are given; but despite the thunder's advice "to give, to sympathize and to control," which projects the possibility of regeneration, the issue is left uncertain at the end.

An Excerpt from Section I: The Burial of the Dead

April is the cruellest month, breeding

Lilacs out of the dead land, mixing

Memory and desire, stirring

Dull roots with spring rain.

Winter kept us warm, covering

Earth in forgetful snow, feeding

A little life with dried tubers.

Summer surprised us, coming over the Starnbergersee

With a shower of rain; we stopped in the colonnade,

And went on in sunlight, into the Hofgarten,

And drank coffee, and talked for an hour.

Bin gar keine Russin, stamm'aus Litauen, echt deutsch.

And when we were children, staying at the archduke's,

My cousin's, he took me out on a sled,

And I was frightened. He said, Marie,

Marie, hold on tight. And down we went.

In the mountains, there you feel free.

I read, much of the night, and go south in the winter.

❧ John Steinbeck (1902–1968)

John Steinbeck, one of the best-known and most widely read American writers of the 20th century, won the Nobel Prize for Literature in 1962. His *Of Mice and Men* (1937) and the Pulitzer Prize-winning novel *The Grapes of Wrath* (1939) examine the lives of the working class and migrant workers during the Dust Bowl and subsequent Great Depression.

John Steinbeck was born in Salinas, California. His father served as the Monterey County Treasurer while his mother, a former school teacher, fostered Steinbeck's love of reading and writing. During summers, he worked as a hired hand on nearby ranches. He then attended Stanford University intermittently until 1925, departing to New York to pursue his dream as a writer. However, he was unable to get any of his work published and returned to California. During World War II, Steinbeck served as a war correspondent for the *New York Herald Tribune*. In 1962 Steinbeck won the Nobel Prize for Literature for his "realistic and imaginative writing, combining as it does sympathetic humor and keen social perception."

Steinbeck's first novel, *Cup of Gold*, based on the privateer Henry Morgan's life and death, was published in 1929. The novel centers on Morgan's assault and sacking of Panama City, sometimes referred to as the "Cup of Gold." Steinbeck followed this with three further novels between 1931 and 1933. *The Pastures of Heaven* (1932) consists of twelve interconnected stories about a valley in Monterey, California, which is discovered by a Spanish corporal while chasing runaway American Indian slaves. *The Red Pony* (1933) is a short 100-page, four-chapter novella, which recollects memories from Steinbeck's childhood. *To a God Unknown* (1933) gives an account of the life of a homesteader and his family in California.

Steinbeck achieved his first critical success with the novel *Tortilla Flat* (1935), which won California Commonwealth Club's Gold Medal. The book portrays the adventures of a group of young men in Monterey who denounce society by enjoying life and wine before U.S. Prohibition in the 1920s. Afterwards, Steinbeck began to write a series of "California novels" and Dust Bowl fiction, set in the Great Depression. These included *In Dubious Battle* (1936), *Of Mice and Men* (1937) and *The Grapes of Wrath* (1939). *Of Mice and Men* is a novel written in the form of a tragedy play. The story is concerned with two traveling ranch workers, George and the dim-witted but physically powerful itinerant farmhand Lennie, trying to work up enough money to buy their own farm. It encompasses themes of racism, loneliness, prejudice against the mentally ill and the struggle for personal independence. Steinbeck followed this success with *The Grapes of Wrath*, based on newspaper articles he had written in San Francisco, and considered by many to be his finest work. The *Grapes of Wrath* is set in the Great Depression and describes a family of sharecroppers, the Joads, who are driven from their land due to the dust storms of the Dust Bowl. The title is a reference to the Battle Hymn of the Republic. It won both the National Book Award and Pulitzer Prize.

Later, some of Steinbeck's writings from his correspondence days were collected and made into *Once There Was a War* (1958). His novel *The Moon is Down* (1942) is about the Socrates-inspired spirit of resistance in a Nazi-occupied village in northern Europe. It is presumed that the country in question was Norway, and in 1945 Steinbeck received the Haakon VII Medal of freedom for his literary contributions to the Norwegian resistance movement. After the war, he wrote *The Pearl* (1947), and traveled to Mexico for the filming. Steinbeck's last novel, *The Winter of Our Discontent* (1961), was critically savaged and commercially unsuccessful.

Amid the gloom and the defeatism which pervade the writing of the decade, Steinbeck manages to keep a refreshing faith in humanity. He often populates his stories with struggling characters, and his fiction draws on real historical conditions and events in the first half of the 20th century. His body of work reflects his wide range of interests, including marine biology, politics, religion, history and mythology.

Selected Reading

The Grapes of Wrath

Released from an Oklahoma state prison for a manslaughter conviction, Tom Joad makes his way back to his family's farm in Oklahoma. He meets Jim Casy, a former preacher who has given up his calling out of a belief that all life is holy. Jim accompanies Tom to his home, only to find all the surrounding farms deserted. Muley Graves, an old neighbor, wanders by and tells the men that everyone has been "tractored" off the land. Most families, he says, including his own, have headed to California to look for work. The next morning, Tom and Jim set out for Tom's Uncle John's, where Muley assures them they will find the Joad clan. Upon arrival, Tom finds Ma and Pa Joad packing up the family's few possessions. Having seen handbills advertising fruit-picking jobs in California, they envision the trip to California as their only hope of getting their lives back on track.

The journey to California in a used truck is long and arduous. Grandpa Joad, who complains that he does not want to leave his land, dies on the road shortly after the family's departure. As the Joads meet more people on their way, they come to realize that the entire country is in flight to the Promised Land of California.

When the Joads are about to reach California, they hear ominous news of a depleted job market. One migrant tells Pa that few jobs are available in California and that his own children have starved to death. Although the Joads press on, their first days in California prove tragic, as Grandma Joad dies. The remaining family members move from one squalid camp to the next, looking in vain for work, struggling to find food and trying desperately to hold their family together. Noah, the oldest of the Joad children, soon abandons the family, as does Connie, a young dreamer who is married to Tom's pregnant sister, Rose of Sharon.

To make matters worse, the Joads are faced with much hostility in California. The camps are overcrowded with starving migrants, who are often nasty to each other. The locals are fearful and angry at the flood of newcomers, whom they derisively label "Okies." Work, either is almost impossible to find, or pays such a meager wage that a family's full day's work cannot buy a decent meal. Fearing an uprising, the large landowners do everything in their power to keep the migrants poor and dependent. While staying in a ramshackle camp known as a "Hooverville," Tom and several men get into a heated argument with a deputy sheriff over whether workers should organize into a union. When the argument turns violent, Casy knocks the sheriff unconscious and is arrested. Police officers arrive and announce their intention to burn the camp to the ground.

A government-run camp proves much more hospitable to the Joads, and the family soon finds many friends and a bit of work. However, one day, while working at a pipe-laying job, Tom learns that the police are planning to stage a riot in the camp, which will allow them to shut down the facilities. By alerting and organizing the men in the camp, Tom helps to defuse the danger. Still, as pleasant as life in the government camp is, the Joads cannot survive without steady work, and they have to move on. Then they are employed to pick fruit, but soon learn that they are earning a decent wage only because they have been hired to break a workers' strike. Tom runs into Casy who, after being released from jail, has begun organizing workers. In the process, Casy has made many enemies among the landowners. When the police hunt him down and kill him in Tom's presence, Tom retaliates and kills a police officer.

Tom goes into hiding, while the family moves into a boxcar on a cotton farm. One day, Ruthie, the youngest Joad daughter, reveals to a girl in the camp that her brother has killed two men and is hiding nearby. Fearing for his safety, Ma Joad finds Tom and sends him away. Tom heads off to fulfill Casy's task of organizing the migrant workers. The end of the cotton season means the end of work, and it is said across the land that there are no jobs to be found for three months. Rains set in and flood the land. Rose of Sharon gives birth to a stillborn child, and Ma, desperate to get her family to safety from the floods, leads them to a dry barn not far away. Here, they find a young boy kneeling over his father, who is slowly starving to death. Realizing that Rose of Sharon is now producing milk, Ma sends the others outside, so that her daughter can nurse the dying man. So the poor try to keep each other alive in the depression years.

An Excerpt from Chapter 1

TO THE red country and part of the gray country of Oklahoma, the last rains came gently, and they did not cut the scarred earth. The plows crossed and recrossed the rivulet marks. The last rains lifted the corn quickly and scattered weed colonies and grass along the sides of the roads so that the gray country and the dark red country began to disappear under a green cover. In the last part of May the sky grew pale and the clouds that had hung in high puffs for so long in the spring were dissipated. The sun flared down on the growing corn day after day until a line of brown spread along the edge of each green bayonet. The clouds appeared, and went away, and in a while they did not try any more. The weeds grew darker green to protect themselves, and they did not spread any more. The surface of the earth crusted, a thin hard crust, and as the sky became pale, so the earth became pale, pink in the red country and white in the gray country.

In the water-cut gullies the earth dusted down in dry little streams. Gophers and ant lions started small avalanches. And as the sharp sun struck day after day, the leaves of the young corn became less stiff and erect; they bent in a curve at first, and then, as the central ribs of strength grew weak, each leaf tilted downward. Then it was June, and the sun shone more fiercely. The brown lines on the corn leaves widened and moved in on the central ribs. The weeds frayed and edged back toward their roots. The air was thin and the sky more pale; and every day the earth paled.

In the roads where the teams moved, where the wheels milled the ground and the hooves of the horses beat the ground, the dirt crust broke and the dust formed. Every moving thing lifted the dust into the air: a walking man lifted a thin layer as high as his waist, and a wagon lifted the dust as high as the fence tops, and an automobile boiled a cloud behind it. The dust was long in settling back again.

When June was half gone, the big clouds moved up out of Texas and the Gulf, high heavy clouds, rain-heads. The men in the fields looked up at the clouds and sniffed at them and held wet fingers up to sense the wind. And the horses were nervous while the clouds were up. The rain-heads dropped a little spattering and hurried on to some other country. Behind them the sky was pale again and the sun flared. In the dust there were drop craters where the rain had fallen, and there were clean splashes on the corn, and that was all.

A gentle wind followed the rain clouds, driving them on northward, a wind that softly clashed the drying corn. A day went by and the wind increased, steady, unbroken by gusts. The dust from the roads fluffed up and spread out and fell on the weeds beside the fields, and fell into the fields a little way. Now the wind grew strong and hard and it worked at the rain crust in the corn fields. Little by little the sky was darkened by the mixing dust and the wind felt over the earth, loosened the dust and carried it away. The wind grew stronger. The rain crust broke and the dust lifted up out of the fields and drove gray plumes into the air like sluggish smoke. The corn threshed the wind and made a dry, rushing sound. The finest dust did not settle back to earth now, but disappeared into the darkening sky.

The wind grew stronger, whisked under stones, carried up straws and old leaves, and even little clods, marking its course as it sailed across the fields. The air and the sky darkened and through them the sun shone redly, and there was a raw sting in the air. During a night the wind raced faster over the land, dug cunningly among the rootlets of the corn, and the corn fought the wind with its weakened leaves until the roots were freed by the prying wind and then each stalk settled wearily sideways toward the earth and pointed the direction of the wind.

The dawn came, but no day. In the gray sky a red sun appeared, a dim red circle that gave a little light, like dusk; and as that day advanced, the dusk slipped back toward darkness, and the wind cried and whimpered over the fallen corn.

Men and women huddled in their houses, and they tied handkerchiefs over their noses when they went out, and wore goggles to protect their eyes.

When the night came again it was black night, for the stars could not pierce the dust to get down, and the window lights could not even spread beyond their own yards. Now the dust was evenly mixed with the air, an emulsion of dust and air. Houses were shut tight, and cloth wedged around doors and windows, but the dust came in so thinly that it could not be seen in the air, and it settled like pollen on the chairs and tables, on the dishes. The people brushed it from their shoulders. Little lines of dust lay at the door sills.

In the middle of that night the wind passed on and left the land quiet. The dust-filled air muffled sound more completely than fog does. The people, lying in their beds, heard the wind stop. They awakened when the rushing wind was gone. They lay quietly and listened deep into the stillness. Then the roosters crowed, and their voices were muffled, and the people stirred restlessly in their beds and wanted the morning. They knew it would take a long time for the dust to settle out of the air. In the morning the dust hung like fog, and the sun was as red as ripe new blood. All day the dust sifted down from the sky, and the next day it sifted down. An even blanket covered the earth. It settled on the corn, piled up on the tops of the fence posts, piled up on the wires; it settled on roofs, blanketed the weeds and trees.

The people came out of their houses and smelled the hot stinging air and covered their noses from it. And the children came out of the houses, but they did not run or shout as they would have done after a rain. Men stood by their fences and looked at the ruined corn, drying fast now, only a little green showing through the film of dust. The men were silent and they did not move often. And the women came out of the houses to stand beside their men—to feel whether this time the men would break. The women studied the men's faces secretly, for the corn could go, as long as something else remained. The children stood near by, drawing figures in the dust with bare toes, and the children sent exploring senses out to see whether men and women would break. The children peeked at the faces of the men and women, and then drew careful lines in the dust with their toes. Horses came to the watering troughs and nuzzled the water to clear the surface dust. After a while the faces of the watching men lost their bemused perplexity and became hard and angry and resistant. Then the women knew that they were safe and that there was no break. Then they asked, What'll we do? And the men replied, I don't know. But it was all right. The women knew it was all right, and the watching children knew it was all right. Women and children knew deep in themselves that no misfortune was too great to bear if their men were whole. The women went into the houses to their work, and the children began to play, but cautiously at first. As the day went forward the sun became less red. It flared down on the dust-blanketed land. The men sat in the doorways of their houses; their hands were busy with sticks and little rocks. The men sat still—thinking—figuring.

Eugene O'Neill (1888–1953)

Eugene O'Neill, an American playwright, is widely recognized as the "founder of the American drama" and even a major figure in world literature. He won the Pulitzer Prize four times and was the only dramatist ever to be awarded the Nobel Prize for Literature.

Eugene O'Neill was born into a family of Irish origin at Broadway, New York, since his father was a well-known actor. In his family, his father suffered from alcoholism and his mother from mental illness. After O'Neill was educated at Catholic boarding schools, in 1906 he attended Princeton University for one year. Then O'Neill spent several years at sea, during which he suffered from depression and alcoholism. Despite this, he had a deep love for the sea and it became a prominent theme in many of his plays. During the 1910s, O'Neill was a regular on the Greenwich Village literary scene. After his experience at a sanatorium where he was recovering from tuberculosis, he decided to devote himself full-time to writing plays. O'Neill had previously been employed by the *New London Telegraph*, writing poetry as well as reporting. In 1914 he entered Harvard University to attend a course in dramatic technique. Then he got involved with the Provincetown Players and some of his early plays gradually moved to Broadway. After achieving success in 1920, O'Neill remained a dominant figure of American theater throughout his life. However, he had numerous personal problems and troubles, including his failed marriage and many health problems. In 1936 he received the Nobel Prize for Literature. Later, after suffering over many years, O'Neill ultimately had a severe tremor in his hands.

O'Neill's first published play, *Beyond the Horizon* (1924), was awarded the Pulitzer Prize for Drama. His first major hit was *The Emperor Jones* in 1920. In the following years, his best-known plays include *Anna Christie* (Pulitzer Prize 1922), *Desire Under the Elms* (1924), *Strange Interlude* (Pulitzer Prize 1928), *Mourning Becomes Electra* (1931) and his only well-known comedy, *Ah, Wilderness!* (1933). After a ten-year pause, O'Neill's now-renowned play *The Iceman Cometh* was produced in 1946. The following year's *A Moon for the Misbegotten* (1947) failed, and it was decades before it began to be considered among his best works. In 1956 his autobiographical masterpiece *Long Day's Journey into Night* was published, which won the Pulitzer Prize in 1957.

The drama *Long Day's Journey into Night*, along with Tennessee Williams' *A Streetcar Named Desire* (1947) and Arthur Miller's *Death of a Salesman* (1949), is often considered as one of the finest American plays in the 20th century. The play is very similar to the family life of O'Neill as a young man. But more importantly, it has become a universal play representing the problems of a family that can not live in the present, immersed in the dark recesses of a troubled past. In the play, Mary, in particular, prefers to dwell on the past so as to escape from the present. As she sinks further and further into the fog of morphine, she relives her childhood at the Catholic girls' school. She also regrets leaving the good home provided by her father to marry a traveling actor. In addition, their family, which is supposed to be happy and enjoyable, turns to be a battlefield on which they attach and counterattack one another. Very soon they are overwhelmed by guilt and regret. Jamie, Edmund and Mary frequently mock penny-pinching James Tyrone for engaging a "quack," who prescribed morphine to alleviate Mary's pain when she was giving birth to Edmund. Tyrone criticizes Jamie for his past and for setting a bad example for Edmund. Meanwhile, Edmund feels guilty about his birth, for it is the indirect cause of his mother's addiction.

O'Neill's style is always associated with Expressionism. In his plays, lighting and music are employed to convey the changes of mood. He also makes use of dialect to amplify the meaning. All these distinguish him from the others in his time.

Selected Reading

Long Day's Journey into Night

After breakfast on a warm summer day in August 1912, Mary, who has recently returned from treatment for morphine addiction, teases her husband, James, a retired actor of modest renown, about his real estate bargains in the living room. When she expresses concern about Edmund's illness, Tyrone reassures her about Edmund's health and compliments her on her own healthy appearance.

After their two sons, Jamie and Edmund, join their parents, the lighthearted family conversation turns increasingly spiteful. A favorite tactic of James is to accuse Jamie of setting a bad example for Edmund, who has apparently picked up many of Jamie's habits, including heavy drinking. Jamie, angry that his parents seem to regard Edmund as the fair-haired boy of the family, attacks Edmund's ambition to become a writer.

Just before lunch, Jamie comes in, and he and Edmund have a whiskey and water the bottle to prevent their father from notice. Jamie becomes upset when he learns that Edmund has allowed Mary to go upstairs alone for fear that she will succumb to a hidden supply of morphine. In fact, Edmund tries to suppress his coughing so as not to disturb her to the extent that might trigger her addiction again. When James comes in for lunch, he pours a whiskey for himself and reluctantly allows Jamie and Edmund to have a shot. He is also devastated to find that Mary is right back on morphine. As the fog outside is becoming thicker and thicker, the family feuding grows worse and worse. Mary scolds James for failing to provide a real home for the family, with no friends to socialize with. Mary also blames James for her addition to morphine, based on the fact that he was so miserly that he would only pay for a cheap doctor who knew of no better way to cure her childbirth pain when Edmund was born. Meanwhile, Mary can not forgive herself for having Eugene, her second baby, died at two years old from measles. Meanwhile, she becomes defensive, whenever questioned about taking morphine and feels guilty from time to time. Nevertheless, she admits that she lies to herself all the time and hopes for redemption one day through the Virgin.

By early evening, Mary is stoned on morphine and full of self-pity. With Cathleen, the maid, as her audience and a foghorn sounding outside, she talks about her past, dwelling especially on her dreams to become a nun or a concert pianist. After Edmund and Tyrone return, Mary warns Edmund that Jamie will only lead him down the path of failure. She also observes that James has set a bad example for them with his drinking. When James is in the cellar fetching more whiskey, Edmund tells Mary that the doctor has confirmed that he has tuberculosis. But Mary refuses to confront this news and thinks that Edmund only desires more attention. Edmund reminds Mary that her own father died of tuberculosis, then retorts that it is difficult having a "dope fiend for a mother." It is time to have dinner, but Mary decides to go upstairs instead, presumably to take more drugs again.

At midnight, the foghorn is heard in the distance. Edmund comes home to find his father drinking and playing solitaire and they argue about keeping the lights on and the cost of the electricity. Actually, Edmund has just returned from a long walk in the cold night and says he loves being in the fog because it lets him live in another world. Arguing with Edmund about the institution where Edmund is to receive treatment, James begins to cry lightly, telling his poor childhood and his terrible father. Finally, James and Edmund, making amends, agree together on a sanatorium for Edmund, a place that is more expensive but substantially better. They hear Jamie coming home drunk, and James leaves to avoid fighting. Jamie and Edmund have their own conversation, and Jamie confesses that although he loves Edmund more than anyone else in the world, he wants Edmund to fail. Then Jamie passes out, dead drunk. When James returns, he wakes up, and then they start to fight again. Mary comes downstairs, by now so doped up she can barely recognize them. She is carrying her wedding gown, lost completely in her past. The men watch in horror and she does not even know they are there.

An Excerpt from Act 3

(The front door is heard closing and Tyrone calls uneasily from the hall.)

TYRONE: Are you there, Mary?

(The light in the hall is turned on and shines through the front parlor to fall on Mary.)

MARY: *(Rises from her chair, her face lighting up lovingly—with excited eagerness.)* I'm here, dear. In the living room. I've been waiting for you. *(Tyrone comes in through the front parlor. Edmund is behind him. Tyrone has had a lot to drink but beyond a slightly glazed look in his eyes and a trace of blur in his speech, he does not show it. Edmund has also had more than a few drinks without much apparent effect, except that his sunken cheeks are flushed and his eyes look bright and feverish. They stop in the doorway to stare appraisingly at her. What they see fulfills their worst expectations. But for the moment Mary is unconscious of their condemning eyes. She kisses her husband and then Edmund. Her manner is unnaturally effusive. They submit shrinkingly. She talks excitedly.)* I'm so happy you've come. I had given up hope. I was afraid you would't come home. It's such a dismal, foggy evening. It must be much more cheerful in the barrooms uptown, where there are people you can talk and joke with. No, don't deny it. I know how you feel. I don't blame you a bit. I'm all the more grateful to you for coming home. I was sitting here so lonely and blue. Come and sit down. *(She sits at left rear of table, Edmund at left of table, and Tyrone in the rocker at right of it.)* Dinner won't be ready for a minute. You're actually a little early. Will wonders never cease. Here's the whisky, dear. Shall I pour a drink for you? *(Without waiting for a reply she does so.)* And you, Edmund? I don't want to encourage you, but one before dinner, as an appetizer, can't do harm. *(She pours a drink for him. They make no move to take the drinks. She talks on as if unaware of their silence.)* Where's Jamie? But, of course, he'll never come home so long as he has the price of drink left. *(She reaches out and clasps her husband's hand—sadly.)* I'm afraid Jamie has been lost to us for a long time, dear. *(Her face hardens.)* But we mustn't allow him to drag Edmund down with him, as he's like to do. He's jealous because Edmund has always been the baby—just as he used to be of Eugene[1]. He'll never be content until he makes Edmund as hopeless a failure as he is.

EDMUND: *(Miserably.)* Stop talking. Mama.

Note [1] Eugene: Mary and Tyrone's second son, who died at the age of two

TYRONE: (*Dully.*) Yes, Mary, the less you say now—(*Then to Edmund, a bit tipsily.*) All the same there's truth in your mother's warning. Beware of that brother of yours, or he'll poison life for you with his damned sneering serpent's tongue!

EDMUND: (*As before.*) Oh, cut it out, Papa.

MARY: (*Goes on as if nothing had been said.*) It's hard to believe, seeing Jamie as he is now, that he was ever my baby. Do you remember what a healthy, happy baby he was, James? The one-night stands and filthy trains and cheap hotels and bad food never made him cross or sick. He was always smiling or laughing. He hardly ever cried. Eugene was the same, too, happy and healthy, during the two years he lived before I let him die through my neglect.

TYRONE: Oh, for the love of God! I'm a fool for coming home!

EMDUND: Papa! Shut up!

MARY: (*Smiles with detached tenderness at Edmund.*) It was Edmund who was the crosspatch when he was little, always getting upset and frightened about nothing at all. (*She pats his hand—teasingly.*) Everyone used to say, dear, you'd cry at the drop of a hat.

EDMUND: (*Cannot control his bitterness.*) Maybe I guessed there was a good reason not to laugh.

TYRONE: (*Reproving and pitying.*) Now, now, lad. You know better than to pay attention—

MARY: (*As if she hadn't heard—sadly again.*) Who would have thought Jamie would grow up to disgrace us. You remember, James, for years after he went to boarding school, we received such glowing reports. Everyone liked him. All his teachers told us that a fine brain he had, and how easily he learned his lessons. Even after he began to drink and they had to expel him, they wrote us how sorry they were, because he was so likable and such a brilliant student. They predicted a wonderful future for him if he would only learn to take life seriously. (*She pauses—then adds with a strange, sad detachment.*) It's such a pity. Poor Jamie! It's hard to understand—(*Abruptly a change comes over her. Her face hardens and she stares at her husband with accusing hostility.*) No, it isn't at all. You brought him up to be a boozer. Since he first opened his eyes, he's seen you drinking. Always a bottle on the bureau in the cheap hotel rooms! And if he had a nightmare when he was little, or a stomach-ache, your remedy was to give him a teaspoonful of whiskey to quiet him.

TYRONE: (*Stung.*) So I'm to blame because that lazy hulk has made a drunken loafer of himself? Is that what I came home to listen to? I might have known! When you have the poison in you, you want to blame everyone but yourself!

EDMUND: Papa! You told me not to pay attention. (*Then, resentfully.*) Anyway it's true. You did the same thing with me. I can remember that teaspoonful of booze every time I woke up with a nightmare.

MARY: (*In a detached reminiscent tone.*) Yes, you were continually having nightmares as a child. You were born afraid. Because I was so afraid to bring you into the world. (*She pauses—then goes on with the same detachment.*) Please don't think I blame your father, Edmund. He didn't know any better. He never went to school after he was ten. His people were the most ignorant kind of poverty-stricken Irish. I'm sure they honestly believed whiskey is the healthiest medicine for a child who is sick or frightened.

(*Tyrone is about to burst out in angry defense of his family but Edmund intervenes.*)

EDMUND: (*Sharply.*) Papa! (*Changing the subject.*) Are we going to have this drink, or aren't we?

TYRONE: (*Controlling himself—dully.*) You're right. I'm a fool to take notice. (*He picks up his glass listlessly.*) Drink hearty, lad.

(*Edmund drinks but Tyrone remains staring at the glass in his hand. Edmund at once realizes how much the whiskey has been watered. He frowns, glancing from the bottle to his mother—starts to say something but stops.*)

MARY: (*In a detached tone—repentantly.*) I'm sorry if I sounded bitter, James. I'm not. It's all so far away. But I did feel a little hurt when you wished you hadn't come home. I was so relieved and happy when you came, and grateful to you. It's very dreary and sad to be here alone in the fog with night falling.

TYRONE: (*Moved.*) I'm glad I came, Mary, when you act like your real self.

MARY: I was so lonesome I kept Cathleen with me just to have someone to talk to. (*Her manner and quality drift back to the shy convent girl again.*) Do you know what I was telling her, dear? About the night my father took me to your dressing room and I first fell in love with you. Do you remember?

TYRONE: (*Deeply moved—his voice husky.*) Can you think I'd ever forget, Mary?

(*Edmund looks away from them, sad and embarrassed.*)

MARY: (*Tenderly.*) No. I know you still love me, James, in spite of everything.

TYRONE: (*His face works and he blinks back tears—with quiet intensity.*) Yes! As God is my judge! Always and forever, Mary!

MARY: And I love you, dear, in spite of everything. (*There is a pause in which Edmund moves embarrassedly. The strange detachment comes over her manner again as if she were speaking impersonally of people seen from a distance.*) But I must confess, James, although I couldn't help loving you, I would never have married you if I'd known you drank so much. I remember the first night your barroom friends had to help you up to the door of our hotel room, and knocked and then ran away before I came to the door. We were still on our honeymoon, do you remember?

TYRONE: (*With guilty vehemence.*) I don't remember! It wasn't on our honeymoon! And I never in my life to be helped to bed, or missed a performance!

MARY: (*As though he hadn't spoken.*) I had waited in that ugly hotel room hour after hour. I kept making excuses for you. I told myself it must be about the theater. Then I became terrified. I imagined all sorts of horrible accidents. I got on my knees and prayed that nothing had happened to you—and then they brought you up and left you outside the door. (*She gives a little, sad sigh.*) I didn't know how often that was to happen in the years to come, how many times I was to wait in ugly hotel rooms. I became quite used to it.

EDMUND: (*Bursts out with a look of accusing hate at his father.*) Christ! No wonder—! (*He controls himself—gruffly.*) When is dinner, Mama? It must be time.

TYRONE: (*Overwhelmed by shame which he tries to hide, fumbles with his watch.*) Yes. It must be. Let's see. (*He stares at his watch without seeing it. Pleadingly.*) Mary! Can't you forget—?

MARY: (*With detached pity.*) No, dear. But I forgive. I always forgive you. So don't look so guilty. I'm sorry I remember out loud. I don't want to be sad, or to make you sad. I want to remember only the happy part of the past. (*Her manner drifts back to the shy, gay convent girl.*) Do you remember our wedding, dear? I'm sure you've completely forgotten what my wedding gown looked like. Men don't notice such things. They don't think they are important. But it was important to me, I can tell you! How I fussed and worried! I was so excited and happy! My father told me to buy anything I wanted and never mind what it cost. She was pious and strict. I think she was a little jealous. She didn't approve of my marrying—especially an actor. I think she hoped I would become a nun. She used to scold my father. She'd grumble, "You never tell me, never mind what it costs, when I buy anything! You've spoiled that girl so, I pity her husband if she ever marries. She'll expect him to give her the moon. She'll never make a good wife." (*She laughs affectionately.*) Poor mother! (*She smiles at Tyrone with a strange, incongruous coquetry.*) But she was mistaken, wasn't she, James? I haven't been such a bad wife, have I?

TYRONE: (*Huskily, trying to force a smile.*) I'm not complaining, Mary.

Part Six

American Literature since 1945

Philosophical and Historical Background

When World War II was over, the United States rose to be the strongest power in the Western world, assuming leadership of the Western capitalist world in opposition to the Soviet Union and the Communist camp in the Cold War. However, what happened immediately after the war exerted a tremendous influence on the mentality of Americans. It changed man's view of himself and the world as well. First of all, the dropping of an atomic bomb over Hiroshima and Nagasaki in Japan, which shocked the whole world, rendered the destruction of the Western civilization possible. The threat of nuclear catastrophe was also looming large in this period. Characterized with fear, the Cold War mentality was manifested both in the Korean War and the Vietnam War, which broadened the gap between the government and the people. Later, that the Cuban missile crisis in 1962 shook the whole American nation was a more explicit manifestation of this fear.

Consequently, the age of the new American empire is sometimes known, quite appropriately, as the age of anxiety. At home, the Cold War mentality was transformed into fear-based domestic politics. McCarthyism, also known as the Red Scare, was the contemporary version of witch-hunt, persecuting artists and writers in the name of fighting Communism and of questioning "un-American" activities. What else contributed to a disquieting society could be found in racism, which survived and even took legal forms one hundred years after the Civil War, for racial segregation was still enforced until the 1960s. The assassination of John F. Kennedy and of Martin Luther King, Jr. and the resignation of Nixon further intensified the terror and tossed the whole nation again into grief and despair. The impact of these changes and upheavals on the American society was so overwhelming that people started to question the role of science in human progress, with the fear of the misuse of modern science and technology spreading. They no longer believed in God and began to reconsider the nature of man and man's capacity for evil. They even began to think of life as a big joke or an absurdity. The world was even more disintegrating and fragmentary and people were even more estranged and despondent.

Despite the widespread fear and anxiety, it was also true that the Unite States did try to promote a civil society, consisting of social forces many of which needed to be distinguished from the government and its policies. The Civil Rights Movement, the continuing feminist movement, as well as the anti-war protests and many social protests suggested that civil forces dissenting from the imperialist and racist ideology never stopped fighting to have their voices heard.

Existentialism   Due to the two world wars and economic crisis, the established beliefs and morality were greatly shaken in the Western world in the first half of the 20th century. Then existentialism, which can be traced back to Nietzsche, Kierkegaard and Dostoevsky, began to surface to offer a better understanding of the prevalent panic and despair. Jean-Paul Sartre (1905–

1980) is generally regarded as one of the important figures in the philosophy of existentialism along with Heidegger and Camus. Sartre's existential theory is mainly illustrated in his *Being and Nothingness* (1943) and "Existentialism is a Humanism" (1946).

A key proposition of existentialism is that "existence precedes essence," which means that the actual life of the individual is determined by his subseqent actions. It is obvious that the existentialists reverse the tradition of Western philosophy and Christianity. According to Platonism and Christianity, there is a predetermined essence that defines what a human is. What man ultimately becomes is the unfolding of his innate nature or essence. However, the existentialists maintain that there is no predetermined essence or transcendent value that controls what man is or what he does. Each individual man is what he makes of himself by a succession of actions taken with the freedom of choice. The world, by itself, is purposeless and absurd, and rebellion against absurdity is the struggle of man's life.

Thus, the idea of absurdity is central to existentialism. To Sartre, the absurdity of human existence is the necessary result of our attempt to live a life of meaning and purpose in an indifferent world. In this world, every man is ultimately alone and feels the absurdity of the world, which results from alienation brought about by capitalist modernization. He tries to achieve proposes, but all will inevitably come to naught in the end, for there is no universally law and absolute values in it. Therefore, the feeling of absurdity, in many cases, may not guide him to find the meaning and propose of his life. This helps to justify the Beat Generation, many of whom turned to drugs, believing the world can not be changed.

In addition, Sartre believes that man is "condemned to be free," endowed with unlimited freedom. Man's freedom originates from man's consciousness or nothingness, which also means man's limitless possibilities. Since existence is prior to essence, man makes himself by acting. Once he comes to the world, he becomes responsible for all he does. So freedom is indispensable with action, and it can only be realized in reality. Sartre further argues that only when man is free can he be a human being.

Deconstruction   Jacques Derrida (1930–2004) made a name for himself as the father of deconstruction in the mid 1960s, distancing himself from the various philosophical movements and traditions that preceded him on the French intellectual scene such as phenomenology, existentialism and structuralism. Deconstruction is primarily concerned with a critique of the Western philosophical tradition and seeks to subvert the various binary oppositions that strengthen our dominant ways of thinking.

Nietzsche once contends that any truth is a linguistic representation of sense and force and that truth is untruthful in origin. Derrida continues to develop this insight with deconstruction, which holds that the textual interpretation involves efforts to intertextualize various texts, considered as a display of curiosity in the indeterminate texts. Once again, Derrida echoes

Nietzsche's belief that the center of Western civilization, a combination of Platonism and Christianity, has been decentered. To subvert logocentrism, which always privileges one and marginalizes the other in an opposition, Derrida intends to deny all ultimate meanings and the immanent signifieds.

Combining "difference" with the French word "différer," différance is coined to mean "difference and deferral of meaning." It is discovered that the difference that can not be heard in speech in French can be discerned in writing. It exactly agrees with Derrida's concept that there is no ultimate referent or foundation. This reversal of the subordinated term of an opposition accomplishes the first of deconstruction's dual strategic intents.

Derrida also makes use of binary opposition, the core concept of Western metaphysics to further deconstruct the "logocentrism." Derrida contends that the relationship of binary dichotomy is not supposed to destroy the other, but to interpenetrate, mutually supplement and depend on each other. When inverting a pair of binary opposition, it is definitely to propose an integrated mindset and enter a new era of pluralism.

Postmodernism　It is generally acknowledged that postmodernism formally comes into being at the end of the 1950s and the early 1960s under the influence of Jacques Derrida, Michel Foucault, Jean-Francois Lyotard, Ihab Hassan, Fredric Jameson and so on. Since it is an interdisciplinary concept that has covered a wide range of fields of study, there is no unifying definition of postmodernism. In the field of theory and philosophy, postmodernism is plural, fluid and open.

The concepts put forward by postmodernists include the dissolution of the grand narratives, the trend of self-unmaking, the loss of the real, the cultural logic of late capitalism, and the indeterminacy, all of which makes postmodernism a complex assembly. While modernism is concerned with the principles such as unity, authority and certainty, postmodernism focuses on difference, plurality and skepticism.

❛ Saul Bellow (1915–2005)

Saul Bellow, a Canadian-American writer, is one of the forerunners in shedding a positive light on the Jewish-American heritage. He was awarded the Nobel Prize for Literature in 1976 and became the first one to win the National Book Award for Fiction three times.

Saul Bellow was born Solomon Bellow in Lachine, Quebec—now part of Montreal. Bellow's parents were both immigrants from St. Petersburg, Russia, who had traveled to Canada in 1913. Life proved to be very difficult in Canada, and thus Bellow's father resorted to bootlegging and other activities. And the small family lived in the most impoverished section of the City of Montreal with other immigrant families.

In 1924 after Bellow's father was beaten almost to death because of his dealings with questionable people, the family decided to leave for America. They moved south, settling in an equally impoverished region in the Chicago slums. Thus, his childhood, far from innocent and carefree, provided Bellow with many materials to draw upon.

To Bellow, a lot of education took place at home. His mother was adamant that Bellow learn Hebrew and Yiddish, as well as English. His desire to read was further developed when he faced many different illnesses that kept him indoors. Although he was bookish by nature, he worked hard at his physical fitness and lived for optimum health. Along with the Bible, he loved other religious texts and they comforted him during many hard times. When Bellow's mother died suddenly, he was emotionally distraught for many months.

In 1924 Bellow moved to Chicago to attend high school and college. The urban landscape began to work on his mind. After attending the University of Chicago for two years, he transferred to Northwestern University where he majored in anthropology. Afterwards, he went to the University of Wisconsin to further his study, but dropped out in order to get married. It was then that he embarked on writing. He finally took an editorial position at *The Encyclopedia Britannica*. His first success as a writer of fiction came in 1941, with the publication of his short story "Two Morning Monologues" in the *Partisan Review*. Meanwhile, Bellow became a naturalized U.S. citizen upon attempting to enlist in the armed forces.

After the attack on Pearl Harbor, he served as a U.S. Merchant Marine during the last year of World War II. When his service ended, he returned to teaching. As he taught at the universities, Bellow constantly worked on his own writing. In 1948 Bellow was awarded a Guggenheim Fellowship, which allowed him to give up teaching temporarily and travel to Europe.

Throughout his life, Bellow was exposed to the economic boom of the forties and fifties, the Cold War, the anti-Semitism of the thirties and forties, the Civil Rights Movement, the end of segregation, and the Vietnam War. He married five times and taught at numerous universities, including the University of Minnesota, New York University, Princeton University, the University of Puerto Rico, and the University of Chicago. He was awarded the Nobel Prize for Literature in 1976. After his death, he was buried at the Jewish cemetery Shir Heharim in Brattleboro, Vermont.

It was while Bellow was serving in the Merchant Marines that he wrote his first novel, *Dangling Man* (1944). It deals directly with emotions and struggles that Bellow saw around him in the various faces of the soldiers he served with, which no doubt, existed in his own psyche. The main character in *Dangling Man* struggled with intellectual and spiritual questions while he waited to be drafted into the war. In 1947 he followed his first novel with *The Victim*. Set in New York City, it was about the complex relationship that develops between a Jew and an anti-Semite. The book addresses the issue of humanity's fate. Does one have a right to choose his fate, or is it chosen for him? This is a theme that echoes in many of Bellow's stories. Saul Bellow's most famous work is *The Adventures of Augie March* (1953). It was with this novel that Bellow let go of previous ideals and restrictions. The novel is concerned with the lives of two brothers who carried on different paths after similar childhoods. The brothers, Augie and Simon, were raised in a fatherless household in the slums of Chicago. Though the novel is comedic in parts, and deftly entertaining, it also portrays Bellow's childhood world in tragic, specific detail. This would be the novel that immortalized Chicago in a specific time.

With three early novels, Bellow made a name for himself. His reputation grew and he was soon regarded as one of the foremost American novelists of the 20th century. In 1965 Bellow was the first American to receive the International Literary Prize for *Herzog* (1964). *Herzog* focuses on the life of a middle-aged Jewish intellectual. The main character, Moses E. Herzog, like Bellow's other characters, is dissatisfied with where his life has taken him. He writes letters to various friends and philosophers, including his ex-wife Madeleine, Martin Heidegger, Nietzsche and God.

Then Bellow became the first novelist to be awarded the National Book Award three times—for *The Adventures of Augie March*, *Herzog* and *Mr. Sammler's Planet* (1970). In 1975 Bellow won the Pulitzer Prize with his novel, *Humboldt's Gift* (1975).

Bellow's strength lies in his faith in man and man's ability to offer a "spirited resistance to the force of our time" (as he puts it). In essence, his works are full of humanism and he is mainly concerned with freedom and love. To him, freedom is the interplay of what is given and what is made in the life of man while love is the interplay between one's identity and his completion in others. In communicating those cultural values, literature and art play a crucial and indispensable role. Bellow also believes that modern man has lived through frustration and defeat, and striven for truth, freedom and wisdom. In most cases, his heroes, Jewish intellectuals or writers, are found to struggle with the absurdity of life and finally overcome it. For example, in *Herzog*, Bellow reacts to the horrors of history in a different way from some other writers do. The Great Depression, World War II, the Cold War and the Vietnam War cause widespread disillusionment, which is well expressed by great artists such as T. S. Eliot. Moses acknowledges the facts of war and death, but he does not become alienated as a result of them. He criticizes the leaders of his country for the war in Vietnam, and condemns an "aesthetic" view of history that ignores death and murder. Bellow believes that modern man can find communion and beauty in midst of the bleakness and isolation of the modern world. Although Moses does feel alienated and the bulk of his novel is about his solitary thoughts, in the end, Moses rejects alienation and solitude. He comes to embrace society and to see the importance of sharing his life with others.

The writing style of Saul Bellow is unique in its descriptive nature, which highlights relevant culture and history. This aspect of his work demonstrates his education in a variety of disciplines, and also gives an added element of depth to his writing.

Selected Reading

Herzog

The novel opens with Moses Herzog in Ludeyville, a town in the Berkshires in western Massachusetts. Herzog, a middle-aged college professor, lives temporarily in his country house and appears to be undergoing a necessary catharsis. He has a habit of writing letters, which are addressed both to intimates and strangers, living and dead, public figures, scientists, philosophers, governments and newspapers, and make up much of the novel.

Then it is disclosed through Herzog's letters, memories and reflections that he has been traumatized by his recent divorce from his second wife, Madeleine, who has an affair with his best friend, Valentine Gersbach. It is also revealed that Herzog has used the money he inherited from his father to pay for the house in the Berkshires, hoping to please Madeleine and allow him peace to write the second volume of his book. However, Madeleine feels suffocated as an isolated country housewife and begins a secret affair with Gersbach. Herzog, oblivious, secures Gersbach a radio job in Chicago, at which point Madeleine presses for a move. Shortly after their relocation, Madeleine ends the marriage, which completely crushes Herzog. Craving a medical diagnosis for his addled state and even sympathy for his plight, he pays a visit to Dr. Emmerich in New York. Dr. Emmerich finds him in good physical health, but suggests an outing with another woman. It is at this point that Ramona, a vivacious student, comes to Herzog's life and they have an affair afterwards.

Worried that Romona takes it too seriously, Herzog decides to visit his friends at Martha's Vineyard. As soon as arriving at the Vineyard, however, Herzog heads to New York, where he spends a night with Ramona. To regain custody of his daughter June, he goes to the courthouse to discuss his plans with his lawyer, Simkin. June's babysitter wrote a letter accusing Gersbach of treating June badly. According to the babysitter, Valentine locked the child in the car while he and Madeleine argued inside the house. While waiting for his lawyer, Herzog happens to witness a series of tragicomic court hearings, including one where a woman is charged with beating her three-year-old child to death by flinging him against a wall.

The next day, Herzog flies to Chicago on impulse, where he gets to his stepmother's house and picks up an antique pistol with two bullets in it, forming a vague plan of killing Madeleine and Valentine and running off with June afterwards. However, he realizes that June is in no danger and changes his mind, when he sees Valentine giving June a bath through a window of their house. He then goes to ask Gersbach's wife for help in gaining custody of June, but is rejected.

Herzog spends the night with his good friend, Lucas Asphalter, with whose help he arranges to meet June. The next day morning, after taking June to the aquarium, Herzog gets into a car accident, in which June is not hurt, but Herzog is knocked unconscious. He wakes up to find himself at the feet of the police, taken to jail on a charge of possession of a weapon. His brother, Will, bails him out and tries to get him back on his feet. So Herzog heads to Ludeyville, where Will meets him and suggests that Herzog allow himself to be taken to a hospital for observed rest under the care of a psychiatrist. But Herzog, who once had the same idea himself, is now coming to terms with his life and rejects it. Much to Will's surprise, Ramona also comes to reunite with Herzog, who starts to make plans to fix up the house, which, like his life, needs repair but is still structurally sound. By the end of the novel, Herzog is contented with his country home and the pleasant weather, and feels no need to write any more letters.

Through Herzog's letters and memory, other details of his life also come to light: He first married Daisy, with whom he had a son named Marco; he was raised in a Jewish immigrant family in LaRoux, Canada and his father failed in many business ventures and eventually became a bootlegger; he constantly makes efforts to be a writer and published one book entitled *Romanticism and Christianity*, which finally gained critical acclaim despite an initially chilly response.

An Excerpt

With Madeleine, several years ago, Herzog had made a fresh start in life. He had won her away from the Church—when they met, she had just been converted. With twenty thousand dollars inherited from his charming father, to please his new wife, he quit an academic position which was perfectly respectable and bought a big old house in Ludeyville, Massachusetts. In the peaceful Berkshires where he had friends (the Valentine Gersbachs) it should be easy to write his second volume on the social ideas of the Romantics.

Herzog did not leave academic life because he was doing badly. On the contrary, his reputation was good. His thesis had been influential and was translated into French and German. His early book, not much noticed when it was published, was now on many reading lists, and the younger generation of historians accepted it as a model of the new sort of "history that interests *us*" —personal, engagée—and looks at the past with an intense need for contemporary relevance. As long as Moses was married to Daisy, he had led the perfectly ordinary life of an assistant professor, respected and stable. His first work showed by objective research what Christianity was to Romanticism. In the second he was becoming tougher, more assertive, more ambitious. There was a great deal of ruggedness, actually, in his character. He had a strong will and a talent for polemics, a taste for the philosophy of history. In marrying Madeleine and resigning from the university (because she thought he should), digging in at Ludeyville, he showed a taste and talent also for danger and extremism, for heterodoxy, for ordeals, a fatal attraction to the "City of Destruction." What he planned was a history which really took into account the revolutions and mass convulsions of the 20th century, accepting, with de Tocqueville[1], the universal and durable development of the equality of conditions, the progress of democracy.

But he couldn't deceive himself about this work. He was beginning seriously to distrust it. His ambitions received a sharp check. Hegel[2] was giving him a great deal of trouble. Ten years earlier he had been certain he understood his ideas on consensus and civility, but something had gone wrong. He was distressed, impatient, angry. At the same time, he and his wife were behaving very peculiarly. She was dissatisfied. At first, she hadn't wanted him to be an ordinary professor, but she changed her mind after a year in the country. Madeleine considered herself too young, too intelligent, too vital, too sociable to be buried in the remote Berkshires. She decided to finish her graduate studies in Slavonic languages. Herzog wrote to Chicago about jobs. He had to find a position for Valentine Gersbach, too. Valentine was a radio announcer, a disk-jockey in Pittsfield. You couldn't leave people like Valentine and Phoebe stuck in this mournful countryside, alone, Madeleine said. Chicago was chosen because Herzog had been there, and was well-connected. So he taught courses in the Downtown College and Gersbach became educational director of an FM station in the Loop[3]. The house near Ludeyville was closed up—twenty thousand dollars' worth of house, with books and English bone china and new appliances abandoned to the spiders, the moles and the field mice—Papa's hard-earned money!

The Herzogs moved to the Midwest. But after about a year of this new Chicago life, Madeleine decided that she and Moses couldn't make it after all—she wanted a divorce. He had to give it, what could he do? And the divorce was painful. He was in love with Madeleine; he couldn't bear to leave his little daughter. But Madeleine refused to be married to him, and people's wishes have to be respected. Slavery is dead.

Note [1] de Tocqueville: (1805–1859) a French politician and historian

Note [2] Hegel: (1770–1831) a German philosopher

Note [3] an FM station in the Loop: a radio station in Chicago

The strain of the second divorce was too much for Herzog. He felt he was going to pieces—breaking up—and Dr. Edvig, the Chicago psychiatrist who treated both Herzogs, agreed that perhaps it was best for Moses to leave town. He came to an understanding with the dean of the Downtown College that he might come back when he was feeling better, and on money borrowed from his brother Shura he went to Europe. Not everyone threatened with a crackup can manage to go to Europe for relief. Most people have to keep on working; they report daily, they still ride the subway. Or else they drink, they go to the movies and sit there suffering. Herzog ought to have been grateful. Unless you are utterly exploded, there is always something to be grateful for. In fact, he was grateful.

He was not exactly idle in Europe, either. He made a cultural tour for the Narragansett Corporation, lecturing in Copenhagen, Warsaw, Cracow, Berlin, Belgrade, Istanbul and Jerusalem. But in March when he came to Chicago again his condition was worse than it had been in November. He told his dean that it would probably be better for him to stay in New York. He did not see Madeleine during his visit. His behavior was so strange and to her mind so menacing, that she warned him through Gersbach not to come near the house on Harper Avenue. The police had a picture of him and would arrest him if he was seen in the block.

It was now becoming clear to Herzog, himself incapable of making plans, how well Madeleine had prepared to get rid of him. Six weeks before sending him away, she had had him lease a house near the Midway at two hundred dollars a month. When they moved in, he built shelves, cleared the garden and repaired the garage door; he put up the storm windows. Only a week before she demanded a divorce, she had his things cleaned and pressed, but on the day he left the house, she flung them all into a carton which she then dumped down the cellar stairs. She needed more closet space. And other things happened, sad, comical, or cruel, depending on one's point of view. Until the very last day, the tone of Herzog's relations with Madeleine was quite serious—that is, ideas, personalities, issues were respected and discussed. When she broke the news to him, for instance, she expressed herself with dignity, in that lovely masterful style of hers. She had thought it over from every angle, she said, and she had to accept defeat. They could not make the grade together. She was prepared to shoulder some of the blame. Of course, Herzog was not entirely unprepared for this. But he had really thought matters were improving.

Tennessee Williams (1911–1983)

Tennessee Williams, the pseudonym of Thomas Lanier Williams, is known as one of the prominent playwrights of the 20th century and has won the Pulitzer Prize twice.

Tennessee Williams was born into the house of his maternal grandfather in Columbus, Mississippi. His father was a traveling salesman who became increasingly abusive as his children grew older. His mother, a descendant of a genteel Southern family, was somewhat smothering. When Williams was three, the family moved to Clarksdale, Mississippi. At five, he was diagnosed with diphtheria, which caused his legs to be paralyzed for nearly two years. Due to his illness, Williams grew withdrawn and his chief solace was writing. In 1918 the family moved again, this time to St. Louis, Missouri, marking the start of the family's decline. During the hard time, Williams was close to his sister Rose, who was diagnosed with schizophrenia and spent most of her adult life in mental hospitals. After various unsuccessful attempts, Rose remained incapacitated for the rest of her life. Unable to get over this hard blow, Williams was driven to alcoholism. Inspired by Rose, the common "mad heroine" appears in many of Williams' plays. At the age of 16, Williams won third prize for an essay published in *Smart Set*. A year later, he published "The Vengeance of Nitocris" in *Weird Tales*. In the early 1930s, Williams attended the University of Missouri, Columbia, where he was a member of the Alpha Tau Omega fraternity. It was there that his friends dubbed him Tennessee for his Southern accent and his father's background in Tennessee. Later Williams transferred to Washington University for a year, eventually taking a degree from the University of Iowa in 1938. During the late 1940s and 1950s, although widely celebrated, Williams was still restless and insecure. He began to travel widely, often spending summers in Europe. To stimulate his writing he moved often to various cities including New York, New Orleans, Key West, Rome, Barcelona and London. Despite great previous success, the 1960s and 1970s brought personal turmoil and theatrical failures to Williams. His decline partly resulted from his addition to alcohol and drugs. In addition, because of McCarthyism, people grew conservative and many attacked Williams for his homosexuality.

In 1944 Williams produced *The Glass Menagerie*, which won instant acclaim and the New York Drama Critics' Circle Award. The play tells the story of a young man, Tom, his disabled sister, Laura, and their controlling mother Amanda, who tries to make a match between Laura and a gentleman. It is obvious that his family relationship serves as inspiration for the play. The huge success of his next play, *A Streetcar Named Desire* in 1947, further established his reputation as a great playwright and won the Pulitzer Prize and the Drama Critics' Circle Award. In the following years, seven of his plays were performed on Broadway: *Summer and Smoke* (1948), *The Rose Tattoo* (1951), *Camino Real* (1953), *Cat on a Hot Tin Roof* (1955) winning another Pulitzer Prize and the Drama Critics' Circle Award, *Orpheus Descending* (1957), *Garden District* (1958) and *Sweet Bird of Youth* (1959).

Although Williams' protagonist in *A Streetcar Named Desire* is the Romantic Blanche DuBois, the play is a work of social realism. In this play, Williams dramatizes the decayed aristocrats of a declining Southern culture. Faced with the decline, the main character, Blanche, finds it difficult to live with the present life. Blanche explains to Mitch that she fibs because she refuses to come to terms with the reality. Lying to herself and to others allows her to make life appear as it should be rather than as it is. Stanley, a practical man firmly grounded in the physical world, disdains Blanche's fabrications and does everything he can to expose them. The relationship between Blanche and Stanley is a struggle between appearances and reality. It propels the play's plot and creates an overarching tension. Ultimately, Blanche's attempts to remake her own and Stella's existences—to rejuvenate her life and to save Stella from a life with Stanley—fail. Throughout the play, Blanche avoids appearing in direct, bright light, especially in front of her suitor, Mitch. She also refuses to reveal her age, and it is clear that she avoids light in order to prevent Mitch from seeing the reality of her fading beauty. In general, light also symbolizes the reality of Blanche's past. She is haunted by the ghosts of what she has lost— her first love, her purpose in life, her dignity and the genteel society (real or imagined) of her ancestors. What highlights the conflict in the play is the sharp contrast between Blanche's educated speech and literary allusions and Stanley's coarse and down-to-earth language clichés.

As a regionalist, Williams makes use of the exotic elements of the Italians and the Creole whites in Louisiana. He is also considered a naturalist in that he has created some of the most debased characters in some of the most sordid settings, yet remains detached from them. However, an air of fantasy and a touch of fairytale is instilled in his plays. As regards aesthetics, he intends to reject the principles of traditional realism.

Selected Reading

A Streetcar Named Desire

On a streetcar named Desire, Blanche DuBois travels to a street named Elysian Fields, in the French Quarter of New Orleans, Louisiana, just after the end of World War II. Blanche is in her thirties and represents the epitome of a Southern Belle, although a faded one. On meeting, Blanche tells her young sister, Stella, that their family plantation, Belle Rive in Laurel, Mississippi, has been lost due to the financial failure and draining after deaths in the family. She also mentions that she has been given a leave of absence from her teaching position because of her nerves.

Blanche is disdainful of the Kowalski's two-room apartment in a noisy working-class neighborhood, which wins her the instant dislike of Stella's husband, a man of Polish descent named Stanley Kowalski. However, it is clear that Stella is happy to leave behind her the social pretensions of her background in exchange for the sexual gratification she gets from her husband, pregnant with his baby. Stanley immediately distrusts Blanche so much so that he suspects her of having cheated Stella out of her share of the family inheritance.

One night during one of his poker parties in the house, Blanche meets Mitch, whose courteous manner sets him apart from the other men, and they are obviously attracted to each other. Unexpectedly, Stanley, drunk and enraged, beats Stella, who escapes to their upstairs neighbor's apartment with Blanche. A short while later, Stanley is remorseful and cries to Stella to forgive him. To Blanche's disbelief and outrage, Stella returns to Stanley and embraces him passionately. Distressed, Blanche leaves with Mitch who tries to console her in the courtyard.

The following day, Blanche attempts to convince Stella to leave her abusive marriage, despite Stella's complete dismissal of the previous night's events. Overhearing the conversation and Blanche's complete disregard for him, Stanley sets out more maliciously to find out more about her past life.

As a few weeks pass by, Blanche and Stanley still fail to get along, but Blanche has hope in Mitch. During a date between the two, Blanche confesses to Mitch that once she was married to a poet, Allan Grey, who turned out to be a homosexual. Later Grey committed suicide, after Blanche taunted him for it. Mitch is touched so much by her honesty that he tells Blanche that they need each other.

One month later, when Stella is preparing a dinner for Blanche's birthday, Stanley comes in to tell her that he has learned news of Blanche's sordid past. He says that she once lived at a hotel known for prostitutes and that she was fired for having an affair with a teenage student. Stella is more disturbed by Stanley's cruelty that Stanley has also revealed it to Mitch, which renders her going into labor and sent to hospital.

Several hours later, Mitch arrives and confronts Blanche about her past and she admits everything. Despite the fact that he will not marry her, Mitch, makes sexual advances towards Blanche and she turns him away, calling out "Fire!" in a loud voice until he's left the building. Then Stanley returns from hospital and Blanche, heavily drunk, tells him that she will soon be leaving New Orleans with her former suitor. In the following confrontation, Stanley overcomes and rapes Blanche, which results in her imminent mental breakdown.

In the end, at another poker game, Stella weeps as she packs Blanche's belongings and prepares to send her away to a mental institution. Although Blanche has told Stella about Stanley's assault, Stella can not allow herself to believe the story. When a doctor and a nurse arrive to take Blanche, Mitch bursts into tears, Stanley comes over to comfort Stella, and the poker game continues uninterrupted.

An Excerpt from Scene One

STELLA: (*Calling out joyfully.*) Blanche!

(*For a moment, they stare at each other. Then BLANCHE springs up and runs to her with a wild cry.*)

BLANCHE: Stella, oh, Stella, Stella! Stella for Star!

(*She begins to speak with feverish vivacity as if she feared for either of them to stop and think. They catch each other in a spasmodic embrace.*)

BLANCHE: Now, then, let me look at you. But don't you look at me, Stella, no, no, no, not till later, not till I've bathed and rested! And turn that over-light off! Turn that off! I won't be looked at in this merciless glare! (*STELLA laughs and complies.*) Come back here now! Oh, my baby! Stella! Stella for Star! (*She embraces her again.*) I thought you would never come back to this horrible place! What am I saying? I didn't mean to say that. I mean to be nice about it and say—Oh, what a convenient location and such—Ha-a-ha! Precious lamb! You haven't said a word to me.

STELLA: You haven't given me a chance, honey! (*She laughs, but her glance at Blanche is a little anxious.*)

BLANCHE: Will, now you talk. Open your pretty mouth and talk while I look around for some liquor! I know you must have some liquor on the place! Where could it be, I wonder? Oh, I spy, I spy!

(*She rushes to the closet and removes the bottle; she is shaking all over and panting for breath as she tries to laugh. The bottle nearly slips from her grasp.*)

STELLA: (*Noticing.*) Blanche, you sit down and let me pour the drinks. I don't know what we've got to mix with. Maybe a coke in the icebox. Look'n see, honey, while I'm—

BLANCHE: No coke, honey, not with my nerves tonight! Where—where—where is—?

STELLA: Stanley? Bowling! He loves it. They're have a—found some Soda! —tournament...

BLANCHE: Just water, baby, to chase it! Now don't get worried, your sister hasn't turned into a drunkard, she'd just all shaken up and hot and tired and dirty! You sit down, now, and explain this place to me! What are you doing in a place like this?

STELLA: Now, Blanche—

BLANCHE: Oh, I'm not going to be hypocritical, I'm going to be honestly critical about it! Never, never, never in my worst dreams could I picture—Only Poe! Only Mr. Edgar Allan Poe! —could do it justice! Out there I suppose is the ghoul-haunted woodland of Weir! (*She laughs.*)

STELLA: No, honey, those are and L & N tracks.

BLANCHE: No, now seriously, putting joking aside. Why didn't you tell me, why didn't you write me, honey, why didn't you let me know?

STELLA: (*Carefully, pouring herself a drink.*) Tell you what, Blanche?

BLANCHE: Why, that you had to live in these conditions!

STELLA: Aren't you being a little intense about it? It's not that bad at all! New Orleans isn't like other cities.

BLANCHE: This has got nothing to do with New Orleans. You might as well say—forgive me, blessed baby! (*She suddenly stops short.*) The subject is closed!

STELLA: (*A little dryly.*) Thanks.

(*During the pause, BLANCHE stares at her. She smiles at BLANCHE.*)

BLANCHE: (*Looking down at her glass, which shakes in her hand.*) You're all I've got in the world, and you're not glad to see me!

STELLA: (*Sincerely.*) Why, Blanche, you know that's not true.

BLANCHE: No? —I'd forgotten how quiet you were.

STELLA: You never did give me a chance to say much, Blanche. So I just got in the habit of being quiet around you.

BLANCHE: (*Vaguely.*) A good habit to get into... (*Then, abruptly.*) You haven't asked me how I happened to get away from the school before the spring term ended.

STELLA: Well, I thought you'd volunteer that information—if you wanted to tell me.

BLANCHE: You thought I'd been fired?

STELLA: No, I—thought you might have—resigned...

BLANCHE: I was so exhausted by all I'd been through my—nerves broke. (*Nervously tamping cigarette.*) I was on the verge of lunacy, almost! So Mr. Graves—Mr. Graves is the high school superintendent—he suggested I take a leave of absence. I couldn't put all of those details into the wire... (*She drinks quickly.*) Oh, this buzzes right through me and feels so good!

STELLA: Won't you have another?

BLANCHE: No, one's my limit.

STELLA: Sure?

BLANCHE: You haven't said a word about my appearance.

STELLA: You look just fine.

BLANCHE: God love you for a liar![1] Daylight never exposed so total a ruin! But you—you've put on some weight, yes, you've just as plump as a little partridge! And it's so becoming to you!

Note [1] God love you for a liar!: May God love you for a liar!

STELLA:　Now, Blanche—

BLANCHE:　Yes, it is, it is or I wouldn't say it! You just have to watch around the hips a little. Stand up.

STELLA:　Not now.

BLANCHE:　You hear me? I said stand up! (*STELLA complies reluctantly.*) You messy child, you, you've split something on that pretty white lace collar! About your hair— you ought to have it cut in a feather bob with your dainty features. Stella, you have a maid, don't you?

STELLA:　No. With only two rooms it's—

BLANCHE:　What? Two rooms, did you say?

STELLA:　This one and—(*She is embarrassed.*)

BLANCHE:　The other one? (*She laughs sharply. There is an embarrassed smile.*)

BLANCHE:　I am going to take just one little tiny nip more, sort of to put the stopper on, so to speak... Then put the bottle away so I won't be tempted. (*She rises.*) I want you to look at my figure! (*She turns around.*) You know I haven't put on one ounce in ten years, Stella? I weigh that I weighed the summer you left Belle Reve. The summer dad died and you left us...

STELLA:　(*A little wearily.*) It's just incredible, Blanche, how well you're looking.

BLANCHE:　(*They both laugh uncomfortably.*) But, Stella, there are only two rooms. I don't see where you're going to put me!

STELLA:　We're going to put you in here.

BLANCHE:　What kind of bed's this—one of those collapsible things?

(*She sits on it.*)

STELLA:　Does it feel all right?

BLANCHE:　(*Dubiously.*) Wonderfully, honey. I don't like a bed that gives[1] much. But there's no door between the two rooms, and Stanley—will it be decent?

STELLA:　Stanley is Polish, you know.

BLANCHE:　Oh, yes. They're something like Irish, aren't they?

STELLA:　Well—

❧ Arthur Miller (1915–2005)

Arthur Miller, who won the Pulitzer Prize and the Jerusalem Prize, has been considered one of the most prominent American playwrights of the 20th century.

Arthur Miller was born into a moderately affluent Jewish-American family in Harlem, New

---

Note [1] gives: bends or stretches under pressure

York. After his father's business failed during the Great Depression, his family moved to humbler quarters in Brooklyn. After graduating in 1932 from Abraham Lincoln High School, he had to work at several menial jobs to pay for his college tuition. At the University of Michigan Miller first majored in journalism, where he became the reporter and night editor on the student paper, *The Michigan Daily*. It was during this time that he wrote his first work, *No Villain* (1936), which won the Avery Hopwood Award. Then Miller changed his major to English, becoming particularly interested in ancient Greek drama and the dramas of Henrik Ibsen. In 1937 Miller wrote *Honors at Dawn*, which also received the Avery Hopwood Award. In 1938 after graduation he joined the Federal Theater Project, a New Deal agency established to provide jobs in the theater, which was closed soon. Consequently Miller began to work in the Brooklyn Navy Yard while continuing to write radio plays, some of which were broadcast on CBS.

During World War II, Miller was exempted from military service because of a high-school football injury to his left kneecap. In 1948 Miller built a small studio in Roxbury, Connecticut, which was to be his long time home. In 1952, Elia Kazan, a director, named eight people from the Group Theater, who had been members of the American Communist Party before the House Un-American Activities Committee (HUAC). Driven by this incident, Miller traveled to Salem, Massachusetts to look into the witch trials of 1692. In 1956 Miller left his first wife Mary Slattery and married Marilyn Monroe. Refusing to identify the writers believed to hold Communist sympathies, Miller was accused of contempt of Congress in 1957, which was overturned the following year.

In 1962 Miller married photographer Inge Morath, after the breakup with Monroe. In 1965 Miller was elected the first American president of International P.E.N.[1] Then Miller dedicated a lot of his time to campaigning against the Vietnam War, leading an American group of writers to Paris in 1968. In 1969 Miller's works were banned in the Soviet Union after he campaigned for the freedom of dissident writers. Throughout the 1970s Miller spent much of his time experimenting with the theater and traveling with his wife. In 1983 Miller traveled to China to direct *Death of a Salesman* at the People's Art Theater in Beijing, which also made a hit.

Miller's life was showered with awards and honors, and in 2001 he was selected for the Jefferson Lecture by the National Endowment for the Humanities (NEH), the U.S. federal government's highest honor for achievement in the humanities. Surrounded by his family and friends, Miller died of heart failure, which coincided with the 56th anniversary of the Broadway debut of *Death of a Salesman* (1949).

Throughout his life, Miller proved to be productive. In 1944 Miller wrote *The Man Who Had All the Luck*, which won the Theater Guild's National Award. In the following years, his

---

Note [1] International P.E.N.: International Association of Poets, Playwrights, Editors, Essayists and Novelists

first published novel *Focus* (1945) got little acclaim. However, in 1947 Miller's *All My Sons* was produced, winning the New York Drama Critics Circle Award and two Tony Awards. The play was directed by Elia Kazan, with whom Miller would have a continuing professional and personal relationship. *Death of a Salesman* in 1949 proved to be a huge success, the first one to win a Tony Award for best play, a New York Drama Critics' Award and a Pulitzer Prize. *The Crucible*, a parable play in which Miller compared the anti-Communism of McCarthyism of the 1950s to the witch-hunt in Salem, opened on Broadway in 1953. In 1955 Miller's verse drama, *A View from the Bridge*, also opened on Broadway. Afterwards, Miller began to work on a film *The Misfits* (1961), starring Monroe. In 1964 *After the Fall* presents Miller's life experience as regards his marriage with Monroe. Meanwhile, his family comedy, *The Price* (1968), turned out to be another success. During the early 1990s, Miller produced three new plays: *The Ride Down Mount Morgan* in 1991, *The Last Yankee* in 1992 and *Broken Glass* in 1994.

After World War II, the United States was faced with profound domestic tensions and contradictions. Although the war had ostensibly engendered an unprecedented sense of American confidence, prosperity and security, the United States became increasingly embroiled in constant anxiety, disorder and confusion. Under the influence of existentialism, Miller fashioned a new version of American Dream in a particular context. *Death of a Salesman*, Miller's most famous work, is concerned not only with the painful conflicts within one family, but also with the indictment of fundamental American values and the American Dream of material success. Willy Loman believes wholeheartedly in what he considers the promise of the American Dream—that a "well liked" and "personally attractive" man in business will indubitably acquire the material comfort. However, in reality his interpretation is at odds with a more rewarding understanding of the American Dream that identifies hard work without complaint as the key to success. Willy's blind faith in his stunted version of the American Dream leads to his rapid psychological decline, when he is unable to accept the disparity between the Dream and his own life.

Miller highlights the psychology of the characters by means of the stream-of-consciousness technique. He also employs vernacular and some other devices to pioneer the literary world.

Selected Reading

Death of a Salesman

As a flute melody plays, Willy Loman, a sixty-year-old salesman, returns home in the evening, exhausted from a failed sales trip. When his wife, Linda, greets him, he tells her that he was delayed because his car kept swerving and he had to drive slowly. Linda is deeply concerned, for he has been in a series of accidents lately. So she suggests that he ask his boss, Howard Wagner, for a job in New York so that he won't have to travel, which Willy agrees to. At the sight of Biff, his older son who has come back home to visit, Willy complains that he has yet to make something of himself.

In fact, Willy and Linda have two grown son, Biff and Happy. Willy always thinks Biff could easily be rich and successful, but is wasting his talents and needs to get on track. Although Happy has a steady job, his own apartment, and a way with women, he also lacks the push and derring-do to rise above mediocrity. Now pleased to see each other, the two brothers reminisce about their high-school days and propose plans for business ventures.

Later that night, Willy starts to hallucinate, talking to imagined images as if they were real people. He's ranting so loudly that Happy and Biff wake up. The brothers are legitimately worried, as they have never seen their father like this. Biff, feeling as though he should stay close to home and fix his relationship with his dad, decides to talk to a former employer, Bill Oliver, about getting a loan to start a business.

In the middle of the night, Willy is talking to himself so loudly that everyone wakes up. Linda admits to her sons that she and Willy are struggling financially and that Willy has been attempting suicide. She is so worried that she accuses Biff of being the cause of Willy's unhappiness. Now Willy joins the family discussion and he and Biff begin to argue, but Happy interjects that Biff plans to see Oliver the following morning, which cheers Willy up and sets everyone to sleep.

The next day, of course, everything goes wrong. Willy feels happy and confident as he meets his boss, Howard. But instead of obtaining a transfer to the New York office, Willy gets fired. Destroyed by the news, he begins to hallucinate, once again speaking with imaginary people, as he heads out to meet his sons at a restaurant.

Waiting for their dad at the restaurant, Biff explains to Happy that Oliver refuses to see him and does not have the slightest idea who he is. Distressed, spiteful and something of a kleptomaniac, Biff steals Oliver's fountain pen. By now, Biff has realized that he is crazy to think he would ever get a loan, and that he and his family have been lying to themselves for their whole lives. When Willy comes into the restaurant demanding good news, Biff struggles to explain what has happened without letting his father down. Willy, who can't handle the disappointment, tries to pretend it isn't true. He starts drifting into the dreamy past again, reliving the moment when Biff discovered his affair with a woman in Boston. While their dad is busy being detached from reality, Biff and Happy ditch him for two girls.

Biff and Happy return home from their dates to find their mother waiting for them, fuming mad that they have abandoned their father at the restaurant. A massive argument erupts. No one wants to listen to Biff, but he makes it clear that he can not live up to his dad's unrealistic expectations and is merely a failure. He's the only one who sees that they've been living a lie, and he tells them so.

The night's fight ends with Willy realizing that Biff, although a "failure," seems to really love him. Unfortunately, Willy can't get over his failure as a husband, a father, a human being and thinks the greatest contribution that he can make toward his son's success is to commit suicide. In doing so, Biff could take advantage of the life insurance money to start a business.

Within a few minutes, there's a loud crash. Willy finally kills himself.

At his funeral, Linda, sobbing, still under the delusion that her husband was a well-liked salesman, wonders why no one comes to his funeral. Having seen through his family's lies, Biff wants to be a better man who is honest with himself. Unfortunately, Happy wants to be just like his dad. Everybody leaves but Linda, who remains at the grave and talks about how she makes the final house payment.

An Excerpt from Act II

BIFF: (*At the peak of his fury.*) Pop, I'm nothing! I'm nothing, Pop. Can't you understand that? There's no spite in it any more. I'm just what I am, that's all.

(*Biff's fury has spent itself, and he breaks down, sobbing, holding on to Willy, who dumbly fumbles for Biff's face.*)

WILLY: (*Astonished.*) What're you doing? What're you doing? (*To Linda:*) Why is he crying?

BIFF: (*Crying, broken.*) Will you let me go, for Christ's sake? Will you take that phony dream and burn it before something happens? (*Struggling to contain himself, he pulls away and moves to the stairs.*) I'll go in the morning. Put him—put him to bed. (*Exhausted, Biff moves up the stairs to his room.*)

WILLY: (*After a long pause, astonished, elevated.*) Isn't that—remarkable? Biff—he likes me!

LINDA: He loves you, Willy!

HAPPY: (*Deeply moved.*) Always did, Pop.

WILLY: Oh, Biff! (*Staring wildly.*) He cried! Cried to me. He is choking with his love, and now cries out his promise: That boy—that boy is going to be magnificent!

(*Ben appears in the light just outside the kitchen.*)

BEN: Yes, outstanding, with twenty thousand behind him.

LINDA: (*Sensing the racing of his mind, fearfully, carefully.*) Now come to bed, Willy. It's all settled now.

WILLY: (*Finding it difficult not to rush out of the house.*) Yes, we'll sleep. Come on. Go to sleep, Hap.

BEN: And it does take a great kind of a man to crack the jungle.

(*In accents of dread, Ben's idyllic music stars up.*)

HAPPY: (*His arm around Linda*) I'm getting married, Pop, don't forget it. I'm changing everything. I'm gonna run that department before the year is up. You'll see, Mom. (*He kisses her*).

BEN: The jungle is dark but full of diamonds, Willy.

(*Willy turns, moves, listening to Ben.*)

LINDA: Be good. You're both good boys, just act that way, that's all.

HAPPY: 'Night, Pop. (*He goes upstairs.*)

LINDA: (*To Willy.*) Come, dear.

BEN: (*With greater force.*) One must go in to fetch a diamond out.

WILLY: (*To Linda, as he moves slowly along the edge of the kitchen toward the door.*) I just want to get settled down, Linda. Let me sit alone for a little.

LINDA: (*Almost uttering her fear.*) I want you upstairs.

WILLY: (*Taking her in his arms.*) In a few minutes, Linda. I couldn't sleep right now. Go on, you look awful tired. (*He kisses her.*)

BEN: Not like an appointment at all. A diamond is rough and heard to the touch.

WILLY: Go on now. I'll be right up.

LINDA: I think this is the only way, Willy.

WILLY: Sure, it's the best thing.

BEN: Best thing!

WILLY: The only way. Everything is gonna be—go on, kid, get to bed. You look so tired.

LINDA: Come right up.

WILLY: Two minutes.

(*Linda goes into the living-room, then reappears in her bedroom. Willy moves just outside the kitchen door.*)

WILLY: Loves me. (*Wonderingly.*) Always loved me. Isn't that a remarkable thing? Ben, he'll worship me for it!

BEN: (*With promise.*) It's dark there, but full of diamonds.

WILLY: Can you imagine that magnificence with twenty thousand dollars in his pocket?

LINDA: (*Calling from her room.*) Willy! Come up!

WILLY: (*Calling into the kitchen.*) Yes! Yes. Coming! It's very smart, you realize that, don't you, sweetheart? Even Ben sees it. I gotta go, baby. 'By! 'By! (*Going over to Ben, almost dancing.*) Imagine? When the mail comes he'll be ahead of Bernard again!

BEN: A perfect proposition all around.

WILLY: Did you see how he cried to me? Oh, if I could kiss, Ben!

BEN: Time, William, time!

WILLY: Oh, Ben, I always knew one way or another we were gonna make it, Biff and I!

BEN: (*Looking at his watch.*) The boat. We'll be late. (*He moves slowly off into the darkness.*)

❚ Toni Morrison (1931–)

Toni Morrison, one of the most important African American writers of the 20th century, was the first African American woman to win the Nobel Prize for Literature.

Toni Morrison was born into a working-class family in Lorain, Ohio. Her parents moved to Ohio to escape Southern racism and instilled a sense of heritage in her by telling traditional African American folktales. She read a lot as a child and among her favorite authors were Jane Austen and Leo Tolstoy. Morrison graduated from Howard University in 1953 and then from Cornell University in 1955. She taught English first at Texas Southern University in Houston for two years, then at Howard for seven years. After the breakup of her marriage, she began working as an editor in Syracuse, going on two years later to Random House in New York, where Morrison helped promote Black literature. In 1993 she was awarded the Nobel Prize for Literature. In 1996 the National Endowment for the Humanities selected Morrison for the Jefferson Lecture.

Morrison began writing fiction, as she got involved in an informal group of poets and writers who met to discuss their work at Howard University. She attended one meeting with a short story about a black girl who longed to have blue eyes. She later developed the story as her first novel, *The Bluest Eye* (1970). In 1975 her novel *Sula* (1973) was nominated for the National Book Award. Her third novel, *Song of Solomon* (1977), brought her national attention. In 1987 Morrison's novel *Beloved* became a critical success. *Beloved* won the Pulitzer Prize for Fiction and the American Book Award.

In addition to her novels, Morrison has written books for children with her younger son, Slade Morrison, who worked as a painter and musician. Slade died of pancreatic cancer in 2010. Morrison's novel *Home*, half-written when Slade died, is dedicated to him. Another novel *God Help the Child* was published in 2015, following her other novels such as *Tar Baby* (1981), *Jazz* (1992), *Paradise* (1999), *Love* (2003), *A Mercy* (2008).

Beloved explores the physical, emotional and spiritual devastation wrought by slavery, a devastation that continues to haunt those characters who are former slaves even in freedom. The most dangerous effect of slavery is its destruction of slaves' identity, and the novel contains multiple examples of self-alienation. Slaves used to be told they were subhuman and were traded as commodities whose worth could be expressed in dollars. After slavery is abolished, the traumatized slaves find it not easy to face a new life and are not sure of their identity. Sethe, for instance, seems to be alienated from herself and filled with self-loathing. Yet her children also have volatile, unstable identities. Denver conflates her identity with Beloved's, and Beloved feels herself actually beginning to physically disintegrate. Paul D is also so alienated from himself that at one point he can not tell whether the screaming he hears is his own or someone else's. Consequently, Paul D is greatly insecure about whether or not he could possibly be a real "man," and he frequently wonders about his value as a person.

Morrison enhances her world by investing it with a supernatural dimension. Her discussions of the main themes similarly resound with biblical allusions. Symbolism also serves as an important method to strengthen the intended subject.

Selected Reading

Beloved

In 1873 Sethe, a former slave, has been living with her eighteen-year-old daughter Denver in a house at 124 Bluestone Road in Cincinnati, Ohio. Because the house is haunted by the ghost of their dead baby sister, Sethe's youngest daughter Denver has been friendless and housebound, and her sons, Howard and Buglar, ran away eight years earlier. Sethe's mother-in-law, Baby Suggs, dies in her bed soon afterward.

The local people refuse to visit Sethe's house and in fact, whenever a wagon passes the house, the driver is more inclined to speed up his horse. However, Paul D, one of the slaves from Sweet Home in Kentucky, the plantation where Baby Suggs, Sethe, Halle—Sathe's husband, and several other slaves once worked, shows up and eventually tries to bring a sense of reality into the house. In attempting to make the family forget the past, he chases out the spirit. Then one day, on their way home from a carnival, they encounter a young woman sitting in front of the house, calling herself Beloved. Paul eventually becomes suspicious of the girl and warns Sethe, who is much devoted to Beloved, and thus turns a deaf ear to it. In the following days, although Denver develops an obsessive attachment to Beloved, Paul D grows to despise her. The girl plays games with him and even seduces him in an apparent attempt to drive him away from Sethe.

When Paul D tells his friends about his plans to start a new family, the reason for the community's rejection of Sethe is finally revealed. Later, Sethe also tells him what happened: After escaping from Sweet Home and reaching her waiting children at her mother-in-law's home, Sethe was found by her master, the schoolteacher, who attempted to reclaim her and her children in the woodshed. To prevent her children from growing up in slavery, Sethe planed to kill them all and finally only had her eldest two-year-old daughter killed by running a saw along her neck. It is too much for Paul D, who then leaves and sleeps in a church that night.

After Sethe comes to realize that Beloved is the daughter she murdered, whose tombstone reads only "Beloved," Sethe begins to spoil Beloved out of guilt. Beloved becomes more and more demanding, throwing tantrums when she does not get her way. Worried about her mother, Denver sets out to search for help from the black community and some of the village women arrive at the house to exorcise Beloved. When they arrive at Sethe's house, they see Sethe on the porch with Beloved, who stands smiling at them, naked and pregnant. At the same time, Mr. Bodwin, who helped Baby Suggs by offering her the house to stay after Halle bought her from their owner, makes his appearance. He has come for Denver who has asked him for a job, which Denver has not shared with Sethe. Mistaking him for schoolteacher who used to treat them cruelly and keep catching her, Sethe runs at Mr. Bodwin with an ice pick. She is restrained, but in the confusion Beloved disappears and never returns.

Afterwards, Paul D comes back to Sethe, who has retreated to Baby Suggs's bed to die. Mourning Beloved, Sethe laments, "She was my best thing." But Paul D replies, "You your best thing, Sethe." The novel then ends with a warning that "this is not a story to pass on." The town and even the residents of 124 have forgotten Beloved "like an unpleasant dream during a troubling sleep."

An Excerpt from Chapter 5, Part I

The woman gulped water from a speckled tin cup and held it out for more. Four times Denver filled it, and four times the woman drank as though she had crossed a desert. When she was finished a little water was on her chin, but she did not wipe it away. Instead she gazed at Sethe with sleepy eyes. Poorly fed, thought Sethe, and younger than her clothes suggested—good lace at the throat, and a rich woman's hat. Her skin was flawless except for three vertical scratches on her forehead so fine and thin they seemed at first like hair, baby hair before it bloomed and roped into the masses of black yarn under her hat.

"You from around here?" Sethe asked her.

She shook her head no and reached down to take off her shoes. She pulled her dress up to the knees and rolled down her stockings. When the hosiery was tucked into the shoes, Sethe saw that her feet were like her hands, soft and new. She must have hitched a wagon ride, thought Sethe. Probably one of those West Virginia girls looking for something to beat a life of tobacco and sorghum. Sethe bent to pick up the shoes.

"What might your name be?" asked Paul D.

"Beloved," she said, and her voice was so low and rough each one looked at the other two. They heard the voice first—later the name.

"Beloved. You use a last name, Beloved?" Paul D asked her.

"Last?" She seemed puzzled. Then "No," and she spelled it for them, slowly as though the letters were being formed as she spoke them.

Sethe dropped the shoes; Denver sat down and Paul D smiled. He recognized the careful enunciation of letters by those, like himself, who could not read but had memorized the letters of their name. He was about to ask who her people were but thought better of it. A young colored woman drifting was drifting from ruin. He had been in Rochester four years ago and seen five women arriving with fourteen female children. All their men—brothers, uncles, fathers, husbands, sons—had been picked off one by one by one. They had a single piece of paper directing them to a preacher on DeVore Street. The War had been over four or five years then, but nobody white or black seemed to know it. Odd clusters and strays of Negroes wandered the back roads and cowpaths from Schenectady to Jackson. Dazed but insistent, they searched each other out for word of a cousin, an aunt, a friend who once said, "Call on me. Anytime you get near Chicago, just call on me." Some of them were running from family that could not support them, some to family; some were running from dead crops, dead kin, life threats and took-over land. Boys younger than Buglar and Howard[1]; configurations and blends of families of women and children, while elsewhere, solitary, hunted and hunting for, were men, men, men. Forbidden public transportation, chased by debt and filthy "talking sheets," they followed secondary routes, scanned the horizon for signs and counted heavily on each other. Silent, except for social courtesies, when they met one another they neither described nor asked about the sorrow that drove them from one place to another. The whites didn't bear speaking on. Everybody knew.

So he did not press the young woman with the broken hat about where from or how come. If she wanted them to know and was strong enough to get through the telling, she would. What occupied them at the moment was what it might be that she needed. Underneath the major question, each harbored another. Paul D wondered at the newness of her shoes. Sethe was deeply touched by her sweet name; the remembrance of glittering headstone made her feel especially kindly toward her. Denver, however, was shaking. She looked at this sleepy beauty and wanted more.

Sethe hung her hat on a peg and turned graciously toward the girl. "That's a pretty name, Beloved. Take off your hat, why don't you, and I'll make us something. We just got back from the carnival over near Cincinnati. Everything in there is something to see."

Bolt upright in the chair, in the middle of Sethe's welcome, Beloved had fallen asleep again.

Note [1] Buglar and Howard: Sethe's two sons

"Miss. Miss." Paul D shook her gently. "You want to lay down a spell?"

She opened her eyes to slits and stood up on her soft new feet which, barely capable of their job, slowly bore her to the keeping room. Once there, she collapsed on Baby Suggs'[1] bed. Denver removed her hat and put the quilt with two squares of color over her feet. She was breathing like a steam engine.

"Sounds like croup," said Paul D, closing the door.

"Is she feverish? Denver, could you tell?"

"No. She's cold."

"Then she is. Fever goes from hot to cold."

"Could have the cholera," said Paul D.

"Reckon?"

"All that water. Sure sign."

"Poor thing. And nothing in this house to give her for it. She'll just have to ride it out. That's a hateful sickness if ever there was one."

"She's not sick!" said Denver, and the passion in her voice made them smile.

Four days she slept, waking and sitting up only for water. Denver tended her, watched her sound sleep, listened to her labored breathing and, out of love and a breakneck possessiveness that charged her, hid like a personal blemish Beloved's incontinence. She rinsed the sheets secretly, after Sethe went to the restaurant and Paul D went scrounging for barges to help unload. She boiled the underwear and soaked it in bluing, praying the fever would pass without damage. So intent was her nursing, she forgot to eat or visit the emerald closet.

Alice Walker (1944–)

Alice Walker, an American novelist, short story writer and poet, has won the Pulitzer Prize and the National Book Award.

Alice Walker was born in Putnam County, Georgia. Since her father earned only $300 a year from sharecropping and dairy farming, her mother supplemented the family income by working as a maid. She worked 11 hours a day for $17 per week to help to pay for Alice to attend college. Living under Jim Crow laws[2], her mother enrolled Alice in the first grade when the girl was four

---

Note [1] Baby Suggs: Sethes's mother-in-law

Note [2] Jim Crow laws: referring to state and local laws enforcing racial segregation in all public facilities in the Southern United States. Enacted after the Reconstruction period, these laws institutionalized a number of economic, educational and social disadvantages and continued in force until 1965. Under such laws, conditions for African Americans were consistently inferior and underfunded compared to those available to white Americans.

years old, even though their landlords expected the children of black sharecroppers to work the fields at a young age. Growing up with a tradition of listening to stories from her grandfather, Walker began writing, very privately, when she was eight years old.

In 1952, Walker was accidentally wounded in the right eye. Because the family had no car, the Walkers failed to take their daughter to a hospital for immediate treatment. By the time they reached a doctor a week later, she had become permanently blind in that eye. When a layer of scar tissue formed over her wounded eye, Alice became self-conscious and painfully shy. Stared at and sometimes taunted, she felt like an outcast and turned for solace to reading and to poetry writing. She later became valedictorian and was voted most-popular girl, as well as queen of her senior class. After high school, Walker went to Spelman College in Atlanta on a full scholarship in 1961 and later transferred to Sarah Lawrence College, graduating in 1965. Walker became interested in the Civil Rights Movement in part under the influence of activist Howard Zinn, who was one of her professors at Spelman College. Continuing the activism that she participated in during her college years, Walker returned to the South, where she became involved in voter registration drives, campaigns for welfare rights and children's programs in Mississippi.

Walker's first book of poetry was written while at Sarah Lawrence. Walker resumed her writing career when she joined *Ms.* magazine as an editor before moving to northern California in the late 1970s. She also renewed her interest in the work of Zora Neale Hurston, an American novelist and short story writer, who inspired Walker's writing and influenced her subject matter in this period. Walker's first novel, *The Third Life of Grange Copeland*, which follows the life of Grange Copeland, an abusive, irresponsible sharecropper, father and husband, was published in 1970. In 1976 Walker's second novel, *Meridian*, was published. The novel dealt with activist workers in the South during the Civil Rights Movement, and closely paralleled some of Walker's own experiences. In 1982 Walker published what has become her best-known work, *The Color Purple*, an epistolary novel that received the 1983 Pulitzer Prize and the National Book Award. In addition, she published a number of collections of short stories, poetry and other writings. Nevertheless, her works invariably focus on the struggles of black people, particularly women, and their lives in a racist, sexist and violent society. Thus Walker proves to be a leading figure in liberal politics.

The Color Purple follows a young troubled black woman fighting her way through not just racist white culture but patriarchal black culture as well. In the story almost none of the abusers are stereotypical monsters who can be dismissed as purely evil. Those who perpetuate violence are themselves victims, often of sexism, racism or paternalism. Harpo, for example, beats Sofia only after his father implies that Sofia's resistance makes Harpo less of a man. Mr. __ is violent and mistreats his family in the way his own tyrantlike father treated him. Celie advises Harpo to beat Sofia because she is jealous of Sofia's strength and assertiveness. At the same time, the characters are largely aware of the cyclical nature of harmful behavior. For instance, Sofia tells Eleanor Jane that societal influence makes it almost inevitable that her baby boy will grow up to be a racist. Only by forcefully talking back to the men who abuse them and showing them a new way of doing things do the women of the novel break these cycles of sexism and violence, making the men who abuse them stop and reexamine their ways. Throughout the story, Walker also portrays female friendships as a means for women to summon the courage to tell stories. In turn, these stories allow women to resist oppression and dominance. Relationships among women form a refuge, providing reciprocal love in a world filled with male violence.

With regard to style, Walker uses the epistolary form to emphasize the power of communication. Symbolism is also employed to deepen relevant implications.

Selected Reading

The Color Purple

Celie, the protagonist and narrator of *The Color Purple*, is a poor, uneducated, fourteen-year-old black girl living in rural Georgia. Celie starts writing letters to God because her father, Alphonso, beats and rapes her. Impregnated by her father, Celie has given birth to a boy and then a girl, both of whom her father takes away. Eventually, Alphonso marries Celie to a man known as Mr. __, which proves to be difficult and joyless on the part of Celie. Shortly thereafter, Nettie runs away from Alphonso and takes refuge at Celie's house, where Mr. __ still makes advances towards her. Consequently, Nettie flees for her own safety and Celie assumes she is dead, never hearing from Nettie afterwards. Harpo, Mr. __'s son, falls in love with a large, spunky girl named Sofia. After Sofia and Harpo get married, Sofia appears to be defiant in the face of Harpo's attempts to beat her into submission, which shocks Celie greatly.

Celie's life changes, when Mr. __ brings home his ill mistress, Shug Avery, a jazz and blues singer, who is everything that Celie isn't: sexy, sassy and independent. Shug is initially rude to Celie, but the two women become friends as Celie takes charge of nursing Shug. Frustrated with Harpo's consistent attempts to subordinate her, Sofia moves out with her children. Several months later, Harpo opens a juke joint where Shug sings nightly. Celie grows confused over her feelings toward Shug. Learning that Mr. __ beats Celie when she is away, Shug decides to stay, which results in a more intimate relationship between Shug and Celie. Sofia returns for a visit and promptly gets in a fight with Harpo's new girlfriend, Squeak. In town one day, the mayor's wife, Miss Millie, asks Sofia to work as her maid. Sofia answers with a sassy "Hell no." When the mayor slaps Sofia for her insubordination, she returns the blow, knocking the mayor down. Thus, Sofia is finally sentenced to work for twelve years as the mayor's maid.

Together with Shug, Celie discovers dozens of letters that Nettie has sent to Celie over the years in Mr. __'s trunk. From the letters, Celie learns that Nettie befriended and traveled with a missionary couple, Samuel and Corrine, to Africa. Based on the fact that their two adopted children, Adam and Olivia, resemble Nettie and Samuel's account of how they adopted them, it occurs to Nettie that the two children are actually Celie's biological children, alive after all. It is also revealed that Alphonso is actually Nettie and Celie's stepfather, who pretends to be their real father because he wants to inherit their mother's house and property. Despite her persistent refusal to accept that Nettie is their children's biological aunt, Corrine feels reconciled before her death. Meanwhile, Celie visits Alphonso, who convinces her of Nettie's story.

Overwhelmed by grief and disillusionment, Celie can't help cursing Mr. __ for his years of abuse and decides to move to Tennessee with Shug and Squeak. In Tennessee, Celie spends her time designing and sewing tailored pairs of pants, eventually turning her hobby into a business. Once, returning to Georgia, Celie finds that Mr. __ has reformed his ways and that Alphonso has died. Consequently, Alphonso's house and land are transferred to Celie, so she moves in. Meanwhile, Nettie and Samuel get married and plan to return to America.

Celie and Mr. __ begin to enjoy each other's company, without strong attachment. Now independent financially, spiritually and emotionally, Celie is no longer bothered by Shug's passing flings with younger men. Released from her servitude, and remarries Harpo and works in Celie's clothing store. Nettie finally returns to America with Samuel and the children. Emotionally drained but exhilarated by the reunion with her sister, Celie believes she and Nettie have just begun the best years of their lives despite their old age.

An Excerpt

First Shug sing a song by somebody name Bessie Smith. She say Bessie somebody she know. Old friend. It call A Good Man Is Hard to Find. She look over at Mr. __ a little when she sing that. I look over at him too. For such a little man, he all puff up. Look like all he can do to stay in his chair. I look at Shug and I feel my heart begin to cramp. It hurt me so, I cover it with my hand. I think I might as well be under the table, for all they care. I hate the way I look, I hate the way I'm dress. Nothing but churchgoing clothes in my chifforobe. And Mr. __ looking at Shug's bright black skin in her tight red dress, her feet in little sassy red shoes. Her hair shining in waves.

Before I know it, tears meet under my chin.

And I'm confuse.

He love looking at Shug. I love looking at Shug.

But Shug don't love looking at but one of us. Him.

But that the way it spose to be. I know that. But if that so, why my heart hurt me so?

My head droop so it near bout in my glass.

Then I hear my name.

Shug saying Celie. Miss Celie. And I look up where she at.

She say my name again. She say this song I'm bout to sing is call Miss Celie's song. Cause she scratched it out of my head when I was sick.

First she hum it a little, like she do at home. Then she sing the words.

It all about some no count man doing her wrong, again. But I don't listen to that part. I look at her and I hum along a little with the tune.

First time somebody made something and name it after me.

Pretty soon it be time for Shug to go. She sing every week-end now at Harpo's. He make right smart money off of her, and she make some too. Plus she gitting strong again and stout. First night or two her songs come out good but a little weak, now she belt them out. Folks out in the yard hear her with no trouble. She and Swain sound real good together. She sing, he pick his box. It nice at Harpo's. Little tables all round the room with candles on them that I made, lot of little tables outside too, by the creek. Sometime I look down the path from our house and it look like a swarm of lightening bugs all in and through Sofia house. In the evening Shug can't wait to go down there.

One day she say to me, Well, Miss Cetie, I believe it time for me to go.

When? I ast.

Early next month, she say. June. June a good time to go off into the world.

I don't say nothing. Feel like I felt when Nettie left.

She come over and put her hand on my shoulder.

He beat me when you not here, I say.

Who do, she say, Albert?

Mr. __, I say.

I can't believe it, she say. She sit down on the bench next to me real hard, like she drop.

What he beat you for? she ast.

For being me and not you.

Oh, Miss Celie, she say, and put her arms around me.

Us sit like that for maybe half a hour. Then she kiss me on the fleshy part of my shoulder and stand up.

I won't leave, she say, until I know Albert won't even think about beating you.

✎ Joseph Heller (1923–1999)

Joseph Heller, one of the best post-World War satirists, is always associated with black humor.

Joseph Heller was born into poor Jewish parents in Brooklyn, New York. After graduating from Abraham Lincoln High School in 1941, Heller went to work as a blacksmith's apprentice, a messenger boy and a filing clerk. In 1942 he joined the U.S. Army Air Corps and two years later was sent to the Italian Front, where he flew 60 combat missions as a B-25 bombardier. After the war, Heller studied English at the University of Southern California and New York University on the G.I. Bill[1]. In 1949 he received his M.A. in English from Columbia University. Following his graduation, he spent a year as a Fulbright scholar at Oxford, England. After returning home, he taught composition at Pennsylvania State University for two years. Then he moved on to become a copywriter for the magazines *Time* and *Look*, and became promotion manager for *McCall's* magazine. He left *McCall's* in 1961 to teach fiction and dramatic writing at Yale and the University of Pennsylvania. After writing *Catch-22*, Heller worked on several Hollywood screenplays. In the 1960s Heller was involved in the Vietnam War protest movement.

Catch-22 (1961) was not a success when first published, but soon this novel has enjoyed steady sales ever since. The novel's title became a standard term in English and other languages for a dilemma with no easy way out. Now Heller's best-selling books include *Something Happened* (1974), *Good as Gold* (1979), *God Knows* (1984), *Picture This* (1988) and *Closing Time* (1994), but his first novel, *Catch-22*, remains his most famous and acclaimed work. *Catch-22* follows Captain John Yossarian, a fictional United States Army Air Force B-25 bombardier, and a number of other characters during World War II. Most events in the book occur while the airmen of the Fighting 256th Squadron are based on the island of Pianosa, west of Italy. Many incidents are described repeatedly from different points of view, so that more and more is revealed. The pacing of *Catch-22* is frenetic, its tenor is intellectual and its humor is largely absurd, but with grisly moments of realism interspersed.

Selected Reading

Catch-22

Captain John Yossarian, a World War II bombardier, is stationed on the island of

---

Note [1] the G.I. Bill: The Servicemen's Readjustment Act of 1944, known informally as the G.I. Bill, was a law that provided a range of benefits for returning World War II veterans, commonly referred to as G.I.s Benefits included low-cost mortgages, low-interest loans to start a business, cash payments of tuition and living expenses to attend university, high school or vocational education, as well as one year of unemployment compensation.

Pianosa. To escape the insanity of the war, he seeks comfort in the hospital, where he simply fakes illness by various means. Other men also begin to take refuge in the hospital, but they are forced to return to the front after the mysterious death of a soldier.

On the front, the other men are equally as crazy as Yossarian. His roommate, Orr, crash-lands every time he goes on a mission and talks about putting apples and horse chestnuts in his cheeks. Hungry Joe has screaming nightmares although he denies them each morning and gets into fistfights with the cat that belongs to his roommate. Likewise, the commanding officers are engaged in squabbles and pointless activities. General Peckem and General Dreedle vie pointlessly for power. Colonel Scheisskopf is so obsessed with winning the weekly parades that he ignores his own wife's sexual overtures.

After a cancelled mission to Bologna, His friend Nately falls in love with a whore from Rome and woos her constantly, despite her continued indifference and the fact that her kid sister constantly interferes with their romantic rendezvous. Finally she falls in love with Nately, but he is killed on his very next mission. When Yossarian breaks the terrible news to her, she blames him for Nately's death and tries to stab him every time she sees him thereafter.

Perhaps the most unusual officer is Lieutenant Milo Minderbinder. He starts his own enterprise called M&M Enterprises and persuades everyone to join his syndicate. Eventually, Milo tries to persuade Colonel Cathcart to relieve him of the enterprise so he can fly missions like everyone else. When Colonel Cathcart realizes how much work there is, he refuses and instead offers Milo all the planes he wants and any medals that may result from the men being killed during the missions.

The war takes an especially harsh toll on the men and their morale. Yossarian continuously opposes the war and Colonel Cathcart's frequent increases in the number of missions that are required to obtain a leave. Yossarian argues with Clevinger that everyone is trying to kill him. He says that anyone who tries to make him fight is just as dangerous as the enemy. Doc Daneeka repeatedly refuses to grant him the privilege, based on "catch-22": If Yossarian is insane, he is supposed not to object to flying the missions. But if he is not insane and does not want to fly the missions, then he is capable of flying them and must do so. Clevinger argues that the war should be fought. He bases this conclusion on the intellectual argument that if they do not fight, others will be killed because of their own cowardice. Meanwhile, all the officers consider Yossarian to be crazy, and they merely dismiss him.

In protest against being forced to fly more than the required number of missions as designated by the Group Headquarters, Yossarian uses various strategies. Despite these tactics, he can not avoid combat entirely and is haunted by his memory of Snowden, a soldier who died in his arms on a mission when Yossarian lost all desire to participate in the war. After this traumatic experience, he walks around naked and watches Snowden's burial from a tree. Then, an otherwise unknown man, Mudd, is killed just two hours after his arrival and is dumped in his tent. Everyone denies the existence of Mudd, so he lies there despite Yossarian's protests.

In the end, Yossarian, troubled by Nately's death, refuses to fly any more missions. He wanders the streets of Rome, encountering every kind of human horror—rape, disease, murder. He is eventually arrested for being in Rome without a pass, and his superior officers, Colonel Cathcart and Colonel Korn, offer him a choice. He can either face a court-martial or be released and sent home with an honorable discharge. There is only one condition: In order to be released, he must approve of Cathcart and Korn and state his support for their policy, which requires all the men in the squadron to fly eighty missions. Although he is tempted by the offer, Yossarian realizes that to comply is to endanger the lives of other innocent men. He chooses another way out, deciding to desert the army and flee to neutral Sweden. In doing so, he turns his back on the dehumanizing machinery of the military, rejects the rule of Catch-22, and strives to gain control of his own life.

An Excerpt from Chapter 5: Chief White Halfoat

Chief White Halfoat was out to revenge himself upon the white man. He could barely read or write and had been assigned to Captain Black as assistant intelligence officer.

"How could I learn to read or write?" Chief White Halfoat demanded with simulated belligerence, raising his voice again so that Doc Daneeka would hear "Every place we pitched our tent, they sank an oil well. Every time they sank a well, they hit oil. And every time they hit oil, they made us pack up our tent and go someplace else. We were human divining rods. Our whole family had a natural affinity for petroleum deposits, and soon every oil company in the world had technicians chasing us around. We were always on the move. It was one hell of away to bring a child up, I can tell you. I don't think I ever spent more than a week in one place."

His earliest memory was of a geologist.

"Every time another White Halfoat was born," he continued, "the stock market turned bullish. Soon whole drilling crews were following us around with all their equipment just to get the jump on each other. Companies began to merge just so they could cut down on the number of people they had to assign to us. But the crowd in back of us kept growing. We never got a good night's sleep. When we stopped, they stopped. When we moved, they moved, chuckwagons, bulldozers, derricks, generators. We were a walking business boom, and we began to receive invitations from some of the best hotels just for the amount of business we would drag into town with us. Some of those invitations were mighty generous, but we couldn't accept any because we were Indians and all the best hotels that were inviting us wouldn't accept Indians as guests. Racial prejudice is a terrible thing, Yossarian. It really is. It's a terrible thing to treat a decent, loyal Indian like a nigger, kike, wop or spic." Chief White Halfoat nodded slowly with conviction.

"Then, Yossarian, it finally happened—the beginning of the end. They began to follow us around from in front. They would try to guess where we were going to stop next and would begin drilling before we even got there, so we couldn't stop. As soon as we'd begin to unroll our blankets, they would kick us off. They had confidence in us. They wouldn't even wait to strike oil before they kicked us off. We were so tired we almost didn't care the day our time ran out. One morning we found ourselves completely surrounded by oilmen waiting for us to come their way so they could kick us off. Everywhere you looked there was an oilman on a ridge, waiting there like Indians getting ready to attack. It was the end. We couldn't stay where we were because we had just been kicked off. And there was no place left for us to go. Only the Army saved me. Luckily, the war broke out just in the nick of time, and a draft board picked me right up out of the middle and put me down safely in Lowery Field, Colorado. I was the only survivor."

Yossarian knew he was lying, but did not interrupt as Chief White Halfoat went on to claim that he had never heard from his parents again. That didn't bother him too much, though, for he had only their word for it that they were his parents, and since they had lied to him about so many other things, they could just as well have been lying to him about that too. He was much better acquainted with the fate of a tribe of first cousins who had wandered away north in a diversionary movement and pushed inadvertently into Canada. When they tried to return, they were stopped at the border by American immigration authorities who would not let them back into the country. They could not come back in because they were red. It was a horrible joke, but Doc Daneeka didn't laugh until Yossarian came to him one mission later and pleaded again, without any real expectation of success, to be grounded. Doc Daneeka snickered once and was soon immersed in problems of his own, which included Chief White Halfoat, who had been challenging him all that morning to Indian wrestle, and Yossarian, who decided right then and there to go crazy.

"You're wasting your time," Doc Daneeka was forced to tell him.

"Can't you ground someone who's crazy?"

"Oh, sure. I have to. There's a rule saying I have to ground anyone who's crazy."

"Then why don't you ground me? I'm crazy. Ask Clevinger[1]."

"Clevinger? Where is Clevinger? You find Clevinger and I'll ask him."

"Then ask any of the others. They'll tell you how crazy I am."

"They're crazy."

"Then why don't you ground them?"

"Why don't they ask me to ground them?"

"Because they're crazy, that's why."

"Of course they're crazy," Doc Daneeka replied. "I just told you they're crazy, didn't I? And you can't let crazy people decide whether you're crazy or not, can you?"

Yossarian looked at him soberly and tried another approach. "Is Orr[2] crazy?"

"He sure is," Doc Daneeka said.

"Can you ground him?"

"I sure can. But first he has to ask me to. That's part of the rule."

"Then why doesn't he ask you to?"

"Because he's crazy," Doc Daneeka said. "He has to be crazy to keep flying combat missions after all the close calls he's had. Sure, I can ground Orr. But first he has to ask me to."

"That's all he has to do to be grounded?"

"That's all. Let him ask me."

"And then you can ground him?" Yossarian asked.

"No. Then I can't ground him."

"You mean there's a catch?"

"Sure there's a catch," Doc Daneeka replied. "Catch-22. Anyone who wants to get out of combat duty isn't really crazy."

There was only one catch and that was Catch-22, which specified that a concern for one's own safety in the face of dangers that were real and immediate was the process of a rational mind. Orr was crazy and could be grounded. All he had to do was ask; and as soon as he did, he would no longer be crazy and would have to fly more missions. Orr would be crazy to fly more missions and sane if he didn't, but if he was sane he had to fly them. If he flew them he was crazy and didn't have to; but if he didn't want to he was sane and had to. Yossarian was moved very deeply by the absolute simplicity of this clause of Catch-22 and let out a respectful whistle.

"That's some catch, that Catch-22," he observed.

"It's the best there is," Doc Daneeka agreed.

Note [1] Clevinger: one of the pilots

Note [2] Orr: one of the pilots

Jack Kerouac (1922–1969)

Jack Kerouac, an American writer and poet, is considered a pioneer of the Beat Generation along with Allen Ginsberg. His life story usually serves as a manifestation of the confused ideology that seeks spirituality with no moral boundaries to guide it.

Jack Kerouac was born in Lowell, Massachusetts and his parents were working-class immigrants from Quebec, Canada. Kerouac's father ran a print shop and published the magazine, which exposed him early to publishing, printing and writing. When Kerouac's elder brother Gerard died at the age of nine, the family, and especially Jack, was overwhelmed by grief. Unable to get over Gerard's death, his mother struggled to seek comfort in Catholicism while his father turned to smoking, drinking and gambling. From then on, Kerouac regarded Gerard as his guardian angel, and followed him throughout his life. This belief, along with his memories of his beloved brother, inspired him to write the novel *Visions of Gerard* (1963). Nevertheless, his family's traditional Catholic values began to fall. He changed from a strong Catholic upbringing to a rebellious lifestyle of no moral boundaries. Kerouac grew up speaking a dialect of French-Canadian and didn't begin to learn English until he was almost six years old. Kerouac played sports extensively, liked to take long hikes, and wrote little diaries and short stories. He was a sociable child but his main companion during his youth and adulthood was the constant notebook he would carry with him wherever he went.

In 1939 he attended Columbia University, but dropped out in 1941 due to his disenchantment with college. Early on in his college days, Kerouac embraced a bohemian lifestyle that urged him to take drug-fueled cross-country trips. Later, he wrote in his personal writings and in his novels that he rejected the values of the time and was seeking to break free from society's restraints. These practices no doubt led to his life-long addictions and habitual drug use. He also rejected traditional ideas about spirituality, and devoted time to Buddhism.

Then he enlisted in the United States Navy, but was discharged for "indifferent disposition." He returned to New York afterwards and sought refuge with his former girlfriend Edie Parker, with whom he got married in 1944. While living in a small apartment, he met and formed strong bonds with Allen Ginsberg, Neal Cassady and William S. Burroughs. These three men made a great influence on him and became the subjects of many of his writings with regard to experimentation with religious practices, sexual preferences and hallucinogenic drugs. It was the experiences Kerouac had while living and traveling with these men that inspired him to describe his friends and his generation as the so-called Beat Generation. Just as Burroughs and Cassady were Kerouac's mentors in his young adulthood, Gary Snyder, an American poet and one of the Beat Generation, took this role later in Kerouac's life. Later *The Dharma Bums* (1958) details Kerouac's newfound devotion to Buddhism and his traveling adventures with Snyder.

In 1952 after the divorce with his wife, Kerouac continued writing and traveling, taking long trips through the United States and Mexico for the next several years. He wrote many of his novels during the 1950s, yet none of them were published immediately. It was only when he and his friends began to get a group of followers in San Francisco that the publishers began to take notice of Kerouac's writing. At that time, Kerouac, Ginsberg and Snyder were underground celebrities because of their constant poetry readings. With the acclaim of *On the Road* (1957), Jack Kerouac soon became a household celebrity. Ironically, this rise to fame coincided with a rapid decline of his personal life. He moved to live with his mother for the rest of his life. As his depression and drunkenness worsened, Kerouac became reclusive and his Buddhist beliefs finally gave in to the devout Catholicism of his mother.

Kerouac's first novel was *The Town and the City*, published in 1950. The novel, like all of Kerouac's novels, is autobiographical and tells the decline of his own family. In 1951 Kerouac took the ideas from various brief writings and in three weeks created *On the Road*, which would eventually be his biggest success despite the initial rejection. In the later period, he finished drafts of more novels, including *The Subterraneans* (1958), *Doctor Sax* (1959), *Tristessa* (1960) and *Desolation Angels* (1965), all of which chronicle many episodes of heavy drinking and depression.

On the Road, as the defining work of the Beat Generation, is an autobiographical account of Kerouac's road trip adventures across the United States and Mexico with Neal Cassady. The main character, Sal Paradise, is modeled after Kerouac and the character of Dean Moriarty is created from the experiences and letters of Neal Cassady. In general, *On the Road* gives voice to a rising, dissatisfied group of the young generation of the late 1940s and early 1950s. It is after the Great Depression and World War II and more than a decade before the Civil Rights Movement and the turmoil of the 1960s. The feelings, ideas and experiences in the novel are remarkably fresh as expressions of restless, idealistic youth who yearn for something more than the bland conformity of a superficially prosperous society.

With his long, stream-of-consciousness sentences and long paragraphs, Kerouac has sought to do no less than revolutionize the form of American prose.

Selected Reading

On the Road

After the breakup of his first marriage, Salvatore Paradise, an aspiring writer, meets Dean Moriarty, who has been released from a reform school prison and has come to New York to take part in its artistic and intellectual scene. Sal is immediately fascinated by Dean, whose life is subject to alcohol, drugs and women. Dean's ideas sparks Sal's own desires for adventure and exploration, so he decides to set out on his own journey after

Dean returns to his hometown of Denver. Sal hitchhikes and takes buses to Denver, meeting different people, among whom are travelers living in the impoverished and ever-moving world of hobos and hitchhikers.

In Denver Sal gets involves with Dean and several other friends, and they spend their time partying, drinking and taking drugs. Afterwards Sal departs for San Francisco to live for a while with his old friend Remi Boncoeur. There Sal works as a security officer until his relationship with Remi deteriorates and he leaves. On his way back to New York, he encounters a Chicano farm girl, Terry, and they work in the cotton fields of California together for several months. Sal thinks he is in love and enjoys becoming a part of this marginalized culture, but the cold weather of winter eventually drives him back to his life in New York.

Sal's second journey begins as Dean comes from San Francisco to Virginia to pick him up at his family's house over Christmas. They drive Dean's Hudson car to New Orleans to visit Old Bull Lee, a mentor and drug addict, who is taking care of the wife of one of their friends. The group travel through Texas and Arizona, stealing gasoline and food as they need it. Finally they reach San Francisco, where Dean abandons Sal and his ex-wife Marylou to live with his current wife Camille. Marylou gets them a hotel room on credit. Soon after this, however, she leaves with a rich man one night and Sal is left alone. Later Dean comes back only to ask about Marylou. Eventually Sal, wearied and broke from his travels, returns to New York.

The third journey begins with Sal in Denver. He has come to start a new life, but he finds that he is lonely and bored without Dean. Then Sal decides to go to San Francisco to meet Dean and the rest of the gang. Dean has been trying to start a new, more domestic life as well, but takes up his careless lifestyle again upon Sal's arrival. As a result, Dean's wife Camille kicks him out of the house, frustrated with his lack of responsibility for his children and family. Thus, Sal and Dean embark on another journey, declaring they will go to Italy. They start their journey in San Francisco with a night of partying and jazz clubs with their old friends. They then catch a ride with a gay and eventually they end up in Denver, where the two spend a wild evening at clubs, taking drugs and getting drunk. After Dean steals someone's limousine, they drive it straight to Chicago without any sleep. Once in Chicago, they wreck it, after which they hitch to New York where Dean falls in love with a new girl, Inez, who becomes impregnated by him.

The fourth and final journey is not a trip West but a trip South. Sal sets out on his own this time to see Mexico, leaving Dean and Inez in New York. But Dean catches Sal in Denver and, with a friend named Stan Shephard, they take off for Mexico together in an old Chevy car, abandoning his new child and lover in New York. They drive through Texas and cross the Mexican border, enchanted by the culture and freedom that Mexico offers. Along the way they stop in several small towns, in one of which, a guide, Victor, gives them drugs and takes them to a whorehouse. In the mountains of Mexico, they encounter the natives of the land and marvel at their impoverished and simple way of life. In Mexico City they find what might have been a kind of Beat haven, but Sal gets sick with dysentery and Dean leaves him there. When Sal is well enough, he leaves Mexico City and returns to New York, where he finds that Dean, having married Inez, leaves her and the child to return to his second wife Camille in San Francisco.

The book ends with Dean traveling to New York to see Sal and Sal's new partner. Sal, despairing over the mess and trouble that such a mad and free lifestyle of travel has brought him, nonetheless remains inspired by Dean's madness. However, he can not follow Dean back to San Francisco and it is the last time that Sal ever sees Dean. As the novel closes, Sal sits by the bank of a river, thinking of the great American landscape that he has seen on his journeys, and thinking of Dean.

An Excerpt from Chapter 6, Part One

In those days I didn't know Dean as well as I do now, and the first thing I wanted to do was look up Chad King, which I did. I called up his house, talked to his mother—she said, "Why, Sal, what are you doing in Denver?" Chad is a slim blond boy with a strange witch-doctor face that goes' with his interest in anthropology and prehistory Indians. His nose beaks softly and almost creamily under a golden flare of hair; he has the beauty and grace of a Western hotshot who's danced in roadhouses and played a little football. A quavering twang comes out when he speaks. "The thing I always liked, Sal, about the Plains Indians was the way they always got s'danged embarrassed after they boasted the number of scalps they got. In Ruxton's Life in the Far Westi there's an Indian who gets red all over blushing because he got so many scalps and he runs like hell into the plains to glory over his deeds in hiding. Damn, that tickled imei!"

Chad's mother located him, in the drowsy Denver afternoon, working over his Indian basket-making at the local museum. I called him there; he came and picked me up in his old Ford coupe that he used to take trips in the mountains, to dig for Indian objects. He came into the bus station wearing jeans and a big smile. I was sitting on my bag on the floor talking to the very same sailor who'd been in the Cheyenne bus station with me, asking him what happened to the blonde. He was so bored he didn't answer. Chad and I got in his little coupe and the first thing he had to do was get maps at the State building. Then he had to see an old schoolteacher, and so on, and all I wanted to do was drink beer.

And in the back of my mind was the wild thought, Where is Dean and what is he doing right now? Chad had decided not to be Dean's friend any more, for some odd reason, and he didn't even know where he lived.

"Is Carlo Marx in town?"

"Yes." But he wasn't talking to him any more either. This was the beginning of Chad King's withdrawal from our general gang. I was had an apartment waiting for me up Colfax Avenue, that Roland Major was already living in it and was waiting for me to join him. I sensed some kind of conspiracy in the air, and this conspiracy lined up two groups in the gang: It was Chad King and Tim Gray and Roland Major, together with the Rawlinses, generally agreeing to ignore Dean Moriarty and Carlo Marx. I was smack in the middle of this interesting war.

It was a war with social overtones. Dean was the son of a wino, one of the most tottering bums of Larimer Street, and Dean had in fact been brought up generally on Larimer Street and thereabouts. He used to plead in court at the age of six to have his father set free. He used to beg in front of Larimer alleys and sneak the money back to his father, who waited among the broken bottles with an old buddy. Then when Dean grew up he began hanging around the Glenarm poolhalls; he set a Denver record for stealing cars and went to the reformatory. From the age of eleven to seventeen he was usually in reform school. His specialty was stealing cars, gunning for girls coming out of high school in the afternoon, driving them out to the mountains, making them and coming back to sleep in any available hotel bathtub in town. His father, once a respectable and hardworking tinsmith, had become a wine alcoholic, which is worse than a whisky alcoholic, and was reduced to riding freights to Texas in the winter and back to Denver in the summer. Dean had brothers on his dead mother's side—she died when he was small—but they disliked him. Dean's only buddies were the poolhall boys. Dean, who had the tremendous energy of a new kind of American saint, and Carlo were the underground monsters of that season in Denver, together with the poolhall gang, and, symbolizing this most beautifully, Carlo had a basement apartment on Grant Street and we all met there many a night that went to dawn—Carlo, Dean, myself, Tom Snark, Ed Dunkel and Roy Johnson. More of these others later.

Vladimir Nabokov (1899–1977)

Vladimir Nabokov, a Russian-American novelist and critic, wrote his first literary works in Russian under the pseudonym of Vladimir Sirin. However, he rose to international prominence, after he began writing in English.

Vladimir Nabokov was born into a prominent aristocratic family in Saint Petersburg, where he also spent his childhood and youth. Since the family spoke Russian, English and French in their household, Nabokov was trilingual from an early age. The Nabokov family left Russia in the wake of the 1917 Russian Revolution for Crimea. Following the defeat of the White Army in Crimea, they left Russia for exile in Western Europe. After emigrating from Russia in 1919, the family settled briefly in England, where Vladimir enrolled in Trinity College, Cambridge, studying Slavic and Romance languages. In 1922 Nabokov's father was assassinated in Berlin, as he tried to shelter the real target. This episode clearly traumatized the young Nabokov so much so that the theme of mistaken, violent death would echo again and again in his works.

In 1923, he graduated from Cambridge and relocated to Berlin, where he gained some reputation as a novelist and poet, writing under the pseudonym of Vladimir Sirin. In 1925 he married Véra Slonim in Berlin, where he lived from 1922 to 1937. Nabokov, like his wife, his son and several characters in his novels, was a synesthete.

Nabokov left Germany with his family in 1937 for Paris and in 1940 fled from the advancing German Nazi troops to the United States. It was here that he met the critic Edmund Wilson, who introduced Nabokov's work to American editors, eventually leading to his international recognition. Nabokov came to Wellesley College in Massachusetts in 1941, founding Wellesley's Russian Department and serving as resident lecturer in comparative literature. He became a naturalized citizen of the United States in 1945. Nabokov left Wellesley in 1948 to teach Russian and European literature at Cornell University. At the same time, Nabokov made a great contribution to lepidoptery, responsible for organizing the butterfly collection of the Museum of Comparative Zoology at Harvard during the 1940s. In addition, he proved to be an outstanding composer of chess problems. Nabokov later lived in Montreux, Switzerland to the end of his life.

Due to his privileged educational background, Nabokov wrote in different languages and his works in English in particular brought him international fame. His main English novels include *Bend Sister* (1947), *Lolita* (1955), *Pnin* (1957), *Pale Fire* (1962) and *Ada or Ardor: A Family Chronicle* (1969), among which *Lolita* is generally regarded as his most important one. In *Pale Fire*, John Shade is mistaken for the king of Zembla and is assassinated. His autobiography *Speak, Memory* (1952) describes his childhood and his exile life.

As a critic, Nabokov translates and comments on Alexander Pushkin's novel in verse, *Eugene Onegin*, published in 1964. Nabokov's collection of lectures at Cornell University published as *Lectures on Literature* also demonstrates his artistic pursuit. He holds that novels should not intend to teach and that readers should not only be identified with characters. Instead, a higher aesthetic enjoyment should be attained, which partly is closely related to its style and structure.

After published in Paris, New York and London successively, *Lolita* quickly attained a classic status and has been seen one of important works of the 20th century literature despite considerable controversy. Throughout *Lolita*, the confrontation between European culture and American culture is clearly presented. Charlotte Haze, an American, is faced with the sophistication and worldliness of Humbert, a European. She admires and is more attracted by Humbert's glamorous background than who he is. On the contrary, Humbert openly mocks the superficiality and transience of American culture and thinks of Charlotte as nothing but a simple-minded housewife. However, he adores Lolita's vulgarities and enjoys the utmost freedom along the open American road. He eventually admits that he has defiled the country rather than the other way around. Though Humbert and Lolita travel together, deep down, they do not understand each other, let alone accept each other. Lolita fails to appreciate Humbert's devotion associated with art, history and culture, while Humbert will never truly recognize Lolita's reluctance to allow him to sophisticate her. Eventually, Lolita leaves Humbert for the American Quilty, who does not bore her with high culture or grand passions.

With *Lolita* Nabokov's ultimate achievement may be that he forces readers to be complicit in Humbert's crimes. In order to uncover the actual story of pedophilia, rape and murder within the text, readers have to immerse themselves in Humbert's words and their shadowy meanings—and thus they must enter Humbert's mind. By engaging so closely with Humbert's linguistic trickery, readers cannot hold him at a far enough distance to see him for the man he truly is.

As to his style, Nabokov believes that the proper language could elevate any material to the level of art. In his works, language effectively triumphs over shocking content and gives it shades of beauty. He uses words to distract, to confuse and to charm.

Selected Reading

Lolita

In the novel's foreword, the fictional John Ray, Jr., Ph.D., explains the strange story that will follow. According to Ray, he received the manuscript, entitled *Lolita, or the Confession of a White Widowed Male*, from the author's lawyer. The author himself, known by the pseudonym of Humbert Humbert, died in jail of coronary thrombosis while awaiting a trial.

In the manuscript, Humbert relates his peaceful upbringing on the Riviera, where he encounters his first love, the twelve-year-old Annabel Leigh. Although Annabel and the thirteen-year-old Humbert never consummate their love, Annabel's death from typhus four months later haunts Humbert ever after. Apart from being a teacher of English literature, he spends time in a mental institution and works a succession of odd jobs. Despite his marriage to an adult woman, which proves a failure, Humbert remains obsessed with sexual desire for young girls. Eventually, Humbert settles down in the house of widow Charlotte Haze in a suburban New England town, the United States, where he becomes instantly infatuated with her twelve-year-old daughter Dolores, also known as Lolita. Humbert follows Lolita's moves constantly, occasionally flirts with her, and confides his pedophiliac longings to a journal. Meanwhile, Charlotte Haze, whom Humbert loathes, has fallen in love with him. When Charlotte sends Lolita off to summer camp, Humbert marries Charlotte in order to be close to his true love. Humbert wants to be alone with Lolita and even toys with the idea of killing Charlotte, but he can't go through with it. However, Charlotte finds his diary and after learning that he hates her but loves her daughter, confronts him. Humbert denies everything and Charlotte storms out of the house. At that moment, a car hits her and she dies instantly.

Humbert goes to the summer camp and picks up Lolita. Only when they arrive at a motel does he tell her that Charlotte has died. In his account of events, Humbert claims that Lolita seduces him, rather than the other way around. The two drive across the country for nearly a year, during which time Humbert becomes increasingly obsessed with Lolita and she gradually learns to manipulate him. When she engages in tantrums or refuses his advances, Humbert threatens to put her in an orphanage. At the same time, a strange man seems to take interest in Humbert and Lolita, and appears to be following them on their travels.

Humbert eventually gets a job at Beardsley College somewhere in the Northeast, and Lolita enrolls in school. Her wish to socialize with boys at her own age results in a strain in their relationship and Humbert becomes more restrictive in his rules. Nonetheless, he allows her to make an appearance in a school play. Since Lolita begins to behave secretively around Humbert, he doubts her faithfulness so much so that he takes her away on another road trip. On the road, Humbert suspects that they are being followed while Lolita does not notice anything.

Lolita becomes ill, and Humbert must take her to the hospital. However, when Humbert returns to get her, the nurses tell him that her uncle has already picked her up. Humbert flies into a rage, but then he calms himself down and leaves the hospital, heartbroken and angry.

For the next two years, Humbert never stops to search for Lolita, unearthing clues about her kidnapper in order to exact his revenge. He halfheartedly takes up with a woman named Rita, but then he receives a note from Lolita, now married and pregnant, asking for money. Assuming that Lolita has married the man who followed them on their travels, Humbert becomes determined to kill him. He finds Lolita, poor and pregnant at seventeen. Humbert realizes that Lolita's husband is not the man who kidnapped her from the hospital. When pressed, Lolita admits that it is Clare Quilty, a playwright whose presence has been felt from the beginning, who has taken her from the hospital. Lolita loves Quilty, but he kicks her out when she refuses to participate in a child pornography orgy. So she ends up in the marriage with her husband, Dick, who knows nothing about her past. Still devoted to Lolita, Humbert begs her to return to him. Lolita gently refuses. Humbert gives her 4,000 dollars and then departs. He tracks down Quilty at his house and shoots him to death. Consequently, Humbert is arrested and put in jail, where he continues to write his memoir, stipulating that it can only be published upon Lolita's death. After Lolita dies in childbirth, Humbert dies of heart failure, and the manuscript is sent to John Ray, Jr., Ph.D.

An Excerpt from Chapter 29, Part Two

Lo-lee-ta: the tip of the tongue taking a trip of three steps down the palate to tap, at three, on the teeth. Lo. Lee. Ta.

...

"Lolita," I said, "this may be neither here nor there but I have to say it. Life is very short. From here to that old car you know so well thee is a stretch of twenty, twenty-five paces. It is a very short walk. Make those twenty-five steps. Now. Right now. Come just as you are. And we shall live happily ever after."

Carmen, voulez-vous venir avec moi?

"You mean," she said opening her eyes and raising herself slightly, the snake that may strike, "you mean you will give us [us] that money only if I go with you to a motel. Is *that* what you mean?"

"No," I said, "you got it all wrong. I want you to leave your incidental Dick, and this awful hole, and come to live with me, and die with me, and everything with me" (words to that effect).

"You're crazy," she said, her features working.

"Think it over, Lolita. There are no strings attached. Except, perhaps—well, no matter." (A reprieve, I wanted to say but did not.) "Anyway, if you refuse you will still get your... trousseau."

"No kidding?" asked Dolly.

I handed her an envelope with four hundred dollars in cash and a check for three thousand six hundred more.

Gingerly, uncertainly, she received *mon petit cadeau*; and then her forehead became a beautiful pink. "You mean," she said, with agonized emphasis, "you are giving us *four thousand bucks*?" I covered my face with my hand and broke into the hottest tears I had ever shed. I felt them winding through my fingers and down my chin, and burning me, and my nose got clogged, and I could not stop, and then she touched my wrist.

"I'll die if you touch me," I said. "You are sure you are not coming with me? Is there no hope of your coming? Tell me only this."

"No," she said. "No, honey, no."

She had never called me honey before.

"No," she said, "it is quite out of the question. I would sooner go back to Cue. I mean—"

She groped for words. I supplied them mentally ("*He* broke my heart. *You* merely broke my life").

"I think," she went on—"oops"—the envelope skidded to the floor—she picked it up—"I think it's oh utterly *grand* of you to give us all that dough. It settles everything, we can start next week. Stop crying, please. You should understand. Let me get you some more beer. Oh, don't cry, I'm so sorry I cheated so much, but that's the way things are."

I wiped my face and my fingers. She smiled at the *cadeau*. She exulted. She wanted to call Dick. I said I would have to leave in a moment, did not want to see him at all, at all. We tried to think of some subject of conversation. For some reason, I kept seeing— it trembled and silkily glowed on my damn retina—a radiant child of twelve, sitting on a threshold, "pinging" pebbles at an empty can. I almost said—trying to find some casual remark—"I wonder sometimes what has become of the little McCoo girl, did she ever get better?" —but stopped in time lest she rejoin: "I wonder sometimes what has become of the little Haze girl..." Finally, I reverted to money matters. That sum, I said, represented more or less the net rent from her mother's house; she said: "Had it not been sold years ago?" No (I admit I *had* told her this in order to sever all connections with R.); a lawyer would send a full account of the financial situation later; it was rosy; some of the small securities her mother had owned had gone up and up. Yes, I was quite sure I had to go. I had to go, and find him, and destroy him.

＼ J. D. Salinger (1919–2010)

Jerome David Salinger, an American writer, won acclaim early in life. He is known for his literary achievement as well as his reclusive nature.

Jerome David Salinger was born into a family of Jewish origin in New York. Raised in Manhattan, Salinger began writing short stories while in secondary school. In 1936 Salinger attended New York University, but dropped out the following spring. Then he went to work in Vienna, Austria and left one month before it was annexed by Nazi Germany in 1938. Afterwards Salinger was educated at Ursinus College in Collegeville, Pennsylvania, but dropped out again after one semester. In 1939 Salinger attended an evening writing class taught by Whit Burnett, longtime editor of *Story* magazine, in which he published his several stories. In 1941 Salinger briefly served as an activity director and possibly as a performer on a Caribbean cruise ship. In 1942 Salinger participated in World War II and was active in several battles. During the campaign from Normandy into Germany, Salinger met Ernest Hemingway and they began corresponding. Based on his experiences in the war, Salinger wrote several stories later.

In 1948 he published "A Perfect Day for Bananafish" in *The New Yorker* magazine, where he also contributed his subsequent works. In 1951 Salinger published his first novel, *The Catcher in the Rye*, which made a hit. The adolescent alienation and loss of innocence in the story was widely read, especially among adolescent readers. After the success of *The Catcher in the Rye*, Salinger became a recluse and offered three collections of short stories: *Nine Stories* (1953), *Franny and Zooey* (1961) and *Raise High the Roof Beam, Carpenters and Seymour: An Introduction* (1963). His last published work, a novella entitled "Hapworth 16, 1924," appeared in *The New Yorker* in 1965.

The Catcher in the Rye is set around the 1950s and is narrated by a young man named Holden Caulfield. It is disclosed that he, now seventeen years old, is undergoing treatment in a sanatorium. The events Holden narrates take place in the few days between the end of the fall school term and Christmas, when he is sixteen years old. *The Catcher in the Rye* is considered a bildungsroman, a novel about a young character's growth into maturity. Holden Caulfield appears to be an unusual protagonist, because he is overwhelmed and can not understand everything around him. Instead of acknowledging that adulthood scares and mystifies him, Holden invents a fantasy that adulthood is a world of superficiality and hypocrisy, while childhood is a world of innocence, curiosity and honesty. The sharp contrast of the two worlds is best shown by his fantasy about the catcher in the rye: He imagines childhood as an idyllic field of rye in which children romp and play, while adulthood is equivalent to death—a fatal fall over the edge of a cliff. However, Holden's various experiences and his encounters with Mr. Antolini and Phoebe in particular, reveal the shallowness of his conceptions. Throughout the novel, Holden seems to be alienated from the world around him, which in his eyes is full of hypocrisy, pretension and shallowness. It is difficult for him to make true friends with anyone, except his little sister, Phoebe, and Jane Gallagher, whom he befriended in childhood. Consequently, he feels lonely and depressed, which drives him to ask for a prostitute and date Sally Hayes. It is his isolation and depression, as well as his inability to face the phoniness of the adult world that finally leads to his mental breakdown.

The story of *The Catcher in the Rye* is told in first-person narration, from the perspective of the protagonist, Holden Caulfield. When presenting the narration and dialogue, the author tries to imitate the language of a teenager struggling to grow up. The style, therefore, is conversational, deliberately intended to contain numerous colloquialisms and clichés. Symbolism is also employed to shed light to the theme of the novel, with "the catcher in the rye" as the main thematic symbol.

Selected Reading

The Catcher in the Rye

Holden Caulfield, sixteen years old, begins his story on the Saturday following the end of classes at the Pencey prep school in Agerstown, Pennsylvania. Pencey is Holden's fourth school, where he has just been expelled after failing four out of his five courses, but he is not scheduled to return home to Manhattan until Wednesday, when his parents expect him to return home for Christmas vacation. So he visits his elderly history teacher, Spencer, to say goodbye, only to become annoyed, when Spencer tries to reprimand him for his poor academic performance.

Back in the dormitory, Holden is further irritated by his unhygienic neighbor, Ackley, and by his own roommate, Stradlater, who has spent the evening on a date with Jane Gallagher, a girl whom Holden used to date and whom he still admires. Holden grows so nervous about their dating that he is thrown into a rage and attacks Stradlater, who overpowers him easily. Holden has had enough of Pencey and decides to go to Manhattan where he plans to stay in a hotel until Wednesday.

On the train to New York, Holden meets the mother of a Pencey classmate. Though considering this student a complete "bastard," he greatly distorts the truth by telling her what a popular boy her son is. In his room at the Edmont Hotel which faces the rooms in the opposite wing, He observes a man putting on silk stockings, high heels, a bra, a corset and an evening gown. He also sees a man and a woman in another room taking turns spitting mouthfuls of their drinks into each other's faces and laughing hysterically. After smoking a couple of cigarettes, he calls Faith Cavendish for sex but gives up when the woman suggests that they meet the next day. Then Holden goes downstairs to the Lavender Room, where he flirts with three women in their thirties, among whom the blonde one attracts him a lot, but ends up with only the check. As Holden goes out to the lobby, he starts to think about Jane Gallagher and recounts how he got to know her.

Holden leaves the Edmont and takes a cab to Ernie's club in Greenwich Village, where he runs into Lillian Simmons, a girl his older brother, D.B. used to date, who compliments Holden in the hope that he can tell his brother about her. Bored and disappointed, Holden walks back to the Edmont. Then Holden agrees to have a prostitute, Sunny, visit his room with the help of Maurice, the elevator operator at the Edmont. Struggling with his heart, Holden makes up an excuse and pays the girl to leave. To his surprise, Sunny returns with Maurice to demand more money, leaving with another five dollars from his wallet.

He wakes up at ten o'clock on Sunday and calls Sally Hayes, a familiar date, and asks her to a play. After checking out of the hotel, Holden has breakfast in a restaurant at Grand Central Station, where he converses with two nuns about *Romeo and Juliet* and donates $10 to help them with their work. He tries to call Jane Gallagher but hangs up, when her mother answers the phone. To look for his younger sister, Phoebe, in Central Park, he ends up going to the Museum of Natural History. When he gets there he decides not to go in and instead takes a cab to the Biltmore Hotel to meet Sally. After the play, Holden and Sally go to Radio City to ice skate. When Holden tries to explain to Sally why he is unhappy at school and actually urges her to run away with him, she leaves. Holden calls Jane again, but there is no answer. He calls Carl Luce, who agrees to meet him for a drink after dinner. After a movie at Radio City to kill time, Holden finally meets Luce, who grows irritated by Holden's juvenile remarks about homosexuals and about Luce's Chinese girlfriend, leaving Holden indulging himself in drinking all by himself.

Quite drunk, Holden telephones Sally Hayes and babbles about their Christmas Eve plans. Then he goes to the lagoon in Central Park, where he used to watch the ducks as a child. Exhausted physically and mentally, he heads home to see his sister. Sneaking into the house and Waking Phoebe up, he tells her his fantasy of being "the catcher in the rye," a person who catches little children as they are about to fall off of a cliff. When his parents return from a late night out, Holden, undetected, leaves the apartment and visits the home of Mr. Antolini, a favorite teacher, where he hopes to stay a few days and fall asleep quickly. Awaking to find Antolini stroking his forehead, he becomes suspicious of Antolini's homosexual overture and leaves hastily, sleeping for a few hours on a bench at Grand Central Station.

Monday morning, Holden intends to say goodbye to Phoebe at lunchtime, but agrees to stay, since she insists on leaving with him. He takes Phoebe across the park and watches Phoebe riding a carrousel in the rain.

In the end, Holden is at the sanitarium in California. He doesn't want to tell us any more. In fact, the whole story has only made him miss people, even the jerks. He also plans to go to a new school and is cautiously optimistic about his future.

An Excerpt from Chapter XXII

That was about all I could think of, though. Those two nuns I saw at breakfast and this boy James Castle I knew at Elkton Hills. The funny part is, I hardly even know James Castle, if you want to know the truth. He was one of these very quiet guys. He was in my math class, but he was way over on the other side of the room, and he hardly ever got up to recite or go to the blackboard or anything. Some guys in school hardly ever get up to recite or go to the blackboard. I think the only time I ever even had a conversation with him was that time he asked me if he could borrow this turtleneck sweater I had. I damn near dropped dead when he asked me, I was so surprised and all. I remember I was brushing my teeth, in the can, when he asked me. He said his cousin was coming in to take him for a drive and all. I didn't even know he knew I had a turtleneck sweater. All I knew about him was that his name was always right ahead of me at roll call. Cabel, R., Cabel, W., Castle, Caulfield—I can still remember it. If you want to know the truth, I almost didn't lend him my sweater. Just because I didn't know him too well.

"What?" I said to old Phoebe. She said something to me, but I didn't hear her.

"You can't even think of one thing."

"Yes, I can. Yes, I can."

"Well, do it, then."

"I like Allie[1]," I said. "And I like doing what I'm doing right now. Sitting here with you, and talking, and thinking about stuff, and—"

"Allie's dead—You always say that! If somebody's dead and everything, and in Heaven, then it isn't really—"

"I know he's dead! Don't you think I know that? I can still like him, though, can't I? Just because somebody's dead, you don't just stop liking them, for God's sake—especially if they were about a thousand times nicer than the people you know that're alive and all."

Old Phoebe didn't say anything. When she can't think of anything to say, she doesn't say a goddam word.

"Anyway, I like it now," I said. "I mean right now. Sitting here with you and just chewing the fat and horsing—"

"That isn't anything really!"

"It is so something really! Certainly it is! Why the hell isn't it? People never think anything is anything really. I'm getting goddam sick of it."

"Stop swearing. All right, name something else. Name something you'd like to be. Like a scientist. Or a lawyer or something."

"I couldn't be a scientist. I'm no good in science."

"Well, a lawyer—like Daddy and all."

"Lawyers are all right, I guess—but it doesn't appeal to me," I said. "I mean they're all right if they go around saving innocent guys' lives all the time, and like that, but you don't do that kind of stuff if you're a lawyer. All you do is make a lot of dough and play golf and play bridge and buy cars and drink Martinis and look like a hot-shot. And besides. Even if

---

Note [1] Allie: Holden's younger brother

you did go around saving guys' lives and all, how would you know if you did it because you really wanted to save guys' lives, or because you did it because what you really wanted to do was be a terrific lawyer, with everybody slapping you on the back and congratulating you in court when the goddam trial was over, the reporters and everybody, the way it is in the dirty movies? How would you know you weren't being a phony? The trouble is, you wouldn't."

I'm not too sure old Phoebe knew what the hell I was talking about. I mean she's only a little child and all. But she was listening, at least. If somebody at least listens, it's not too bad.

"Daddy's going to kill you. He's going to kill you," she said.

I wasn't listening, though. I was thinking about something else—something crazy. "You know what I'd like to be?" I said. "You know what I'd like to be? I mean if I had my goddam choice?"

"What? Stop swearing."

"You know that song 'If a body catch a body comin' through the rye'? I'd like—"

"It's 'If a body meet a body coming through the rye'!" old Phoebe said. "It's a poem. By Robert Burns."

"I know it's a poem by Robert Burns."

She was right, though. It is "If a body meet a body coming through the rye." I didn't know it then, though.

"I thought it was 'If a body catch a body,'" I said. "Anyway, I keep picturing all these little kids playing some game in this big field of rye and all. Thousands of little kids, and nobody's around—nobody big, I mean—except me. And I'm standing on the edge of some crazy cliff. What I have to do, I have to catch everybody if they start to go over the cliff—I mean if they're running and they don't look where they're going I have to come out from somewhere and catch them. That's all I'd do all day. I'd just be the catcher in the rye and all. I know it's crazy, but that's the only thing I'd really like to be. I know it's crazy."

Old Phoebe didn't say anything for a long time. Then, when she said something, all she said was, "Daddy's going to kill you."

"I don't give a damn if he does," I said. I got up from the bed then, because what I wanted to do, I wanted to phone up this guy that was my English teacher at Elkton Hills, Mr. Antolini. He lived in New York now. He quit Elkton Hills. He took this job teaching English at N.Y.U. "I have to make a phone call," I told Phoebe. "I'll be right back. Don't go to sleep." I didn't want her to go to sleep while I was in the living room. I knew she wouldn't but I said it anyway, just to make sure.

While I was walking toward the door, old Phoebe said, "Holden!" and I turned around.

She was sitting way up in bed. She looked so pretty. "I'm taking belching lessons from this girl, Phyllis Margulies," she said. "Listen."

I listened, and I heard something, but it wasn't much. "Good," I said. Then I went out in the living room and called up this teacher I had, Mr. Antolini.

References

Baym, Nina *et al.*, eds. *The Norton Anthology of American Literature*. 3rd edition. New York: W. W. Norton, 1989.

Cunliffe, Marcus. *The Literature of the United States*. Baltimore: Penguin Books, 1954.

Evans, Mari. *Black Women Writers*. New York: Anchor Press, 1984.

Hart, James D. *The Oxford Companion to American Literature*. 5th edition. Oxford: Oxford University Press, 1983.

Hassan, Ihab. *Contemporary American Literature 1945–1972: An Introduction*. New York: Frederick Ungar, 1973.

Horton, Rod W. & Edward, Herbert W. *Backgrounds of American Literary Thought*. 2nd edition. New York: Appleton Century Crofts, 1967.

Lawrence, D. H. *Studies in Classic American Literature*. New York: Doubleday, 1960.

Mack, Maynard *et al.*, eds. *The Norton Anthology of World Masterpieces*. New York: W. W. Norton, 1986.

Pizer, Donald. *Realism and Naturalism in Nineteenth-Century American Literature*. Carbondale and Edwardsville: Southern Illinois University Press, 1966.

Quinn, Arthur Hobson. *A History of American Drama: From the Civil War to the Present Day*. New York: F. S. Crofts & Co., 1943.

Stafford, William T. *Twentieth-Century American Writing*. New York: The Odyssey Press, 1965.

Waller, George M. *Puritanism in Early America*. Boston: D. C. Heath and Company, 1950.

Ward, Alfred C. *Longman Companion to Twentieth Century Literature*. 3rd edition. Harlow: Longman, 1981.

常耀信. 美国文学简史（第三版）. 天津：南开大学出版社，2008.

童明. 美国文学史. 南京：译林出版社，2005.

张伯香. 英美文学选读. 北京：外语教学与研究出版社，1998.

图书在版编目(CIP)数据

新编美国文学史及选读：英文 / 朱玉英主编. — 杭州：
浙江大学出版社，2016.12
ISBN 978-7-308-16301-9

Ⅰ．①新… Ⅱ．①朱… Ⅲ．①文学史－美国－英文②文
学－作品－介绍－美国－英文 Ⅳ．①I712.09

中国版本图书馆CIP数据核字(2016)第243535号

新编美国文学史及选读

朱玉英　主编

策划编辑	徐　霞	
责任编辑	陈丽勋	
责任校对	董　唯　魏钊凌	
封面设计	春天书装	
出版发行	浙江大学出版社	

（杭州市天目山路148号　　邮政编码　310007）
（网址：http://www.zjupress.com）

排　　版	杭州林智广告有限公司
印　　刷	富阳市育才印刷有限公司
开　　本	787mm×1092mm　1/16
印　　张	11.75
字　　数	330千
版印次	2016年12月第1版　2016年12月第1次印刷
书　　号	ISBN 978-7-308-16301-9
定　　价	28.00元